THE ROAD THROUGH RUSHBURY

MARTHA KEYES

Cover design by Martha Keyes and Ashtyn Newbold.

Martha Keyes
http://www.marthakeyes.com

CHAPTER 1

Ten thousand.

That was the number of pins Georgiana Paige estimated she'd had stuck in her hair since her coming out eight years ago. She winced as her maid placed another one, the edge of it prodding the crown of her head in much the same way the heel of a boot prods at a reluctant horse.

Georgiana relaxed as her maid stepped back, making a final adjustment to the coiffure. It was not Georgiana's preferred way to wear her hair, but she didn't care enough to dispute it. One could only muster so much opinion on such a matter. She dismissed the maid and was left alone with her younger sister Daphne.

"You look magnificent!" Daphne's voice was almost reverent as she stepped forward and surveyed Georgiana in the mirror in front of them.

Georgiana looked up at her with a twinkle in her eye. "I look too old for this hairstyle, that's what I look." She stood and smoothed her skirts.

"Nonsense," Daphne said. "You mustn't think that way, Georgie." She pursed her lips together in a manner entirely at odds with her youthful naiveté. "You must consider tonight's ball as though it were your very first—and you freshly arrived in Town."

Georgiana took stock of herself in the long mirror. "I *feel* as though I have been here an eternity." She said it softly, almost to herself. She was every bit as plain as she had been upon her coming out—hair a nondescript shade of brown, a nose too long to convey the delicacy so valued in Society—and her face was showing subtle signs of the years that had passed: light wrinkles at the outer edges of her eyes and on her forehead, and a few pale freckles on her nose.

Utterly forgettable. Those were the words she had once overheard applied to her appearance. They had stung at the time, but there was truth to them, no doubt. She turned from the mirror and smiled at her sister.

"I cannot imagine tiring of London," Daphne said with a sigh, plopping down on the bed and pulling a pillow into her arms.

"Well, let us hope, then, that you haven't occasion to spend as many Seasons as I have here, for I assure you that eight of them is *more* than ample time to give you a distaste for Society." Georgiana held out the crook of her arm, and Daphne rose to take it, accompanying her out of the bedchamber and down the corridor.

"But," Daphne sputtered, "with all the balls, routs, evenings at the theater—"

"All begin to blend together."

Daphne frowned. "But surely there are enough new people each Season to provide plenty of variety?"

Georgiana smiled. She remembered being on the cusp of her first Season, just as Daphne was—the fluttering nerves as she prepared for her first ball, the anticipation of making a smart match. Never would she have imagined that she would be doing all the same things nearly a decade later, no closer to marriage than when she had been in the schoolroom.

"I'm afraid *they*, too, begin to blend together, Daph. I have found that there is not much to choose amongst the gentlemen here—they are very much the same." She patted Daphne's arm. "But you mustn't listen to me, you know, for I am nothing but a jaded spinster."

A gasp came from Daphne, and Georgiana glanced at her amusedly before rushing on. "I am determined to begin wearing caps and warm shawls and perhaps even adopt a cat to keep me company, in which case I shall forever be carrying it in my arms and saving it scraps of food from the dinner table."

Daphne let out a giggle and elbowed her as they came to the dining room. "Stop being ridiculous, Georgie. You are not a spinster. We will find someone for you yet!"

"Thank you, my dear, but for some time now, I have thought that nothing would suit me better than living out my life in some solitary cottage, far from the sights and smells of Town." They broke arms, and Georgiana turned, looking down at Daphne and shedding her humor. "I am terribly sorry that you find yourself having to wait for your turn at London because of me. I hardly think that Papa realized what he was agreeing to when he said he didn't want two daughters out in Society at once. I believe he meant it as a way to spur me to action, but it has instead merely served to hurt *you*."

Daphne managed a smile. "It isn't your fault, Georgie. And I only have to wait another year, even if you *don't* make a match this Season."

Georgiana shut her eyes briefly. The likelihood of her marrying in the next few months was so negligible as to be ridiculous. And to someone like Daphne, a year was an eternity. Daphne should not be punished for Georgiana's inability to elicit an offer.

Footsteps sounded, and their parents entered the dining room, her father glancing around.

"Where is Archibald?" He looked more grave than usual.

Georgiana shrugged her shoulders. It was rare that they knew her brother's whereabouts. "I imagine he will arrive halfway through dinner as he often does."

Her father pursed his lips and motioned for them all to take their seats.

Daphne looked at Georgiana consideringly as she pulled at her glove fingertips to remove them. "How is it that Archie can spend even more Seasons than *you* in London and yet still find plenty of enjoyment and to spare?"

Georgiana's eyes flitted to her father, who was listening with a slight crease to his brow. He worried over Archie's unceasing ability to enjoy London—and the corresponding ability to spend money. No doubt Georgiana would have found more pleasure in London if she enjoyed the freedom that her brother did.

"Well, as to that, Archie has always been odd, hasn't he?" She raised her brows enigmatically, hoping Daphne would let the subject rest. She had no desire to set the tone for dinner with a discussion of Archie's antics. She loved her brother dearly, but he knew just how to get under their father's skin with his carefree and thoughtless attitude.

She glanced at the folded letter her father set next to his plate, and his eyes lingered on it for a moment.

"Is that from Aunt Sara?" Georgiana was happy for a reason to change the subject. And nothing was surer to bring a bit of joy to her father than talking about his younger sister.

He nodded, but his brow only furrowed further.

Georgiana glanced at her mother, who grimaced and put a hand on her husband's.

"What news does Aunt Sara send from Granchurch House?" Georgiana kept her voice light, determined to fight against the glum mood that her father was bringing to the room.

"Nothing good, I'm afraid. Miss Baxter succumbed to what appeared at first to be nothing but a cold."

Georgiana's hands stopped in the act of cutting a carrot.

Aunt Sara and her cousin Miss Baxter had been living together for nigh on two decades now, seemingly happy in their mutual spinsterhood.

Her father picked up the letter and opened it, scanning its lines and shaking his head with a sigh. "Your aunt is in very poor spirits, as you might imagine. She wrote this the day before the funeral was held." He held up the letter, and Georgiana thought she could see a few spots where tears had perhaps fallen, smudging the ink.

"Poor Aunt Sara," Daphne said. "She must be terribly lonely."

Their mother nodded and squeezed her husband's hand. "Yes. But if she can only find a companion quickly, I think it will do wonders to prevent her from descending into a melancholy."

Their father shook his head. "But what companion? I am afraid that she will find any replacement sadly lacking indeed, for there is no company like one's own family. Who could ever replace Miss Baxter?"

Georgiana stared at her father, her wrists resting on the edge of the table. Her chest heaved at the enormity of the thought that assailed her. *Could* she?

Her father set the letter down again so that the edge of it was tucked under his plate. Georgiana sensed the fading of an opportunity and seized the moment.

"I could."

All eyes turned toward her, and she felt her muscles tense, even as energy pulsed through her with her speeding heartbeat.

"You could what?" her father asked, perplexed.

She wet her lips. "I could be her companion. Aunt Sara's."

There was an unwieldy pause. Georgiana didn't know if she had been wise to put forth the idea so rashly, but the more she considered it, the more it appealed to her.

"What, and move to Yorkshire indefinitely?" He looked as though she had just suggested moving to the moon.

Georgiana had never been to Yorkshire, but she had heard enough about it from friends who had traveled there during summers to know that it was thought to be a magnificent place. The thought of leaving London and seeing somewhere entirely new made her skin tingle. It spoke volumes about the monotony of her life that playing companion to her aunt could elicit such a reaction.

She shrugged. "Why not?"

Her father scoffed lightly. "Well, I think that should be obvious, my dear." Just what should be so obvious, though, he declined to say, instead tugging at his cravat and avoiding her eye.

Georgiana smiled wryly. "Father, if someone were going to offer for me, I think we can confidently say that it would have happened sometime during the legion Seasons I have spent in London and the many between-Seasons I have spent in Brighton and Bath."

Georgiana had no doubt that each one of her family and friends had their reasons for believing her to still be unmarried. It was a matter she herself had pondered on for years, at times anxiously. Had she some glaring flaw that was apparent to everyone except herself? She *did* sometimes offer her opinion too readily. And she had certainly never been counted among the Incomparables, but she felt herself no less marriageable than many of the young women who had made matches over the years.

Perhaps it was merely a function of ill luck? After all, Georgiana had never yet met a man who had made *her* wish to marry, agreeable as many of them were. Was it so difficult to believe that the reverse was also true? That she had not inspired that type of reaction in any of the gentlemen she had met, through no fault of her own?

She lifted her chin and straightened her shoulders at the pitying look she noted in her mother's kind eyes.

Her mother only wanted to see her cared for and established, but pity was one thing Georgiana would leave behind with gusto if she went to Yorkshire. Wishing to see anything but that sorrowful compassion, she glanced at Daphne, who was still looking at her incredulously.

Daphne. She was more than ready to be a part of the London scene. Since her arrival in Town a few weeks before, not a night had passed without Georgiana returning home to find Daphne sitting upon her bed, waiting anxiously for her to recount the events of the evening. Waiting until the beginning of the next Season would be torture for her. And entirely unnecessary.

What Daphne needed was to enter Society unencumbered by the constant presence of Georgiana and the shadow she inevitably cast over the family, a shadow that lengthened its reach with every year she failed to make a match.

Her father was watching her through considering eyes, shadowed by bushy eyebrows. He hadn't said "no" yet, and it was time to press home her advantage if Georgiana wished to spend the most crowded and suffocating part of the Season anywhere but London.

"I am certainly not Miss Baxter," Georgiana said, "but I believe that I could be a very helpful and agreeable companion to Aunt Sara, knowing and loving her as I do. She was always very fond of me, you know."

She watched her father's frown relax slightly and the way his jaw worked in tandem with his thoughts.

"And what's more, this could be the perfect opportunity for Daphne."

Daphne's eyes swelled in horror. "Going to Yorkshire?"

Georgiana laughed. Leaving London for a place like Yorkshire would feel like a death sentence to Daphne. To Georgiana, though, it felt like freedom.

"No, of course not, silly!" She placed her hands in her lap and looked back to her mother and father. They were glancing between their two daughters, who were separated by nearly a decade in years and yet the dearest of friends despite it. "It is March, and the most promising part of the Season is still before you. If I leave to be with Aunt Sara, Daphne might be brought out after Easter instead of waiting for next year."

Daphne's hand grasped Georgiana's under the table and directed a gaze at her so painfully hopeful that Georgiana determined that, whether or not her parents agreed to the idea, she would find a way to ensure Daphne had her come-out before the Season ended.

"Well..." said her father, obviously finding it hard to refute the sense in the argument. He was terribly fond of his sister Sara and would go well out of his way to ensure her comfort, but to agree to Georgiana's plan would mean acknowledging the unlikelihood of her making a match, and he was far too kind to do such a thing.

"Let me think on it," he said evasively. He shot a smile and wink at Georgiana. "I do my best thinking over a bottle of port."

When the women rose to leave him to the bottle—with still no sign of Archie—Daphne immediately linked her arm with Georgiana's.

"Georgie!" she whispered urgently, leaning in so that Georgiana had to push back on her to keep from stumbling. "What in heaven's name are you thinking?"

"What do you mean?"

"Yorkshire? Aunt Sara? Papa has said that she lives in the most remote village. I imagine there isn't a young gentleman to be found within miles."

Georgiana smiled. "It sounds delightful. I would be content never to see a marriageable gentleman again." She'd had enough talk of marriage and prospects to last her a lifetime—and thinking of the lack of *actual* offers she had received brought on the familiar desire to curl up in a dark corner.

Daphne shook her head slowly, disbelieving. She would

likely never understand the appeal that a life in the countryside held for Georgiana.

Georgiana hadn't seen Aunt Sara in years, but even if her aunt were a terribly difficult woman, her vagaries would likely be outweighed by the freedom Georgiana would gain—freedom from every expectation and every pitying grimace that currently filled her days and nights.

There was something terribly humiliating about watching her parents' ambitions progressively shift from the wealthy lords they had hoped for during her first Season, to the simple but well-off gentlemen during Seasons three and four, to today, when they rarely mentioned her prospects at all. Georgiana suspected that they would be relieved by almost any decent man who could put a roof over her head and food in her belly.

The door opened, and Archie strode in with a smile and quick, confident movements.

"Archibald," their mother said, striding over to him for a quick embrace. "How good of you to come. Your father is still in the dining room if you'd like to join him."

Archie returned her embrace and shook his head. "When I can spend time with you three dashing beauties?"

Their mother tried to look severe, but Archie's good humor was too difficult to resist, and her mouth stretched into a smile even as she shook her head at his flattery.

"What have I missed?" he asked, disposing himself in a chair so that his legs stretched in front of him, crossed at the ankles.

The door opened again, and their father entered—apparently too restless to linger long over his port—his eyes immediately finding Archie and then moving to Georgiana. He held the letter from Aunt Sara in his hands, and his thumbs rubbed it as his eyes rested on Georgiana.

She met his gaze, feeling her heart trip as she waited for him to say something.

"Very well," he said with a decisive nod.

Georgiana's brows shot up, and she blinked three times. "You mean that I may go?"

He looked down at the letter. "I will not be at peace until I know Sara is in good hands, and I can think of no one I trust more than you to ensure her well-being. I think she will benefit greatly from your presence."

Georgiana stepped toward him, taking his hands in hers and smiling gratefully as her heart pounded and her mind tried to wrap itself around the ramifications of what he was saying.

She was leaving London.

"But," he said significantly, "this is only a temporary situation, Georgie. I hope that, whatever influence you manage to gain over your aunt, you will exercise it in trying to convince her to sell Granchurch House and move nearer to us. What in heaven's name she and Miss Baxter found to love about such a far-flung place as Rushbury, I can't fathom. But it is only sensible with Miss Baxter gone that Sara return somewhere less distant from her remaining family—as things stand, she could hardly be further."

Georgiana nodded quickly, more than happy to agree to whatever terms her father attached to her freedom. Such details could be sorted out later. For now, she had the most childish desire to run from the room and fling her arms in the air, twirling and dancing at the prospect of the wide-open space and independence Yorkshire would afford her.

"What's all this about?" Archie asked, looking at Georgiana with his head tipped to the side.

"Papa," Daphne interjected, "does this mean that…" She trailed off, her hands clasped in front of her, her eyes full of that same painful hope Georgiana had seen at dinner.

Their father stared at Daphne for a moment before a smile broke over his face and he nodded.

Daphne ran over, wrapping her arms around him with such force that Georgiana was obliged to grab hold of his arm.

Daphne apologized over and over. "I am just so terribly excited!" She turned to Georgiana, her smile fading slightly as her brows furrowed. "But surely you needn't leave in order for me to have my come out?"

"Would someone mind telling me what in the deuce is going on?" Archie said with an exasperated chuckle.

Informed of the developments that had happened over the course of the dinner he had missed, Archie pushed himself to a stand and walked over to Georgiana. Daphne was already anxiously making plans with their mother and father about all the things that would need to happen before she could make a proper come out.

"Georgie," Archie said, wrapping an arm about her shoulders, "what is all this nonsense? Yorkshire?"

She laughed and nodded.

He pulled his arm from her shoulders and faced her, waiting for an explanation. He didn't say anything, just looking at her with his round eyes and shaking his head. It was as unfathomable for him as it was for Daphne. Archie lived for London.

"Oh, Archie," she said, "you know that I have little love for London and life on the Marriage Mart."

"Yes, of course, but…*Yorkshire*? You might as well move to an isle on the sea. Everything I know about Rushbury paints a very —" his lips pushed into a thin line, as if debating over what word to choose "—*provincial* picture, and much as you say you dislike London—" he nodded at her dress, a green satin with embellished sleeves and hem "—you are hardly provincial, Georgie."

She laughed, but he only grimaced. "I mean it. You are consigning yourself to living in a remote village with an aunt I imagine has become an eccentric after so much time in such a forsaken place."

Determined not to let Archie take away the sense of victory and anticipatory freedom still coursing through her, she said,

"Well, you may turn your nose up at Rushbury and Aunt Sara, but perhaps you will be singing a different tune when she leaves her money to me, since none of her other family will venture abroad to visit her." She winked at him teasingly.

Archie looked very struck by this comment. "Perhaps I should come with you." He leaned in toward her, his eyes shifting to their father. "Between me and you, I've been spending the blunt a bit too freely."

Georgiana laughed. "If you think that is news to Papa, then you are sorely mistaken." She raised one brow. "Indeed, I don't think it could be news to anyone."

"Hmph. Well, I doubt Yorkshire would suit me anyway."

"No, I don't think it would. But it will suit *me* very well indeed."

Georgiana was sure of it. She could picture it now: solitary walks—without even a maid to trail her—where she might hold up her skirts to avoid muddying them up without occasioning the least comment, for there would be no one around to see; where no one would make remarks about her husbandless state because there was no way to change it amongst a village of married men; where fresh air and stillness awaited after years of breathing in dust and town smells.

Yes, the more she thought on joining Aunt Sara in Yorkshire, the more she felt certain that it would be just the thing.

CHAPTER 2

Samuel Derrick scraped at the ground with a hand, but the dirt didn't yield to his insistent fingers. He shook his head. "Still too early, I'm afraid."

His friend and the parish constable, Michael Burke, stood leaning against the fence that surrounded the glebe garden, one hand resting on Samuel's coat, which was draped over the gate. For years, Burke had been taking on the task of farming the small plot of land attached to the parsonage—except for the little garden Samuel cared for himself.

"Can't say I'm surprised after the winter we've had," Burke said. "Only time will tell what havoc the weather has wreaked upon the crops. I fear we may have more pests to deal with than usual."

Samuel stood and brushed his hands off, a few stray specks of dirt that had come loose falling to the hard ground below. "We must pray for the best."

He looked down at the dirt again and grimaced, his dark brows furrowing. It wasn't too late to begin planting the earlier crops, but he wished he knew when the ground would loosen enough to make it possible. He had a number of pots inside the parsonage that he had planted weeks before, some containing little sprouts trying mightily to grow with the limited sunlight of a Yorkshire March.

Burke clapped him on the back and handed him his coat. "It will all work out. It always does."

Samuel shrugged on his black coat, and they began walking toward the front of the parsonage. "We cannot afford another harvest like last year's, Burke." It had been a difficult winter for Samuel's parishioners. He prayed that they would be better prepared for the next one, that the weather would be kinder this year. He glanced up at the blanket of gray clouds covering the sky and took in a breath, smiling at Burke. "But you're right. We will all manage it together, whatever comes."

The rumbling of carriage wheels sounded, and they both looked up at the smart coach passing by, heading in the direction of the manor house.

"Have you spoken to them?" Burke asked, watching the carriage travel down the bumpy lane.

"No, but they only arrived three days ago. I imagine they are still settling in. I sent a note yesterday, though, expressing my intention of making a visit tomorrow."

"What do we know about them?"

Samuel took in a deep breath. "Sir Clyde Gilmour. For now, I believe it is just him and his wife who will be staying at Amblethorne. A fairly young couple—she younger than he." He wished he knew more, and yet he was anxious about what he might learn when he did pay them a visit.

"Let us hope that their stay will be longer than any of the past tenants."

Samuel turned from the road. "I imagine it will, for they aren't renting, you know. They have purchased the manor."

Burke chuckled. "Yes, but how many times have we had a new purchaser of Amblethorne in the past few years?"

Three. Samuel could recall all three owners—and the renters in between purchases—with perfect clarity. One didn't forget the people who exerted such influence over Rushbury. "Let us hope that they stay only as long as will be good for Rushbury."

"They and whoever is coming to take Miss Baxter's place at Granchurch."

Samuel chuckled humorlessly. "Yes. We look to have an interesting spring approaching, don't we, with all these newcomers?"

Burke cleared his throat. "Precisely. Who knows what Miss Paige's new companion will bring?"

"Indeed." Samuel became aware of Burke's eyes on him, a mischievous smile on his face. He turned his head toward the constable and frowned. "What? Why do you look at me so?"

Burke shrugged in faux-innocence. "No reason. I only mean to say that Miss Paige's new companion might be a wonderful addition to Rushbury. And that I hope you will ensure that she feels *very* welcome among us."

Samuel scoffed. "Oh, Burke. Have done with your plotting and your machinations. Do you truly intend to try making a match between me and someone old enough to be my mother?"

Burke kept his eyes on the rural scene before them rather than meeting Samuel's gaze. "Perhaps she won't be so old after all." It was said as a mere suggestion, but Samuel was no fool.

"Burke," he said suspiciously, turning toward him at the gate that led from the parsonage to the village lane. "Do you know something I don't?"

Burke grinned widely, and Samuel shut his eyes and shook his head. "Never mind. It hardly matters."

"Oh, come, Sam," Burke said, his smile replaced by a look of exasperation. "You can't keep every outsider at arm's length." He put up a finger which he shook at Samuel. "I'll laugh unabashedly at you if the day comes that you fall headlong in love with one of these strangers."

Samuel put a hand on Burke's shoulder. "Don't hold your breath, my friend."

"You *do* realize that you will never marry if you refuse to look beyond Rushbury for a wife."

Samuel kept his eyes on the village lane where one of his parishioners crossed to the house opposite his, a bundle in his arms. Burke was right: there were no women of marriageable age in Rushbury.

But Miss Baxter had been a member of the gentry, just like Miss Paige. Whoever replaced the poor woman would also undoubtedly belong to that class, and Samuel had no desire to enter their ranks. Of course, he himself could technically be considered a gentleman, but he felt much more at home with his hard-working parishioners than he did with any of the people who flitted in and out of Amblethorne Park or Granchurch House.

"Yes. But why need I look for a wife at all? I am perfectly content as I am."

Burke raised his brows censoriously. *"Nevertheless neither is the man without the woman, neither the woman without the man in the Lord."*

Samuel controlled the unruly smile that formed on his lips and narrowed his eyes at Burke. "I dislike nothing so much as when you use my own calling against me. A constable shouldn't know scripture nearly as well as you do."

Burke shrugged. "Someone has to reprimand the reprimander."

Samuel reared back. "You refer to me? *I* am the reprimander?"

Burke nodded.

Samuel let his head drop back, chuckling. "Yes, and that *someone* is the bishop."

Burke's brows drew together dramatically, and he shook his head. "Ah, but how often does he come to Rushbury? Not with nearly enough frequency to issue reprimands as often as *you* stand in need of them." He chuckled and put a hand on Samuel's back. "Are you off to Granchurch again?"

"Yes," Samuel said, trying to stifle a sigh. "I will be glad of it once Miss Paige's new companion arrives." Seeing the enigmatic and hopeful expression forming on Burke's face, he rushed to add, "*Only* because, whoever she is, she will be able to take on some of the burden of buoying the woman's spirits. I am running out of scriptures to give comfort to the woman. Miss Baxter's death rattled her considerably." He frowned. "Though she has been relying on me as much for my medical knowledge as for my spiritual knowledge."

Burke set his hat atop his head with a smile. "The trial of having had a doctor for a father, eh?"

Samuel let out a scoffing laugh. "Only in a place like Rushbury would *I* be considered knowledgeable enough to act as a sort of doctor." He shook his head. "Perhaps her new companion will be able to convince her to seek medical wisdom from someone qualified."

He was glad to provide help wherever he could, but he wished that the apothecary who served the area were nearer. Samuel's training and knowledge were both lacking and highly informal, coming as they did from observing and accompanying his father on visits.

"You're a good man, Sam. May Miss Paige's replacement arrive swiftly." Burke opened the gate, wished Samuel good day, and was off toward home down the village lane where his wife was no doubt preparing him a hearty supper.

Samuel watched his friend's form grow smaller and smaller then sighed, turning back toward the parsonage.

The following day, Samuel eyed the grand exterior of Amblethorne Park across its manicured lawns, his eyes scanning the row of tall, white-bordered windows that lined the first floor of the manor. He didn't particularly relish being there. How many times over the course of his life would he be obliged to welcome new tenants or owners to the area? Would Sir Clyde and his wife even attend church? Or would they make Amblethorne the *home* at which they spent only three weeks of the summer?

He scoffed lightly. For better or for worse, Londoners and the gentry seemed unable to withstand the winters of the Yorkshire West Riding. He was frankly surprised to find Sir Clyde here as early as March, even if it was only to transport some of his belongings and get a feel for the place.

Samuel continued up the dirt path toward the front door, where he was admitted by a liveried servant and led to the morning room.

Sir Clyde and his wife glided into the room a few minutes later, Lady Gilmour smiling benevolently upon him as her eyes took in Samuel's serviceable but well cared for clothing. She was young, likely not much older than Samuel's thirty-one years, but she carried herself with the confidence and poise of a well-seasoned matron.

"Mr. Derrick," Sir Clyde said. "Allow me to introduce you to my wife, Lady Gilmour."

She inclined her head regally, and he executed a bow.

Sir Clyde gestured for him to take a seat. "Very kind of you to come visit us here at Amblethorne. I was quite happy to receive your note, for we had been wondering when we would have the opportunity to make the acquaintance of Rushbury's vicar."

Samuel took a seat on the soft, embroidered chair indicated by Sir Clyde. "You are very kind, sir. I hope you don't feel at all neglected—I didn't wish to disturb you while you were arranging things here and settling in."

"Not at all, not at all," Sir Clyde said with a smile. "Though we are very much looking forward to getting better acquainted with the area"— he leaned in toward Samuel with a knowing gaze —"and hopefully making some improvements."

Samuel felt himself stiffen and forced his shoulders to relax.

Sir Clyde leaned back and set a hand on each of his knees. "I was led to understand by the previous owner that Rushbury is somewhat...behind, shall we say, in many areas of advancement."

Samuel cleared his throat, trying valiantly to control the way his fingers clenched against his palms. "Certainly we are not like London, Sir Clyde, but I have often found that to be to our credit rather than to our detriment."

"Ah, yes," said Lady Gilmour with a sugary sweet smile. "There are certainly advantages to life in the nether regions of the country, I imagine. But"— she inclined her head — "some matters must be addressed. We are fortunate to have someone as obviously capable as yourself serving as vicar, so we need not concern ourselves with *that* responsibility."

Samuel frowned. "Am I to understand that you have purchased the advowson of Rushbury along with Amblethorne Park?"

She nodded enthusiastically as the tea tray arrived, which she began preparing with her fluid, graceful movements. "Yes. Mr. Corbyn was very loath to part with it, was he not, Sir Clyde? But as we know the bishop very well indeed, he was...*persuaded.*"

Though Amblethorne Park had passed through many hands during Samuel's life, the advowson had always remained with the same man who, though he preferred not to keep Amblethorne Park itself, seemed to care for the fate of Rushbury enough to preserve control over the living. Samuel had no rational reason to fear the Gilmours. He was already installed in the living, and only the bishop could change that. But if the Gilmours had managed to persuade—Samuel didn't at all like Lady Gilmour's intonation as she had said the word—the bishop into making the purchase of the advowson possible, might they not find a way to oust Samuel if they didn't like his way of running the parish?

"Matters of safety, too, must be attended to, such as the appointing of a constable."

Samuel laughed, but it sounded nervous even to him. "Thankfully we have a very able man who holds that position—Mr. Michael Burke."

Lady Gilmour again smiled her overly sweet smile. "I think you will understand that we would like to meet the man who plays such a significant role in preserving the safety of us all."

Samuel's throat constricted, but he nodded. "Of course." The threat implied in her words was that, if Burke did not meet their expectations, he would be replaced.

"In any case," Sir Clyde said, "we hope to bring Rushbury into the new century and grow it into the great hub of activity it deserves to be, for it has wonderful potential, I am sure you will agree."

Nausea filled Samuel's stomach and, to keep his mouth occupied, he took a large gulp of tea, which he found to have the same cloying factor that he found in Lady Gilmour's demeanor.

She and her husband clearly intended to take the reins in Rushbury and exercise their influence to the fullest extent possible—and certainly not with any regard for how the community had been doing things for decades. The only hope Samuel had was that the Gilmours would spend too little time in the village to do as much damage as they seemed intent upon doing. Or that they would find life in Yorkshire not at all to their taste and let Amblethorne Park to tenants.

"Well," Samuel said, trying to keep his tone cordial and light as he stood and smiled, "I do not wish to keep you from the myriad of things you no doubt have to do. I merely wished to make myself known to you and welcome you to Rushbury."

The Gilmours rose with him. "We are delighted to make your acquaintance, Mr. Derrick."

He bowed, and Sir Clyde saw him to the front door, with Samuel only half-listening to the polite small-talk as he accompanied him.

His pace as he returned to the parsonage was brisk, his brows drawn together, and his eyes on the ground. He had spoken the day before of the eventful spring they were likely to have with so many newcomers among them, but he had hardly realized how true his words were likely to be.

"And what's got you in a brown study today?"

Samuel looked up and halted in his tracks, confronted with Burke. He sighed. "I've just come from Amblethorne."

Burke nodded his understanding and began walking next to him. "I take it Sir Clyde is not the type of person you were hoping he would be?"

"No, nor the type of person *you* were hoping for."

Burke's brow puzzled, and his head tilted to the side in a question as they came upon the gate to the garden.

"If they don't take to you and your approach," Samuel said, "I fear they will have no compunction at all in replacing you with someone they *do* like—an outsider, no doubt." He shook his head and sighed.

Burke entered the garden gate, folding his arms and staring at the ground. He brought up a hand to rub his chin.

"I had the distinct impression," said Samuel, "that their good humor extends only to those who do not cross them."

CHAPTER 3

For a journey that promised to change Georgiana's life in almost every respect, the first three-quarters of it were surprisingly dull. Nothing of account happened between London and Rotherham, and there was only so much conversation to be had with her father when he was constantly nodding off to sleep between every change of horses.

Her mother had been very concerned that she employ a maid immediately upon arrival at Granchurch, but Georgiana had every intention of taking her time. If the village of Rushbury was as rural as she had been led to believe, there could be no reason to hurry. Perhaps she would even find that the cost was unnecessary.

When she and her father parted ways at The Crown in Rotherham, she watched the sad light that gleamed in his misty eyes and felt the reluctance in her father's arms as they pulled away from their embrace.

He sniffed and blinked rapidly, putting a finger behind his glasses to rub at his eyes. "I know, Georgie, that your life has not taken the path that you or I had perhaps anticipated it would, but I want you to know that a part of my heart has been grateful that you have not yet married." He smiled pathetically and put a gloved hand to her cheek. "It has meant that I have had more time with you myself, and I cannot find it in me to regret that."

Georgiana emitted a tearful laugh and pulled him in for another embrace. "Nor I."

"Give Sara my love," he said, planting a kiss on her cheek and pulling away. "I know you will take care of her."

He helped her into the post-chaise, where Jane sat waiting. One of the side pockets inside bulged at the bottom, heavy with the weight of the pistol Georgiana had promised her mother she knew how to use.

The chaise pulled away from The Crown and onto the lane north toward York.

Jane was an easy companion, following Georgiana's lead in conversation and silence, and the first two stages of the day passed without incident.

Turning north at Rastrick, though, brought them onto roads so choppy that Georgiana and Jane were both required to stabilize themselves using the sides of the carriage to keep from sliding all about.

Five miles after the last change of horses, a deafening blast sounded, and the carriage came to a halt.

Georgiana shared wide-eyed glances with Jane as a loud voice sounded.

"Hand over the gee-gaws!" Footsteps approached the chaise, and Georgiana slid over on the seat toward the side pocket, pulling out the cold, hard metal handle of Archie's spare pistol with trembling hands.

The door to the chaise opened—less violently than Georgiana had expected it to—and a man whose face was covered and whose hat was pulled down deep onto his forehead peered in. His hat tugged upward with his eyebrows as his gaze settled on the occupants inside the chaise. Apparently he was not accustomed to finding two women alone in such equipages.

Jane cowered, curled up in the very corner, with her legs pulled up onto the seat, an arm pulled up to her chin, and the other arm extended with Georgiana's reticule in hand. No wonder Mama had been hesitant to allow Georgiana to finish the journey with no one but Jane for company.

But Georgiana was not going to allow some ruffian to send her into the wilds of Yorkshire without her reticule or, if Jane had her way, likely all of Georgiana's most valuable possessions.

Forcing her hands to remain steady, she leveled the pistol at the man. "I assure you that I *will* pull this trigger if you so much as flinch."

The man's eyes widened and his hand drew back from the outstretched reticule as he moved his head back out of the chaise.

"I am a very fine shot," she said, perjuring herself as she forced away thoughts of her questionably fruitful lessons with Archie last summer. "But you may put my words to the test if you wish."

The man swallowed, his eyes crossing slightly as he stared at the pistol barrel she pushed closer toward him.

"If I'd've known it were two ladies, ma'am," he said, backing up more, "I wouldn't've...." He swallowed again.

She didn't believe him for a second. If she hadn't been pointing a pistol at him, she believed he would have gladly run off with everything he could manage to hold in his arms. And his calling her "ma'am" stoked her temper dangerously.

"Go," she said, pleased with how stable her voice sounded. "You have ten seconds before I shoot this pistol."

He stepped back and turned, moving out of sight. A moment later, a clucking noise sounded, followed by galloping hooves, the sound of which grew more faint with every passing second.

Georgiana's hands shook as she laid the pistol down on the seat beside her, shutting her eyes to compose herself.

A sob sounded, and Jane crumpled in half, sobbing into her hands.

"It's all right, Jane," Georgiana said, unable to prevent the clipped quality to her voice. She moved to sit beside the maid and laid a comforting hand on her back.

The postilion appeared at the door, looking very flustered. He looked little more than a youth, no doubt new to his position, and his throat bobbed. "Are you well?"

Georgiana bit her tongue to keep from asking why in heaven's name he hadn't used the blunderbuss in his possession. "Yes, thankfully my brother had the forethought to send his pistol with me—" she nodded her head toward it "—or else I think we must have been quite done up."

The postilion nodded, swallowing again so that the lump in his throat dipped behind his cravat and then reemerged. "Beggin' your pardon, miss, but the blunderbuss jammed when I pulled the trigger—" he held up the offending article in his hand, and Georgiana reared away from the open end, which pointed toward her and Jane in the postilion's careless hand "—and then, before I knew what was happening, there was a man pointing his own pistol at me so that I hadn't a moment to check what might have kept it from working."

Georgiana took in a breath and manufactured an understanding smile. He was clearly shaken up by the encounter, and taking out her fears and frustrations on him would do no good at all. "I am sure none of us anticipated such a thing to happen. But we are all safe, and that is what matters. Please forge on. I would like to arrive at Granchurch before dinner if at all possible."

He nodded and bowed deeply, shutting the chaise door firmly.

Jane had composed herself somewhat, but her body convulsed with a large, irrepressible sniff every few seconds.

Georgiana didn't know whether to comfort her or wring her

neck. Where would they be if Georgiana had been as poor-spirited as her maid had been?

The bumpiness of the road did nothing to assuage her temper, and the worst of it was that she knew that she had only herself to blame, so confident had she been that the journey would occur without hiccups.

The roughness of the current road gave way to one worse—impossible though it had seemed to Georgiana that any track of road could be more neglected. Her only consolation as she jostled to and fro, unable to anticipate the movements of the chaise, was that they were within a couple miles of Granchurch House. The end was in sight, and not a moment too soon, for she didn't know how she could abide much more of such a rough journey.

A particularly large and unexpected dip sent Georgiana off her seat, her head hitting the carriage roof, crushing her bonnet. The jolt was accompanied by a creak and then the unmistakable sound of splintering wood. The chaise tipped precariously before toppling over. Georgiana and Jane collided against the side, smashed up against the window, with the door above them.

Georgiana was not the type to utter cursings, but she had to bite her tongue in this one instance, as she tried to hold herself in a way that prevented her crushing Jane.

The door opened above them, and the postilion's pallid face appeared. A bit of the color returned when he saw both women conscious inside the chaise, but he gave another large swallow, and Georgiana was sure that the skin covering the large knob in his throat would begin to chafe against his cravat if he insisted on doing so any more.

"I…I…the road…it—"

Georgiana reached a hand up to him, keeping a tight rein on her temper. "Never mind that. It is an atrocious road and certainly not your fault that whoever runs this parish has no care at all for the poor souls required to travel upon it."

He assisted her and then Jane up through the door, where the three of them surveyed the damage to the chaise.

Georgiana grimaced at the sight of the snapped wheel. One of the spokes jutted out awkwardly, broken as it was near the inner hub. Her eyes moved to the valises and portmanteaux, some of which had managed to stay in the box behind the chaise, others which had tumbled onto the road where clouds of dirt were still settling. She put a hand to her temple and shut her eyes, taking in a large breath before speaking. Perhaps Daphne and Archie had been right. This had been a huge mistake.

"How far are we from Rushbury, sir?" she asked the postilion, who was surveying the damage with the most pitiable fear in his eyes. "Sir?"

He tore his eyes away from the carriage. "I believe it is but a half mile or so, though I have never been there."

"There is nothing for it, I fear," she said on a resigned sigh. "We must walk the remaining distance to Granchurch House, though you"—she looked to the postilion—"will need to go to the village to find the nearest wheelwright."

He nodded.

"We must all carry as much as we can manage, for it is quite clear"—her nostrils flared—"that we cannot trust anyone who might come upon this wreckage to be the decent sort of people who would leave the things be."

The postilion took up the largest of the valises, and Georgiana selected one of the mid-sized portmanteaux to carry in one hand and a larger one for the other hand—both containing articles of clothing and other items she had no wish to part with.

Perhaps Archie had been right when he told her she was not provincial enough for Yorkshire. She certainly hadn't packed as though she were, and she was already coming to regret it. But as the alternative was to leave her belongings to whatever dubious figures frequented such an excuse for a road, she steeled herself to the prospect of carrying the heavy bags the remaining distance to Granchurch.

Georgiana found herself repenting of her ingratitude for the ride in the chaise. However bumpy and uncomfortable it had been, surely it was much better than trudging the distance as they were now obliged to do.

CHAPTER 4

Samuel sat on the edge of the chair next to Miss Sara Paige's large, four-poster bed. She wore a cap to cover her gray hair, and she coughed into her hand.

"I do think that you would benefit from a bit of mild exercise, Miss Paige—a gentle, short walk outside, even."

Miss Paige looked toward the window, a glint of sadness in her blue eyes. "It will seem silly to you, no doubt, but I cannot help thinking of Matilda. She was recovering—I am sure of it—until she ventured outside for such a walk, and it was but a week later that...."

Samuel grimaced and nodded. He doubted Miss Baxter's death was related to her venturing outside—he suspected that it had more to do with the medieval practices of the apothecary who attended her—but he was too kind to say such a thing. Miss Paige was no hypochondriac, but he suspected that her cousin's death had made her feel much more vulnerable than usual, and she had plenty of time to dwell on such thoughts now that she had no companion to direct them elsewhere.

"I hope you may get some good rest this evening," he said, rising from his chair. "May I return tomorrow? To ensure that your cough is not worsening?"Another visit to Granchurch

House was the last thing he wanted to be doing on a day as busy as the morrow promised to be, but he couldn't help feeling compassion for the woman.

"Though I must remind you that I am no doctor—just a vicar who happens to have a bit of knowledge of such things. If you are truly concerned for your health, I think it behooves us to have the apothecary sent for."

She waved a dismissive hand. "A bumpkin with no knowledge at all of what makes people ill or well."

He chuckled softly. He couldn't argue with her assessment. Mr. Wilson was decades behind in his care, and his brusque manner did little to endear him to those under his care.

He set his hat atop his head. "Well, I shall hope you are feeling better tomorrow. I cannot allow you to be ill for much longer. I am counting on you to assist me in welcoming the newest residents of Amblethorne to Rushbury."

A gentle knock sounded on the half-open door of Miss Paige's bedchamber.

A footman stepped into the room. "A Miss Georgiana Paige has arrived from London, ma'am."

Miss Paige's expression brightened, and she instructed the footman to have her sent up.

"I will leave you to your…" Samuel paused.

"Niece. My brother's daughter," Miss Paige replied.

"I will leave you to your niece, Miss Paige."

"Thank you kindly. You are the very best of vicars. And doctors."

He bowed and turned to leave.

He let out a gush of air through his nose as he strode down the hall. The arrival of Miss Paige's niece was very fortunate—it was nearing dinnertime, and he could eat an ox.

"It is just up this way, miss." The voice of the footman sailed up the stairs, and Samuel, pausing at the top, glanced at the woman following behind the servant, though she was mostly concealed by the footman's form.

The newcomer was here. The new Miss Baxter.

Samuel's curiosity warred for a moment with his desire to avoid interaction with strangers, particularly those from London —indeed, how long would this one last in Rushbury?

But his curiosity won out in the end. He needed to know how this woman would shift the balances of the village. Would she keep to herself, as the old Miss Baxter had done? He certainly hoped so—he hardly needed any more to worry about than the Gilmours had given him.

The footman and the woman approached the top of the stairs, her hands empty while his were laden with a valise and two portmanteaux. Samuel noted two more valises at the base of the stairs.

He nodded at the footman. "Hello, Andrew."

Andrew smiled back and bowed deferentially.

"How is your mother?" Samuel asked. Her gout was always worst in the spring.

Andrew grimaced. "On the mend, we hope, though she still cannot walk without great pain." His eyes shifted as if he remembered the woman behind him.

"Can I assist with your other belongings, ma'am?" Samuel asked.

The footman paused and glanced behind him. The woman moved so that she could see Samuel, and his eyebrows went up at the sight before him.

She was no *ma'am*. She was young—indeed, certainly younger than thirty—and even taking into account her brown hair which was both crushed and frazzled, there was something about her he found alluring. He was no judge of the latest fashions, but he had little difficulty concluding that her traveling dress—dusty and wrinkled as it was—was of the first stare. She was no great beauty, and he puzzled for a moment over what it was about her that he liked.

There was a hard set to her jaw, her face was red, and her hairline looked to be damp, a strange thing indeed given the cool March air.

She donned a very manufactured smile. "That is very kind of you, sir. I would carry them myself, you see, but I confess that I am a bit fatigued from having done so for the past mile and more." There was a decided bite to her voice.

"Good heavens," he said. "Did your coachman mistake the address? Or did you ride the Mail to the village?" He could hardly believe either of his own suggestions, though, for only the silliest of coachmen could make such a mistake in an area as sparsely inhabited as this, and it was far less than a mile to the village from Granchurch. Perhaps the woman was simply exaggerating. She would not be the first woman to do so, by any means.

She certainly did *not* look like she belonged on the Mail, though.

"No," she said. "The fault, I'm afraid, lies entirely with these things you in Yorkshire apparently call *roads* but which bear greater resemblance to a war zone."

Samuel blinked twice. "Have you *been* to a war zone?" Samuel couldn't help but ask the question. He didn't know whether to be amused or exasperated by the woman before him.

She only narrowed her eyes irritably in response to his question, but he could have sworn that the slightest twitch trembled at the corner of her mouth, producing in him the strangest desire to make her laugh.

But it appeared that she had not yet finished her tirade.

"I don't know what type of equipages you manage to build here in Rushbury—" her voice dripped with sarcasm "—but the post-chaise I hired in Rotherham was clearly not of the required caliber, as its wheels failed to withstand the crater-sized holes in the road."

Samuel's desire to laugh began to dissipate. It was clear that the woman was laboring under a great sense of abuse, but he hardly cared to hear Rushbury and its surroundings disparaged by yet another Londoner. The woman had no idea what she was talking about, no idea how difficult it was to maintain roads with the variable weather they received in their corner of Yorkshire—and deprived of a surveyor to take on the enormous task of their upkeep in hand.

"I am sorry you were put to such trouble, miss," he said, noting the way her eyes sparkled in anger and looking away. She was one of those uncommon people who managed to look even more captivating when animated by such strong emotion. "I imagine that you will accustom yourself to it after a short time here."

She scoffed, brushing harshly at some dirt on her sleeve. "And, pray, just how many carriages shall I be required to keep on hand to ensure I always have a working one? I imagine your wheelwright must live very high indeed for all the business he has. I had heard that Rushbury was very rural—provincial, even—but one can hardly wonder at this, I think, for what people can be expected to frequent the place when the roads are in such a state?"

Samuel's smile, already devoid of humor, disappeared entirely. Who in the world did she think she was to say such things? "Perhaps you might simply consider going at a slower pace? Whatever pressing need you felt to make a timely and grand entrance to each ball in London, I assure you that no one here will be put out if you arrive belatedly—or not at all."

He clenched his jaw, busying himself with stepping down the stairs to take the valises in hand, torn between horror at what he had just said and satisfaction that he had momentarily bereft the woman of speech. She was obviously not the type that could be expected to adapt to Rushbury's ways—she was making it very clear that she expected Rushbury to conform to *her* standards.

But Samuel would not let her do so without a fight. In his experience, people like the woman before him were all-too-ready to air their grievances but hardly ever willing to take any real action to address them.

"Well," she finally said, "I shall certainly bear that in mind the next time I consider risking my life by going out."

"It is apparent that your feelings on the matter are strong indeed. If you wish to channel your indignation at our provincial ways"— he tried to match her sarcastic tone —"into a more practical avenue, you could attend the vestry meeting on Thursday where we will be discussing such matters. Or perhaps you prefer to simply air your grievances at every opportunity—and to every stranger you meet."

She blinked as though he had thrown something in her face, and he knew a moment's guilt.

But she raised her chin defiantly. "No, indeed. Perhaps I *shall* attend."

"Very good," said Samuel, confident that she would do no such thing. They held one another's eyes for a long moment, neither willing to be the first to break the challenge implicit in the action, until the footman cleared his throat.

"Shall I convey these to your bedchamber?"

Samuel thought he saw her mouth twitch as if suppressing a smile, but he must have imagined it, as her face remained as stony as ever, softening only the slightest bit as she nodded to Andrew—who hung back from them uncomfortably—and thanked Samuel in an icy voice.

Andrew continued up the stairs, and Samuel couldn't blame the young man for being anxious to beat a hasty retreat.

. . .

Miss Paige reached for the valises in Samuel's hands, and he instinctively pulled away from her.

Her brows shot up, and she stared at him in disbelief.

Realizing that it appeared strange indeed for him to keep Miss Paige from her own valises, he cleared his throat. "I am more than happy to follow Andrew and leave them in your bedchamber."

She put out an expectant hand for one of the valises. "Thank you, but no. You will forgive me, I hope, but I find it difficult to trust anyone with my belongings after today's experiences."

He chuckled dryly. "You cannot trust me to carry your belongings because your carriage met with an accident? I assure you, I shall take every care not to throw them about between here and your bedchamber. Our ways may be provincial here, but we are not barbarians."

"The carriage accident is hardly the reason for my distrust."

"Then what *is* the reason for it?"

"It needn't concern you," she said. "I assure you I shan't *air my grievances* to you anymore—nor trouble you to take my belongings." She reached for the valises again.

My, but she was stubborn. He could hardly do anything but relent, given the circumstances, and he returned her things to her wordlessly.

She winced as one of the valises bumped against her leg. Setting it down for a moment, she reached into the pocket of her traveling dress, pulling out a pistol.

Samuel drew back. "Good heavens!"

She narrowed her eyes, checking the pistol to ensure it wasn't cocked, then glancing up at him. "What? I shan't shoot you, if that's what you're worried about."

He gave a wry chuckle. "I thank you." It was all he could do not to inquire about the thing, but he had the feeling that it would only provoke her ire further—indeed, *everything* seemed to do so.

She bent down, opening up the valise and setting the pistol within. Rising to her feet, she dipped her head. "I thank you, Mr...?"

"Derrick," he said with a bow. "Samuel Derrick. I hope you will give Rushbury a chance to alter your opinion of us."

"I fear that would be quite a feat at this point."

She was captivating, even in her derision, confound her.

He smiled tightly. "We shall try, nevertheless. I think you will find that there isn't a better place nor a better set of people in the world—if you have eyes to recognize it." He bowed and turned to go, looking over his shoulder to say, "I shall see you in the vestry on Thursday, Miss Paige. Four o'clock."

He wasn't sure whether he hoped that she would prove him wrong by attending or prove him right by missing it.

CHAPTER 5

Georgiana shut the door to her bedchamber, pausing for a moment to take a breath. She shut her eyes in consternation.

Certainly the last fifteen minutes had not been her finest—and not exactly the first impression she had hoped for with the people of Rushbury village. She had fully intended to seek out her room once she arrived at Granchurch House, a private space where she could exhaust her anger by yelling into a pillow or scribbling an irate letter to whatever imaginary soul she could blame for both of the unfortunate events she had met with in the last miles of her journey. She had even given orders for Jane to rest before coming to help with the unpacking of Georgiana's things.

Instead, she had been met with the very last thing she wished to see: a man of marriageable age. And a strikingly handsome one, at that, with his defined, dramatic brow line and the uncommon stubble that lined his jaw. And that hint of a Yorkshire accent? She found that she rather liked it. But no sooner had the sight of him fanned the flames of her irritation and suppressed anger than she realized that he was very likely already married.

For whatever reason, this thought had *not* improved her mood. Such a perfect storm had resulted in Georgiana losing her hold on her temper, finding Mr. Derrick its object.

She let out a little groan as she remembered some of the things she had said and how disagreeable she had been.

In London, she might simply hope that she and Mr. Derrick would never cross paths again, but she'd had a glimpse of the village as they passed by its crossroad on the way to Granchurch House, and she was far too realistic to believe that avoiding *anyone* would be a possibility in such a small place. Much smaller than she had anticipated, in fact.

When Archie and others had referred to the rural quality of Rushbury, she had been imagining a place more like Rotherham: a fraction of the size of London, certainly, but with a selection of shops and a number of inns. Rushbury was not even near that, though. She had noted only one road running through it. She hoped that, when she had a chance to walk its length, she would perhaps find a few streets branching off from the main road, perhaps with a haberdasher or a linen draper.

Granchurch House at least was a very respectable estate, with its four small, crenulated turrets and dirt-darkened cream façade. Aunt Sara was well enough off that she could afford a decent-sized estate, as Granchurch looked to be.

Even if she *had* been able to avoid Mr. Derrick, she was conscious of a sense of relief that such a course was not open to her. She *did* hope to see him again, and she decided to ascribe this strange feeling to a very natural desire to ensure that she was not thought badly of. Well, if she attended this vestry meeting—whatever that was—she would have the chance to redeem herself, perhaps. Now it only remained to discover what a vestry meeting was. She had heard the term before, but she hadn't the faintest idea what occurred at such a meeting or what she might accomplish by attending.

Georgiana turned to the small mirror on the wall and stifled a yelp. Her hands rushed to calm the mess—her hair was matted down in places from her bonnet while in others, clumps jutted out at strange angles.

She shut her eyes. No, she had certainly not presented her best side to Mr. Derrick. All the anger and frustration she had been storing inside, unable to unleash it upon Jane or the postilion, had erupted upon hearing him refer to her as *ma'am*.

She knew it was silly to take offense at such a thing—had she not teased Daphne about her own status as a spinster just a week ago?—but once her temper had flared up, she had found the words spewing forth. She might have been able to shift course after the initial eruption but for Mr. Derrick's unhelpful responses, teasing her about the war zone she had compared Yorkshire to and then provoking her into agreeing to attend the vestry meeting of all things.

This was not a promising beginning to her new life.

Finishing repairs to her hair and attire as best she could, she let out a determined breath and went to seek out her aunt, wondering with a grumbling stomach when she might find dinner—and horrified at the sudden thought that she might have missed it. How early *did* people dine in Yorkshire?

She found her aunt lying abed, dressed in a vibrant dressing gown of puce with turquoise flowers and a lace cap atop her head.

"My dear Georgiana!" she said, putting her arms out in invitation for an embrace.

Georgiana leaned over the bed to submit to it, and found that her aunt smelled strongly of lavender.

"You have come!" Aunt Sara said, patting the bed beside her.

Georgiana sat down.

"I am sorry to welcome you in my bed of all places," Aunt Sara said. "I have come down with a small cold. I trust you had an agreeable journey?"

Georgiana hesitated a moment, and then nodded her head

with the brightest smile she could muster, shooing away the image of the cracked wheel and the dark cloth pulled over the highwayman's face. She needn't trouble her aunt with such things. Her father had presented a picture of Aunt Sara that was very fragile. "I am *very* glad indeed to be here at Granchurch House with you rather than on the road, though." That at least was true. "How are you, Aunt Sara? I was so very sorry to hear of Miss Baxter's death."

Aunt Sara's chin trembled, and she attempted a smile. "It was a great blow, and I find it has affected me in no small way. But I am very glad for your company, my dear. I hope you will feel at home at Granchurch and in Rushbury."

Georgiana smiled, wondering how likely such a thing was. The contrast of London to Rushbury could hardly have been more stark, and she found the relative silence of Granchurch strange. No muffled sound of rumbling carriage wheels or raised voices of coachmen and street traders came through the walls of Granchurch. Georgiana had certainly spent time in the Paige's country estate, but as it was only twelve miles outside of London and but half a mile from a good-sized town, it couldn't really be compared.

Besides, the great majority of her time had been spent between London, Bath, and Brighton—it would certainly be a new experience to stay for an extended period in a place like Rushbury.

"We shall be quite cozy here when Rachel arrives," Aunt Sara said, smoothing her bed linens with a content smile.

"Rachel?" She knew a moment of misgiving. Had Aunt Sara gone to the trouble of hiring a maid for Georgiana already?

"Rachel," Aunt Sara said, as if that might clarify things for Georgiana. "She is the widow of my cousin John—he died just a few days after Matilda." She sighed but then brightened. "In any case, she has agreed to come live at Granchurch. I wrote to her when I heard the news of John's death. But I thought you knew this!"

Georgiana shook her head slowly

Aunt Sara waved a hand. "Ah, well, the mail is quite slow from here—I imagine your father didn't receive it before you set out. But it is no matter, after all. I am very content to have both of you here." She grasped Georgiana's hand and squeezed it.

Georgiana suddenly felt sheepish. There had been a comfort in knowing that she was going where she would be needed. But not only was Aunt Sara clearly not the needy woman Georgiana's father had made her sound, she already *had* a replacement for Miss Baxter.

She cleared her throat. "When shall she arrive?"

"Oh, not for another month or so. She has to attend to all of John's affairs first."

Georgiana nodded, unsure what to make of the news. At least Aunt Sara hadn't seemed surprised or dismayed to see her. Surely that was something.

"Aunt," she said, suddenly frowning. "Can you tell me something?"

Aunt Sara smiled and waited expectantly.

"Do you know what a vestry meeting is?"

Samuel walked the quarter mile to the vicarage with a deep frown, reviewing again and again his encounter with Miss Paige. He felt the unmistakable pricking of his conscience as he did so—it had been some time since he had lost control of his temper. But the woman had been insufferable. And beneath his anger, he felt fear and worry. How many antagonistic outsiders could they manage in Rushbury?

Whether Miss Paige's sharp tongue was a pillar of her character or merely the result of having passed a bad day of travel, he couldn't be certain. He was determined, though, that either way, she would quickly learn that Rushbury would not change to suit her ideas of what was acceptable. She could adapt to their ways or else take herself off, just as every woman of her sort had in the past.

His jaw tightened as Miss McIntyre's face flitted through his mind. It had been four years—no, almost five—since she had left without a word, and though Samuel hadn't allowed himself to become attached to any of the families that had since moved to Amblethorne, he had watched them each depart with predictable rapidity, inevitably reminding him of her.

Miss Georgiana Paige too would likely leave as quickly as she had come, and so much the better. With any luck, she would remain a stranger.

"I was a stranger, and ye took me in."

Samuel's head whipped around, but there was no one near as he approached the parsonage.

He turned back around and closed his eyes, chuckling softly at himself. It wouldn't be the first time Burke's voice had sounded so loudly in his head that he had thought it real.

The man delighted in hurling scripture at him, and he would certainly push back against Samuel's reluctance to welcome a stranger—and a Londoner—like Miss Paige. Who needed a conscience when they had Michael Burke to keep them in line?

He sighed, pulling the creaky wooden gate toward him and walking up the stone path to the parsonage.

Samuel tugged at a new weed attempting to hide amongst the plants in the garden. It resisted, and he stumbled a bit as the leaves suddenly yielded to his grip.

He scoffed, eying the remaining root with annoyance and pitching the bit he held in his hand over the glebe fence. If only his own plants were as quick to grow and as stubbornly resilient as the weeds. He spotted a few more of them and made a mental note to attend to them later. It was time to head to the vestry meeting, and he didn't want to dirty himself. He just wanted to check on the garden's progress.

He removed his gloves and tossed them beside the glebe gate as footsteps approached.

"Thought I'd come fetch you for the meeting."

Samuel laughed. "Afraid I'd forget?"

Burke only smiled. He made it a habit of walking by the parsonage once a day to talk with Samuel, but he always offered some flimsy excuse—as if Samuel wasn't just as desirous for a bit of friendly companionship.

Burke slipped into the garden, running his eyes along the rows of small sprouts. "I heard Andrew Smith telling his father that Miss Paige's niece has arrived—a Miss Georgiana Paige."

Samuel let out a puff of air from his nose. "Yes, I had the doubtful pleasure of making her acquaintance yesterday." He narrowed his eyes at Burke. "You *knew* she was a young woman, didn't you?"

Burke grinned and nodded. "Miss Paige told me herself a few days ago."

"You could have told me as much."

Burke gripped his shoulder. "Ah, but that would have sapped all the fun out of it!"

Samuel raised his brows significantly. "Fun? There was nothing *fun* about our encounter. A veritable firebrand she is. And I can tell you that we provincial Yorkshire folk have *not* found favor with her."

"Oh dear," Mr. Burke said, a slight chuckle making his shoulders shake. "How have we managed to provoke her ire so soon?"

Samuel's own mouth resisted his attempts to fight off a smile. "She had an eventful arrival. A broken carriage wheel, the blame for which she places squarely on our shoulders and the dismal state of the roads."

"What? And no blame left for whatever fool of a driver failed to slow down?"

Samuel raised his brows significantly.

"She sounds worse than the Gilmours. I retract my suggestion for a match between the two of you and ask your pardon."

Samuel chuckled. "Even had you not, I'm afraid the prospect was doomed from the start, as she has an opinion of me no higher than she has of our village."

Burke clapped him on the back. "Her mistake. Fear not, though. We won't let these Town folk ruin what we have here."

Samuel pointed at the garden dirt, narrowing his eyes in contemplation. "I fear that what I have *here* is being ruined—just as you predicted—by an inordinate number of slugs." He kicked at one with the toe of his boot, but it stuck in place.

Burke squatted down and squinted at the tender leaves, parting a couple of the larger ones with a finger. "Ah. There's one—no, two."

A small black beetle scurried out of the nearest plant, away from the slugs, and Samuel let out a frustrated gush of air, lifting his foot and smashing it.

"Ho!" Burke cried, watching the action with dismay.

Samuel moved his boot and cringed at the remains of the insect. "The garden is overrun with all manner of critters. With every passing year, I become more convinced that I am no gardener and never shall be."

"Well, you certainly won't be if you're forever smashing things!"

Samuel chuckled. "What, you want me to let the slugs and beetles have free rein?"

"Slugs? No! Beetles?" He shrugged. "That depends. If it's like the one you just stepped on, then yes."

Samuel reared back. "Beetles don't belong in my garden,

Burke. I remember your lecture on the subject very well from the first year I attempted to grow anything in this miserable plot of land."

"And I was telling you the truth. *Most* beetles are enemies to these plants of yours. But not him." Burke pointed to the remnants of the critter. "The more you see of him, the less you see of the slugs."

Samuel tilted his head to look up at Burke through narrowed eyes. "How in the world do you come by such obscure facts?"

He gripped Samuel by the shoulder. "They're not obscure when your livelihood depends on them. And now that you've killed your only friend in this garden"—his eyes twinkled —"shall we head to the vestry?"

CHAPTER 6

Georgiana pulled at her lip thoughtfully as she sat in the parlor at Granchurch House. Jane was already on her way back to London on the stagecoach, and Aunt Sara was resting in her room. Apparently she never came down for breakfast, so Georgiana had paid her a visit in the late morning.

She found Aunt Sara to be both amusing and difficult to understand. She was kindness itself, but it was clear that she had no desire for constant companionship.

Unneeded as Georgiana was, she was left to puzzle out the wisdom of attending the vestry meeting she had assured Mr. Derrick she would attend. When Aunt Sara had made it known that Mr. Derrick was the vicar, Georgiana's shame at the way she had treated him and spoken of his parish was compounded.

To be sure, she still found herself at a loss to understand why the village would allow the roads to remain in such a deplorable state, but she was usually not so forward with her criticisms, and it was apparent that the vicar had not appreciated her words. Indeed, how could he have?

Part of her wished to stay indoors and hope to heaven that the vicar would forget her behavior. But she had assured him that she would be in attendance, and she hardly wished to add to his ill opinion of her—and as a result, the ill opinion of the village—by disregarding that promise.

She glanced at the ticking clock on the mantel. She had just enough time to slip on a pelisse and make her way to the church. Perhaps she would even have time for a word with the vicar if she moved quickly—a chance to set at rights his opinion of her. Why she found that to be such a pressing matter, she couldn't say—or preferred not to pursue.

She hurried up the stairs to her bedchamber, chose a crimson pelisse to wear over her pale yellow muslin, and slipped on her bonnet and gloves on her way down the stairs. It would be her first time venturing out of Granchurch House, and she was curious about what she would find in this mysterious village. She had been too agitated on the walk to Granchurch to appreciate her surroundings. Besides, this was an opportunity to revel in precisely the freedom she had been anticipating in coming to Rushbury: a solitary walk.

Granchurch House was set at the top of a narrow lane leading down toward the village, the dirt track up to it flanked on both sides by drystone walls, which were blanketed in most parts by a thick layer of lichen and moss. Georgiana determinedly pushed aside the memory of traipsing up the hill with two heavy portmanteaux in hand—she would give Rushbury a fair chance to charm her.

The gray skies and somber hues of a landscape still struggling to climb out of winter surrounded her. It was a bit dreary, particularly compared to the sunny, blue skies and emerging daisies of London. She chafed her arms and then pulled her pelisse more tightly around her. The cold had much more bite to it here.

It made sense, of course. The descriptions she had heard of Yorkshire were all given by those who had visited during the summertime. March in Yorkshire looked much like January in London and Surrey.

The church came into view, the cemetery covered by a canopy of large, leafless branches from two trees that must have been there for well over a hundred years. A small lane curved around one side of the church. Georgiana squinted to see through the trees and thought she recognized the outline of what must be the parsonage—it was quite a bit larger than Georgiana would have expected in a village as small as Rushbury. Its gray stones perfectly complemented the darker patches of cloud in the skies above.

She followed the lane leading up to the church door, her nerves fluttering in a way they hadn't since her first Season in London. How ironic that it would be the prospect of meeting a small group of rural, working villagers that would strike fear into her heart, when she could have waltzed into the grandest of London balls with complete calm.

She pulled open the door, wincing as its creaking echoed throughout the nave. The church was cold inside, even colder than the outside air, and she walked as quickly and noiselessly as she could in the direction she expected to find the vestry.

A man stepped out from a doorway nestled between a break in the pews, his eyes finding Georgiana and his brows raising slightly. He wore a well-used brown greatcoat with just one cape and a tricorn hat, which he removed as he stepped out into the stone path.

"Good day, miss," he said with a bow. "How may I help you?"

She clasped her gloved hands together, successfully stopping their tendency to tremble, and smiled. "I am looking for the vestry—I understood that the meeting was to begin at four o'clock?"

His jaw opened wordlessly for a moment, as though he didn't know what to make of what she had said.

"Georgiana Paige, sir," she offered, and his eyes widened slightly. "I am newly arrived here and shall be staying with my

Aunt Sara at Granchurch House." She paused. "Do you know her?"

The man chuckled. "Aye, miss. In a place like this, one cannot help but be known, for better or for worse." He took a step toward her and bowed. "The name is Michael Burke. I serve as the constable here in Rushbury. I understand you had a bit of an ordeal arriving."

"Oh dear," she said, untying the ribbons of her bonnet with a self-deprecating laugh. "It is just as I feared. My reputation precedes me—as a difficult, grumbling faultfinder, no doubt."

Mr. Burke shook his head. "Losing a wheel would try anyone's patience, miss."

She smiled at him. "I think I might have borne that well enough if it hadn't been for the encounter before it."

"Encounter?"

"Yes, with a highwayman. But happily, he was no match for my pistol, so it did not end so terribly, after all."

Mr. Burke looked at her, blinking slowly. "You shot the man?"

She gave a little laugh. "No. I think my courage might have failed me if he had persisted enough to require that. I merely pointed it at him."

"Well," Mr. Burke said, looking very much struck, "I think even a saint would be hard put not to grumble after the likes of what you were put through, and I am very sorry for it. Come." He gestured for her to follow him. "Everyone is in the vestry."

Her heart quickened again. Who precisely was *everyone*? She had never attended a vestry meeting before, but she imagined that all of the most important people in the village would be in attendance. And if Mr. Burke's words were any indication, they were already aware at least of the irregularity of her arrival in their village.

She tried to still the silly nerves that made her feet suddenly feel awkward, and she ran a hand down her dress, glad to be holding her bonnet in the other hand, if only for something to keep her hands occupied.

Her eyes had no trouble at all finding Mr. Derrick in the room, for he was the only person unseated. He leaned against the square wooden credens which contained the vestments and hangings and held an account book in his hand, supporting it with one hand and running a finger along one of the pages.

Something about him held her gaze. What was it? Certainly he was handsome—though with his low-set, thick brows and the shadow of stubble around his angular jaw, his attraction was more rugged than Georgiana was wont to admire. But that was not it.

She felt a prickling at the nape of her neck that let her know that she was the center of attention at that moment. Mr. Derrick looked up, at which point not a pair of eyes was directed anywhere but Georgiana's face.

"Everyone, I am pleased to introduce you to Miss Georgiana Paige," said Mr. Burke. "She is the niece of our own Miss Paige and will be staying with her at Granchurch House."

Mr. Derrick stared at her, only one long blink interrupting his focus until Mr. Burke cleared his throat. Mr. Derrick shut the account book with a loud snap, flinching a bit, and strode toward her.

"Miss Paige," he said. "How very pleased I am to see you here."

Georgiana rubbed her lips together, but she couldn't stop a smile. "I somehow find that hard to believe." She kept her voice low.

His lip twitched. "Ah, you must learn not to believe the worst of us here."

"*Touchée,*" she said, taking a seat in the empty chair he indicated.

Mr. Burke shot a mysterious but significant look at Mr.

Derrick, who returned it with the briefest of exasperated expressions before leaning against the sacristy credens again.

"Welcome, friends," he said, his eyes flitting to Georgiana, who resisted shifting in her chair. She did not fall under that umbrella term, and she had a hard time believing that she ever *would* as she looked around at the other faces in the room.

For the first time in her life, she felt uncomfortably conscious of her clothing—that her pelisse and the dress beneath had only been worn a few times, that it was obscenely colorful in a place so uniformly gray and muted as were Rushbury and its people, who were all attired in various shades of brown and gray. It was impossible to tell whether some of the brown she saw was simply the color of the fabric or caused by dirt and much wear.

Everyone chuckled at a comment made by Mr. Derrick, and Georgiana glanced at him, her heart skipping a beat at the unexpected sight of his smile.

The rugged soberness was completely displaced as his mouth stretched into a large grin and his eyes wrinkled at the sides. And she suddenly knew what it was about him that had struck her.

He looked at home— so very comfortable and relaxed, so perfectly meant to be exactly where he was, as if the church and the room would have been incomplete without him.

Georgiana blinked. What strange thoughts to have about someone she knew not at all.

But no. There was no doubt at all how very much he belonged exactly where he was.

A pang of jealousy rang in her heart.

"What of the new folk at Amblethorne?" asked one of the villagers, a tall, lanky man with a dirty face and tousled, sandy hair. "What do ye make of 'em, vicar?"

Mr. Derrick glanced at Mr. Burke, and Georgiana adjusted in

her seat. If she had not been there, no doubt the people would have inquired after *her* as well—if they hadn't already, of course.

"I visited Sir Clyde and Lady Gilmour the other day, though for only a few minutes. I think," he said slowly, "that we will all do well to tread carefully around the Gilmours. They seem to have *plans* and *visions* for Rushbury, and I would not wish for any of you to make an enemy of them."

He was obviously choosing his words carefully.

The low rumble of murmuring sounded. They were clearly nervous at Mr. Derrick's words.

"May they go the way of all the rest who've lived at Amblethorne, then!" said a short, plump woman, swiping at the air with her hand. "Only more quickly. For we don't want 'em!"

Grumbles of assent were uttered by the others, but Mr. Derrick shook his head.

"We must do our best not to alienate them, but rather help them understand the way things are done in Rushbury."

"They won't listen to the likes of us!" said the sandy-haired man. "Gentry morts only care for the opinions of their own kind."

Mr. Derrick's eyes found Georgiana, and she fiddled with the edge of her kid glove. It seemed a very unfair characterization of her fellows, but she could hardly say so here.

"Well, I'm afraid we have no choice but to do our very best to win them over—"

The plump woman scoffed.

"—or *at least,*" Mr. Derrick continued determinedly, "not give them any reason to take us in dislike. Let us move on to other matters, though. I know that Miss Paige had a very particular reason for wishing to attend today's meeting."

Georgiana's head came up, feeling everyone's eyes once again upon her, both curious and wary.

She looked at Mr. Derrick, her nostrils flaring. It was terribly rude of him to put her back at the center of everyone's notice when she was a stranger amongst them—and an unwelcome one, by all appearances.

"Not at all," she said through a smile of clenched teeth, hoping he took the warning in her eyes.

She had the distinct impression that Mr. Derrick was enjoying her discomfiture. Perhaps he felt she deserved it after the way she had treated him yesterday. She had never had as much control over her tongue as she wished, but it had been particularly unruly after the difficult journey. Any remorse she had felt, though, began to dissipate under his treatment of her now.

"Did you not wish to speak to the matter of our roads?" he said with a puzzled brow that looked forced.

She cleared her throat. "I merely thought that the state of the roads might be prioritized as an issue, as it is clear they are in need of repair." She smiled and looked around the room. "I cannot be the only one to have had such thoughts."

Murmurs sounded, punctuated by sidelong glances from the whispering villagers, and warmth seeped into her cheeks. Perhaps she shouldn't have said anything. Surely the villagers didn't believe their roads to be above reproach?

"I believe there was another phrase you used to refer to our roads…what was it?" Mr. Derrick squinted and tapped his fist against his lips.

War zone. She had said the roads near Rushbury resembled more of a war zone than anything. She held his eyes, as if the heat flooding her cheeks might somehow transfer to him and scald him. He would deserve it. If he repeated her words, she might bid farewell to any hope of making a good impression amongst the village.

"Ah, well," he said, brushing the thought away with a careless hand. "I cannot for the life of me remember. But we are all very anxious, nonetheless, to hear whatever you have to say about the improvement of our roads, are we not?" He looked around at the group expectantly, but only Mr. Burke nodded decisively, while the others shifted their gazes from one to another and then back to Georgiana.

She smiled nervously at the villagers.

"No, we are not," said a woman. "She's been here a day and thinks to tell us how to manage our affairs, does she? Just like the Gilmours, no doubt. Just who are any of them to tell us about how things should be done here?" The squat woman with a hand on her hip let her evaluative gaze travel over Georgiana. "Yet another gentry mort trying to bring London where no one wants it."

Georgiana's muscles tensed. She had anticipated that the villagers would need time to thaw to her, but she had not expected outright hostility. Was every village so opposed to newcomers?

Mr. Derrick glanced at Georgiana, and she thought she saw an almost apologetic glint appear in his eyes, as if he had awoken a monster and felt responsible. "Hardly, Mrs. Green. I think that she merely believes the roads could use more tending to."

Mrs. Green laughed, her bosom shaking along with her belly. "And I suppose she's ready to shovel and smooth the dirt herself?" She nodded her head at Georgiana's crimson pelisse.

A few chuckles sounded around the room, and Georgiana glanced down at her clothing. Only for a moment did she consider lashing back. She would not repeat her behavior from the day before. And she could hardly blame the people for laughing. The image of her with a shovel in hand must have been preposterous. "I certainly cannot vouch for my abilities with a shovel" — she smiled sheepishly at the villagers — "but I would like to help in whatever way I can."

Mr. Derrick was watching her with narrowed eyes, the beginnings of a smile pulling at one side of his mouth. He doubted her sincerity—that much was obvious. "In that case," he said, "perhaps you would like to assume the role we need filled since Mr. Wood's departure for Leeds." He looked down at the paper he held in hand. "It is one of our main items of business today."

A disbelieving scoff sounded, and Georgiana turned toward it, finding that it had come from Mr. Burke. "You cannot truly mean to ask a lady to take on the role of surveyor of the highways, Sam."

"Why not?" said Mrs. Green. "She said herself that she would like to be of help, and she wouldn't be the first woman to do so—in Honley parish, Mrs. Peterson did so after the death of *her* husband. And it ain't paid, so it can't offend her *fine* sensibilities." She chuckled, and the woman next to her gave a little snigger.

Georgiana held Mr. Derrick's eyes, and he met them with a smiling challenge in his own. He had certainly put her in a corner. To turn down the role would be to confirm the view he had no doubt taken of her already: a woman of the Town, all too ready to criticize anything that inconvenienced her, but loath to lift a hand herself.

Delight and victory shone from the vicar's eyes, and it struck at Georgiana's contrary side. She *needed* to show him—and the village—that they were wrong about her.

"I should be happy to accept such a position, providing it doesn't interfere too greatly with my role as companion to my aunt," she said, letting her eyes linger on Mr. Derrick for a moment. She turned to the villagers. "That is, if you will have me. I fear you will have to have a great deal of patience, for I am not only new to Rushbury but a great novice when it comes to the administrative and practical concerns involved in maintaining roads."

"Well, as to that, we must all start from somewhere, miss," said Mrs. Green, seeming to thaw a bit toward her.

"True words," chimed in Mr. Burke. "And I'm sure Mr. Derrick will be more than happy to teach you our ways. It is *his* responsibility to choose the surveyor, after all, and no one knows the parish better than he. I shouldn't think your duties will take up much more than two or three hours a week."

Georgiana smiled graciously, putting aside the thought that the only reason she was accepting the role of surveyor—whatever that title entailed—was that *their* ways hardly seemed to be working.

Mr. Derrick cleared his throat, his eyes resting on Mr. Burke for a moment. "Indeed."

It was Georgiana's turn to smile pleasantly at Mr. Derrick. He could hardly have imagined that in his attempt to teach Georgiana a lesson, she would be consigned to his responsibility.

She sat through the rest of the vestry meeting, hands in her lap, listening with interest to the inner workings of the small Yorkshire village. Mr. Derrick seemed to be very skilled as guide of the conversation, and the villagers quite clearly held him in great esteem based on the way they deferred to him when any small conflict arose. Though Georgiana had never been present at any such meeting before, she suspected that this one was accomplished with much less tension or clashing of wills than would be the case elsewhere.

As the group stood to leave, Georgiana found herself next to Mr. Burke.

"Regretting having attended, are you, miss?"

She laughed, gripping her bonnet in her hands as she shook her head. "No, I actually found it quite fascinating to listen in, for I have never attended such a meeting."

"Well, there'll be plenty of opportunity. We hold them more frequently than most parishes. Sam—Mr. Derrick, I mean—believes that the more time between vestry meetings, the more time there is for matters to pile up and get out of hand."

Georgiana's eyes moved to Mr. Derrick as he shook hands, smiling genially, with Mrs. Green. The woman appeared much less intimidating interacting with the vicar than she had when taking stock of Georgiana. Like the vicar, her face transformed when she smiled.

"I imagine he is quite right," Georgiana said. "In any case, it was very kind of you to welcome me when I know nothing at all of the village yet—something I hope to remedy."

The last of the villagers headed for the door, and Mr. Derrick turned toward Mr. Burke and Georgiana.

"Sam," said Mr. Burke, "were you not saying that you were meant to visit Miss Paige's aunt today to see how she was getting along?"

Mr. Derrick glanced at Mr. Burke and then manufactured a smile at Georgiana. "Indeed. I promised her a visit, though it will need to be short—the dinner hour approaches."

"Oh, Aunt Sara will quite understand," Georgiana said. "She wouldn't wish to keep Mrs. Derrick waiting."

Mr. Burke looked to Mr. Derrick and then back to Georgiana, his mouth widening into a grin. He set a hand on the vicar's shoulder and squeezed. "While Sam has the staid and steady disposition that's the mark of a winning husband, there is not as yet a Mrs. Derrick."

Georgiana's heart leapt inside her, and she tried to swat it down immediately. And unsuccessfully. What in the world was happening to her? Rushbury was bringing out the fool within her.

"Thank you for that, Burke," said Mr. Derrick in anything but a gracious tone.

Mr. Burke stared at Mr. Derrick, still grinning and then finally clearing his throat.

Mr. Derrick turned to Georgiana. "May I escort you home, Miss Paige?"

"I imagine the two of you will have plenty of parish matters to discuss," said Mr. Burke. "Sam, could I have a quick word before you leave?"

Mr. Derrick smiled politely at Georgiana and moved with Mr. Burke out into the nave.

Georgiana sighed, unsure how to feel at the prospect of the walk home with Mr. Derrick. She felt a flutter of nerves and an impatient curiosity to hear his reaction to the turn of events.

She hated the recognition of those feelings within her.

They didn't bear considering. Rushbury was the place where she was meant to put the idea of marriage behind her once and for all. She had not come all this way only to fall in love with someone.

CHAPTER 7

Samuel braced himself for an earful as he followed Burke out of the vestry door. The man turned toward him, an accusatory expression on his face.

"What is the subject of today's lecture, Bishop Burke?" Samuel asked.

"Dishonesty." Burke's tone was censuring, but there was a touch of humor in it.

Samuel frowned, nonplussed.

Burke moved in closer, his eyes flitting to the doorway of the vestry. "You failed to mention that the new Miss Baxter was a beautiful young woman."

Samuel scoffed, rubbing at his chin. "My deepest apologies. I wasn't aware that it was relevant."

"So, you agree?" Burke said, smiling mischievously.

"Oh, have done, Burke."

"You made her sound like a miserly old woman, man! When the truth is that Rushbury has never seen the likes of anyone as beautiful as her—saving my Molly, of course. And perhaps Miss McIntyre."

The last words were said with slight hesitation, and Samuel felt his stomach clench. Yes, Miss McIntyre had been undeniably beautiful, and Samuel had allowed himself to be made a fool for that beauty. It had been a hard-won lesson about outsiders, and it was only now, years later, that he felt himself capable of wishing the woman well. She had toyed with his heart, making him believe she would welcome an offer of marriage from him, only to disappear in an instant. It was village gossip that had put Samuel out of his misery, informing him of her sudden match with a baronet in Derbyshire.

"Sorry," Burke said, head dipped in remorse. "Beauty isn't everything, is it? My Molly is one of those rare treasures whose inner beauty eclipses the outer."

Samuel managed a chuckle. Molly Burke was entirely average in her appearance, but Burke truly believed her to be unmatched in every regard. "You certainly married up when you managed to convince Molly to marry you." He raised his brows. "Is that all you wished to say, then. Here *I* was, certain you wished to chastise me for appointing Miss Paige as surveyor."

"I admit that I was opposed to it at first," Burke acknowledged, "but I have changed my mind. I think it a very good idea —one of your better ones."

Samuel twisted his mouth to the side. "Because I shall be obliged to take her in hand?"

Burke grinned widely.

Samuel grasped his friend by the shoulder. "Stick to your constable duties, Burke. You make a wretched matchmaker." He turned back toward the vestry, but Burke grabbed his arm.

His face was sincere, the humorous light gone from his eyes. "You know that she didn't *just* lose a wheel on her journey the other day?"

Samuel shook his head. "What do you mean?"

"The carriage was intercepted by a highwayman."

Samuel's eyes scanned Burke's face, and he thought back on his encounter with her. "So *that's* what the pistol was for."

Burke nodded. "You might extend a bit of compassion her

way, Sam. I can only imagine what it must have been like to receive such a welcome to a new place."

Samuel's conscience squirmed. He had only compounded the inhospitable reception with the things he had said to her.

"And don't take out the past on her. I happen to like her—and I think you do, too."

Samuel felt his cheeks warming and opened his mouth to retort, but Burke talked over him. "One more thing. I've captured three beetles for you to let loose in your garden. But *only* if you promise me you'll be kinder to them than you were to the last one."

Samuel chuckled. "Very well, but in truth, I am not entirely convinced that this isn't some malicious attempt on your part to ruin my garden, Burke."

Burke scoffed. "What, so I can add that hard bit of dirt to my duties farming the glebe? No, thank you."

Samuel smiled. "I will do my best not to step on any of your precious beetles."

Burke nodded approvingly, then pushed him toward the vestry, giving him a look that said, "Go on, now."

Samuel stepped back into the room, putting out a hand to invite Miss Paige to precede him back out into the nave. She certainly *was* handsome—and decidedly more so now that she didn't wear the scowl she had been wearing upon their meeting the day before and now that her hair was coiffed—but that fact was still entirely irrelevant.

Their footsteps echoed loudly in the nave as he followed her out of the church.

"So," he said, closing the door behind him and blinking in the brighter light of the outdoors. "Surveyor Paige." He debated offering her his arm but settled upon clasping his hands behind his back.

She laughed lightly. "Yes, and I am afraid you have no one but yourself to blame for that, Mr. Derrick."

He looked down at the ground, trying not to smile. "I am sure I haven't any idea what you mean."

"Ah," she said, one of her eyebrows creeping up. "I must have been mistaken, but I was convinced that you were trying to teach me a lesson back there."

He frowned and shook his head. "That would have been very presumptuous of me. I can't imagine that you would have any need of a lesson. And certainly not from me."

"Because you believe I think myself above you and your village?"

He raised his brows and put up his hands in a gesture of innocence. "*I* never said such a thing."

She pursed her lips and narrowed her eyes at him, and he couldn't help but grin in response.

"Well," she said, her eyes lingering suspiciously on him, "I meant to have a word with you before the meeting began, but I hadn't any idea just how punctual people were here."

"Used to London manners, no doubt." He was struggling to control his mouth. There was something thoroughly enjoyable about sparring with Miss Paige.

She sent him a playful glare. "Yes, if you must know. But the point is"— she lifted her chin slightly — "I wished to beg your pardon for my behavior yesterday." She glanced at him quickly and then back down to her hands. "I hope you can forgive me for taking out my anger upon you. I had been obliged to hold it in on account of the extraordinarily tender feelings of both my maid and the hired postilion who was present for both mishaps." She looked at him with something between a smile and a grimace. "You just happened to be the first person who looked strong enough to withstand my ire."

He laughed. "I *think* that is meant to be a compliment?"

"Mr. Derrick!" a voice called to them from the seat of an approaching donkey cart.

"John," Samuel said with a wide grin.

The donkey cart pulled up beside them, and the man looked to Miss Paige. Samuel recognized the wary look in his eyes. It was the same look he had seen in everyone's eyes at the vestry meeting— and he had little doubt that Miss Paige recognized it too. She was no fool.

"John, allow me to present you to Miss Georgiana Paige, the niece of Miss Paige. She has come to stay at Granchurch House. Miss Paige, this is John Reed. He is the most talented stockinger in the West Riding."

John nodded briskly. "How do ye do, miss?"

"Very well, I thank you," she said. She shivered slightly and clamped her teeth together with a chattering smile.

Mr. Reed glanced at her gloves and clothing. "Miss ain't dressed for a Yorkshire spring, not with a cotton pelisse and kid gloves."

"Oh dear," she said with a shaky laugh, looking up at the overcast sky. "Is this what I should expect for the next few months? I was rather hoping that you were experiencing an irregular burst of cold temperatures."

Mr. Reed let out a reluctant laugh, and Samuel sent her a look of commiseration. "Yorkshire springs—and particularly those of Rushbury—are late to bloom. But well worth the wait, I assure you. You should let Mr. Reed here make you a few things more suitable to living in the North. A pair of wool gloves, at least."

Mr. Reed opened his mouth—to decline, no doubt—but Samuel directed a significant glance at him, and he clamped his mouth shut.

"Would you?" Miss Paige asked hesitantly. "I would be terribly indebted to you, for I assure you that I am the weakest of creatures when it comes to the cold and in the end shall likely need to be fitted for an entire wardrobe of wool." She chafed at her arms, and Samuel wished he had thought to wear his great coat to offer her. He was far too accustomed to Yorkshire winters to bat an eye at the relative briskness of the end of March.

Mr. Reed nodded. "Come by tomorrow morning, miss. Third house from the end, on the right."

"I shall come," she replied, giving another shiver, "wearing every last article of clothing I possess."

Approaching hoofbeats and carriage wheels sounded, and Mr. Reed tipped his hat at them, tossing the reins and continuing on his way to make way for the equipage.

A well-sprung chaise appeared around the bend, drawn by four sturdy, black horses whose wavy manes flowed with the wind. It was the Gilmours.

Samuel took Miss Paige gently by the arm and guided her to the edge of the road so that they came up against the drystone wall behind. "You have no doubt noticed that our roads are somewhat narrow here."

She tossed him an arch look tempered by the slight smile tugging the corner of her mouth upward. "That was the least of the issues I noticed."

He chuckled. "Touché."

The chaise drew up beside them, and Samuel took in a steadying breath, reminding himself that it was in the entire village's best interest if he could manage to stay on good terms with the Gilmours.

"Mr. Derrick!" called Sir Clyde, his head and arm appearing through the window. "How good to see you again so soon. And who have we here?" He looked at Miss Paige, and Lady Gilmour's head appeared behind him, attempting to see of whom he spoke. A nudge from her resulted in his opening the chaise door, allowing for a greater field of vision.

Mr. Derrick began performing the introductions, but he had gotten no farther than Miss Paige's surname when Lady Gilmour cut in.

"Paige," she said with a wrinkled brow. "Are you any relation of Albert Paige?"

"Yes," Miss Paige replied, "very close in fact. He is my father."

Lady Gilmour covered her mouth with one very elegantly gloved hand. "We are acquainted with your father, you know." She frowned slightly. "But then, where do you fall amongst the children? For I thought that he had only one daughter out in Society, though quite firmly on the shelf, poor thing."

Miss Paige's lips pinched together as pink seeped into her cheeks. She smiled. "*I* am that poor thing, in fact, but the shelf suits me."

Samuel's eyes widened in sympathetic embarrassment on Lady Gilmour's behalf. There was only good humor in Georgiana's voice, but Samuel hadn't missed the way she had shifted her weight before responding, nor the way one of her hands clutched at her skirts.

"Oh!" Lady Gilmour said, blinking. "But you do not look at all as if you have been out for ten Seasons, my dear!"

"Only because I haven't," she replied with an amused smile. "I fear the reports you have heard have been *far* exaggerated, for I have been out a mere *eight* Seasons, my lady."

Samuel's shoulders shook at the look of dismay on Lady Gilmour's face. He might have felt sorry for a woman in Miss Paige's position—indeed it seemed incredible that such a woman would have managed to go so long without being married—only *she* didn't seem terribly bothered by it. She wasn't like any woman he'd ever known.

"Well," said Sir Clyde, stepping into the awkward pause, "you positively *must* come pay us a visit at Amblethorne tomorrow, miss."

"I should be delighted," Miss Paige said.

They moved back onto their seats, shutting the chaise door, and it tumbled forward along the bumpy lane.

Miss Paige let out a sigh as she watched it disappear. "So *those* are the Gilmours."

Samuel smiled down at her and began walking toward Granchurch House. "Yes. Somehow they were even more charming to you than they were to me earlier today."

She tried in vain to suppress a smile. "So very charming that I shall have to think of an excuse to prevent my visit tomorrow."

The lane began to turn up on an incline, the dirt still a deep brown from the rain they had received two days before, and he offered her his arm. The last thing he needed was for Miss Paige to slip on the road on her first day in the village.

"Yes, thank you," she said, taking his arm, "for who knows what type of accident I might have on these Rushbury roads."

How in the world had she known exactly what he was thinking?

"Well," he said, "you now hold the power—nay, the responsibility, even—to address the plethora of faults to be found in these lanes, Surveyor Paige. In the future, when new faces arrive in Rushbury, they will have only *you* to blame for their carriage wheels cracking or their axles breaking. And I," he said, taking in a full breath so that his chest rose, "shall watch in blissful contentment."

She sent him a hostile glare. "And how, pray, am I to fulfill that responsibility? What precisely *are* my powers?"

Samuel tipped his head from side to side. "Well, the surveyor of the highways can levy a rate for the upkeep of the parish roads. He—or in your case, *she*—is also at liberty to require six working days from the villagers each year for the labor required to maintain the roads at an acceptable level or working order."

Miss Paige squeezed his arm, a gesture which caused his heart to trip.

"Well, come now! That is wonderful news indeed!" she said. "No one could mind so terribly if they were asked to pay just a bit more to ensure passable roads."

Samuel smiled at her enthusiasm. "It might seem so, but I am afraid that you will have quite a time of it trying to wring even a farthing from the village. They see nothing wrong with the way things are. They are accustomed to it, you see." He cringed slightly at the downtrodden look on her face. "I admit that I have known a fair bit of guilt since you accepted the position—I never truly imagined you would. And I only suggested it to—"

"To prove a point to me," she said with a knowing expression. "Yes, I was very aware of that."

"I am certain I could find a way for you to be relieved of the position without any fine—particularly given that you are not the typical person to fill the position."

"Thank you," she said. "But I am grateful for the opportunity to prove my mettle."

"And to teach me a lesson in the meantime?" he teased. "I certainly deserve it."

The way she looked up at him with a twinkle acted like a spur to his heart.

"Well, I shan't argue that," she said. She narrowed her eyes in thought. "Perhaps if you and I set out together to persuade them of the benefits?"

He grimaced his doubt.

"Well," she said, her tone still bright but slightly deflated, "if they won't pay, they can still assist with the labor, surely."

Samuel's grimace transformed to one of clenched teeth, and he shrugged. "You are, of course, welcome to do as you please, Surveyor Paige, but I can tell you that on the last occasion that the village was meant to labor on the roads—when Mr. Wood was still here—none but Burke, Mr. Wood, and I put in an appearance."

"How terrible!" Miss Paige said, indignant. "And how very unfair. It seems very shortsighted and selfish for such a close-knit community to serve you so."

Samuel pursed his lips and stopped, turning to Miss Paige, who let her arm drop from his, looking up at him expectantly, though her brow was still wrinkled with displeasure.

"Imagine for a moment, Miss Paige," he said, "that you are required to work six days a week—at the very least—to simply feed your family and put a roof over their heads. That you spend your days laboring in the fields or perhaps using a framework knitter as does Mr. Reed, until your hands are calloused or even bleeding. That even when you return home for the day, the labor is not done, for children must be tended to, dinner must be prepared, and nothing is ever done at home." He paused. "How anxious would *you* be to give up some of that meager income—to risk your children going hungry—so that you could spend a day of back-breaking labor on roads that will undoubtedly have craters and mounds from the rains within a fortnight?"

She stared into his eyes, her forehead drawn down so that two wrinkles appeared above the bridge of her nose. "I see." Her voice was quiet and subdued.

Why did he feel as though he had just kicked a puppy? But it was only the truth he was telling her. It was better for her to know how things worked in Rushbury or else she would be forever disappointed. And for some reason, Samuel didn't want her to be disappointed.

She turned back to the road, reaching absently for his arm, and they continued walking the last bit to Granchurch House.

"Perhaps I can convince the Gilmours to take on the labor," she said, looking up at him with a twinkle in her eye. "Lady Gilmour in particular looks like she would be valuable."

Samuel nodded, unable to suppress a grin. "You can suggest it to them at your visit tomorrow, though I will very much regret being absent for the look on their faces if you do."

She laughed and then looked around at their surroundings. What did she think of Rushbury? Why was it so difficult for outsiders to see its beauty—to see why Samuel couldn't imagine home being anywhere else?

"Everyone at the vestry meeting seemed very concerned about the Gilmours' arrival," Miss Paige said. "Why is that? Apart from Lady Gilmour's *charming* demeanor, I mean. For it was apparent that no one had met them, and yet everyone was anxious."

They arrived at the door to Granchurch House, and Samuel pulled it open for her to pass through. How could he explain to her why the presence of any member of the gentry was looked on as unwelcome by the parish? And how he had regarded her arrival with almost the same dismay as he had the Gilmours'?

They stepped into the entry hall, and Miss Paige undid the buttons on her pelisse, which Samuel assisted her in removing, well paid by the grateful smile she sent him over her shoulder as he did so.

"We have not had particularly good luck with the residents of Amblethorne in the past." He noted the little edge in his own voice, and Miss Paige looked up at him as if she too had remarked it.

He forced a smile. He would leave it at that. She needn't know all of the ways in which the gentry at Amblethorne had affected his personal life. "We as a village are rarely in agreement with them, and unfortunately, they hold a great deal of power over things. The Gilmours look more than ready to wield that power. They spoke to me yesterday of improvements to be made here and of *bringing Rushbury into the current century*."

She rolled her lips together. "Well perhaps we might make them allies instead of enemies with a bit of care."

He smiled wryly.

"What?" she asked. "Is that such a preposterous idea?"

"There is enough of a gap in status and class between us in the village and those who reside at Amblethorne that…." He grimaced and raised up his shoulders.

"But *you* are a gentleman," said Miss Paige. "Surely they feel a kinship with *you* at least?"

He bit his lip. "I am a lowly vicar in a village so small that we could cease to exist without causing inconvenience to almost anyone. I fraternize too freely with those considered below me—indeed, I feel more comfortable and easy with a baker or a lowly farmer than I do with the likes of the Gilmours. I don't dress in the height of fashion, by any means, and I stoop to fulfilling some of the duties of a physician when those services are urgently needed here. It is not precisely a recipe for respect from genteel families."

The footman Andrew approached them, bowing and then looking at Samuel. "Here to see the mistress, Mr. Derrick?"

Samuel nodded, turning back to Miss Paige. "Perhaps we can discuss your duties more soon."

She nodded. "I fear that I will require a fair amount of instruction to understand not only the duties but the *realities* of my role, since there is quite obviously a gap between them."

He nodded with feigned gravity. "It is only natural that you would need more instruction than usual. I will try my best to be patient, as I know how slow to learn you London types can be." His mouth broke into a grin, and he winked at her as her mouth twitched, acknowledging his hit.

"It was a pleasure, Miss Paige." He bowed and followed Andrew toward the stairs.

It *had*, very unexpectedly, been a pleasure.

CHAPTER 8

Georgiana chose a dress for dinner that night that wouldn't require the help of a maid—she didn't wish to deprive Aunt Sara of her maid, and she wanted to test her own limits. But even *that* dress she found difficult to manage on her own, with the ties at the top and waist in the back.

She had looked on the prospect of her new and independent life with great anticipation, certain that she would relish not having a maid to follow her on errands and such. But certainly there were very practical considerations like dressing that required such help.

As she reached her arms back to tie a simple bow at her waist, she looked in the long mirror with an appraising gaze. Lady Gilmour had not believed her old enough to be out ten Seasons, but Georgiana would look the part of a spinster sooner than later, she suspected.

But what of that? No one in Rushbury would care that she was seven-and-twenty. And she would have little occasion to care for anyone's opinion but that of the villagers while she remained at Granchurch House. The thought was liberating in many ways and frightening in other ways. Gaining the good opinion of the village seemed a more difficult cause than she had anticipated.

She smiled sardonically as she thought on the first impression she must have made at the vestry meeting, letting her arms drop and rolling her shoulders to relieve them of the ache occasioned by tying the stubborn bow.

Mr. Derrick had spoken of the effect his interaction with the villagers had upon his reputation with people like the Gilmours. What, then, would they make of Georgiana's new position as surveyor of the highways?

She bit her lip at the thought. It was so absurd as to be comical. Lady Gilmour would be scandalized, no doubt, as would Georgiana's own family—Aunt Sara, too, more than likely. She could keep the knowledge from her family—indeed, there seemed little purpose in telling them about something they would hardly understand—but she could not hide it from Aunt Sara. She would have certain duties associated with the position, and it would be best to ask her aunt whether they would interfere with keeping her aunt company.

She left her bedchamber to seek out her aunt. Perhaps Mr. Derrick would still be with her?

But Mr. Derrick had gone when Aunt Sara's maid opened the door to Georgiana—a fact which caused a slight feeling of disappointment within her. Aunt Sara was dressed and ready for dinner, though.

"I am feeling much more the thing today," Aunt Sara said, sweeping toward the doorway in a fluid motion.

She seemed to have regained her energy—and her appetite too, based on the number of helpings she took from the platter of roast duck and potatoes. She chattered energetically throughout the meal on topics ranging from the weather to the health of the Prince Regent.

It wasn't until the servants were removing the covers and set down a few sweetmeats that Georgiana had the opportunity to broach the subject of her new position in the village.

Aunt Sara stared, hand suspended in the act of reaching for one of the desserts. "Surveyor of the highways!"

Georgiana held her breath. "Do you dislike it terribly?"

Aunt Sara blinked and took one of the bite-sized cakes from the tray. "Dislike it? No. It is not that. It is just...well, I assumed that such a role would be filled by one of the farmers in the village, perhaps? I cannot think that it was meant to be taken up by a young lady of your position."

"No, I imagine not," Georgiana said, tilting her head from side to side. "But it is not as though I shall be required to dirty my hands, you know. And it is not a paid position—merely a way to assist the parish and the county at large by taking in hand a nuisance that people are obliged to confront on a daily basis."

She sat back in her chair and smiled. If Aunt Sara continued so energetically, how much companionship would she stand in need of? It would be good for Georgiana to have something to occupy her and, unlike with needlework or sketching, her time could be spent in benefit to the community.

"Hmm," Aunt Sara said, devouring the last of the cake and reaching for a tart. "You shall have to appear before the Justices, if I am not mistaken, to give an account of the roads in the parish."

Georgiana's jaw opened and then shut. She had not realized that. "Well, I need to speak with Mr. Derrick about the various duties that comprise the position, but I cannot think it would be such a terrible thing for the Justices to be confronted with me rather than a farmer. They might be more likely to take me seriously."

"What, a woman?" Aunt Sara said with a furrowed brow. She shrugged, popped the tart into her mouth, and chewed for a moment. "Well, you are old enough to know your own mind, my dear, so I shan't try to dissuade you from it. But do have a care. I shouldn't wish for your father to be angry with me for allowing such a thing."

"Aunt," said Georgiana with a laugh, "I did not come here for you to be inconvenienced with the role of acting as chaperone to me, you know. I came so that we could act as friends and companions to one another."

"You are very kind, Georgiana," Aunt Sara said, "but I am hardly a fit companion for a young lady like you."

Georgiana opened her mouth to counter her aunt's words, but Aunt Sara plowed on.

"Whatever you may say or think, you are *not* a spinster, my dear. And I hope that you will not feel obligated to stay at Granchurch all day on my account. Someone to talk to at dinner, someone to share in the management of the household, someone to receive visitors with—that is the type of companionship I hope we may provide for one another."

Georgiana smiled and nodded. There was relief at the knowledge that Aunt Sara didn't wish for her constant company, and yet somehow Georgiana found herself a bit somber. Her father had clearly overestimated his sister's fussiness and particularity when it came to a companion. It rather seemed that any woman —young or old—might have provided the type of companionship Aunt Sara was looking for. And Rachel would arrive in a few weeks, making Georgiana even superfluous.

"You mention visits, Aunt Sara," said Georgiana. "I wonder if you might wish to accompany me—if you are feeling well, that is—to visit Sir Clyde and Lady Gilmour tomorrow. They are the new residents at—"

"At Amblethorne, yes," said Aunt Sara, looking full of interest and anticipation.

"They happened upon Mr. Derrick and me as we were

walking back from the vestry meeting, and Lady Gilmour requested a visit tomorrow."

"I will most certainly accompany you," she said, rising from the table decidedly, as if they were set to leave right then. "I have been very curious indeed to know what sort of people would be taking up residence at Amblethorne."

Georgiana woke to a crisp and frosty morning, and while the thought of venturing outside in such cold made her shiver in anticipation, it was precisely to combat such cold that she had agreed to visit Mr. Reed in the village.

She took in a large breath of the warm air inside Granchurch House and then stepped outside, noting how the short blades of grass lining the pebbled drive had frosted tips. She grasped her arms at the elbows and forged ahead.

It was not yet spring, of course, but living in the south had given her a false sense of that season, with its milder weather and early-budding snowdrops, bluebells, and daffodils. She walked along the drystone wall that ran the length of the lane from Granchurch, hoping that the grass that skirted the lane would keep her from slipping in the layer of mud that coated the road. If she had known she was opting to reenter winter in coming to Rushbury, she might have delayed her journey a few weeks.

No. The thought of four more weeks of social engagements did not at all appeal to her. A little cold and a little dreariness—well, a great deal of dreariness—was a price she was willing to pay for more freedom.

She took in a breath of cold air, feeling it fill her lungs and invigorate her. As if to reward her for choosing not to regret her decision, the sight of a patch of unopened daffodils met her eyes. They hung somewhat limp, chilled and lined with frost. Did the sun ever come out in Rushbury to warm such plants and give them a direction to face?

Approaching the third door from the end on the right, Georgiana felt her heart begin to race again. Mr. Reed was a distrustful fellow from what she had seen, and she had the distinct impression that he had not been thrilled to meet her. In fact, no one seemed thrilled at her presence in Rushbury. Of anyone she had met, Mr. Burke had been the most welcoming.

But perhaps the villagers were much like the frozen daffodils she had just seen—in need of a bit of warmth and coaxing to unfurl their petals and show the more inviting side of their natures.

Before setting a hand to the door, she glanced at the window and noted the wide-eyed faces of two little children pressed up against the small pane. She smiled and waved at them before knocking on the door.

It was Mrs. Reed who opened the door to Georgiana. Unlike her husband, she was smiling and kind, inviting Georgiana in with a baby boy on her hip and an apron covered in flour. It was a humble house, simple and small, and Georgiana thought about Mr. Derrick's words—the labor it required to feed the mouths of the Reeds and keep this roof over their heads.

A large framework knitting machine sat on one side of the main room in the house with the kitchen on the other side. A few woolen products—gloves, stockings, and a scarf—lined the window so that passing villagers could see them. Bunches of raw wool sat beside the knitting machine, and the two children who had watched Georgiana from the window stood next to it, their eyes fixed upon her. An older girl who looked to be near the age of Daphne bustled about the kitchen, hands covered in flour and dough, her red hair tied back with a string.

"Come, children," said Mrs. Reed. "Stop your ogling of Miss

Paige and mind the wool. If Papa is going to make something warm for her, the wool must be carded, you know."

Georgiana shifted uncomfortably, feeling slightly embarrassed that it was her need that required the young children to be put to work.

Both of them nodded and obediently picked up the carders on the floor.

"That's Sarah and Jane," said Mrs. Reed. She indicated her older daughter in the kitchen. "And this is Patience."

Patience wiped her hands on her apron and smiled kindly at Georgiana, curtsying prettily. "Pleased to meet you, miss."

Mr. Reed walked in and inclined his head at Georgiana. "Good morning, miss. Very glad I am to see you." His stern face contradicted his words, but Georgiana refused to let that dampen her spirits. Mr. Reed must surely be accustomed to a bright disposition and tone, based on his wife's demeanor, so she needn't adapt her manner to match his.

"It is very kind of you to let me come, Mr. Reed. I feel very foolish for coming to Yorkshire so ill-prepared."

"No matter, miss," he said. "Better that you buy things here than in London. At least *here* you can be sure that they are fit for the climate. We make our products out of only the finest wool. Handmade, just as they should be." The last words came out with an extra dose of harshness.

"John," said Mrs. Reed in a warning voice. She pursed her lips and raised a brow at him. "That'll do."

"Come, Mary. It's only the truth." The arrhythmic sound of wool being carded filled the silence as Mrs. Reed let out a displeased huff and sent an apologetic glance at Georgiana.

"Isn't it, girls?" Mr. Reed asked. The carding stopped. "What do we always say about wool?"

"If done by hand, through time 'twill stand," the children repeated in synchrony.

Mr. Reed nodded proudly. "Right you are."

"Perhaps you can focus your attention on Miss Paige's needs now?" Mrs. Reed said, though a smile played at her lips.

Mr. Reed cleared his throat. "What might we do for you, miss?"

Georgiana smiled, fascinated as she watched the family's interaction. "I hardly know. I think I must surely have a pair of gloves and stockings, for no matter how hot the fire burns in my bedchamber, my toes are always frozen. And"— she glanced at the two girls, who had resumed their carding. She hesitated to make more work for them, but she knew, too, that this was their livelihood. More work meant more money. "I thought of perhaps inquiring whether you could make me a pelisse? I imagine I won't have need of it for too much longer this year, but I should like to be prepared for the next winter."

Mr. Reed's head tipped from side to side. "You *may* not need it much longer this year, but there's no telling. There've been years when we've had snow well into May."

Georgiana's eyes widened. "You terrify me."

Mr. Reed shook his head. "With our wool, you'll be well-equipped for such cold."

She left the Reed home with a pair of brown gloves, a pair of white stockings, and the promise of a wool pelisse, which she imagined would be very much a family endeavor. She had learned that the children were responsible for cleaning and spinning the wool; Mr. Reed was responsible for operating the knitting machine; and Mrs. Reed acted as the clothier to sew the wool together.

She shivered again as she made her way back to Granchurch House, glancing at the full and rolling dark clouds above. Whatever the finished pelisse looked like, Georgiana would certainly think differently of it, knowing the people whose labor had produced it. It made one wonder just whose hands—how young, how old, how calloused—had been involved in making the abundance of clothing she owned.

A few raindrops dropped onto her bonnet, and she sighed, tucking the stockings and gloves under her arm to protect them. If Mr. Reed was to be believed, it was possible that she would be wearing the wool pelisse for weeks to come.

CHAPTER 9

Georgiana held her saucer and teacup on her lap as she sat on the soft blue velvet chaise longue with Aunt Sara.

"We were so very relieved to learn that there was another genteel family in Rushbury," said Lady Gilmour with a hand to her chest and a significant look. "I told Sir Clyde that, if it was just to be us, with naught but a few poor stockingers and farmers to speak to, I would be obliged to leave him here alone within the week, for I positively must have female company, you know."

Georgiana managed a smile, stirring her tea again. It had become clear within a few short minutes of their arrival why the villagers would look askance at the residents of Amblethorne Park. It was not that there was anything to dislike in Lady Gilmour's personality. But she was clearly accustomed to having things done her way, and she and Sir Clyde seemed to be full of ideas about how things should be done in Rushbury.

"I understand what you mean, of course," said Aunt Sara. "My own dear cousin lived with me for nigh on twenty years. When she died a few weeks ago, I realized how terribly I had come to take her presence for granted." She sent a warm glance at Georgiana. "I am very grateful indeed that my niece has come to stay with me, for there is nothing that can compare with female company, as you say."

"Well," said Lady Gilmour, "Sir Clyde and I have every intention of making Rushbury into a place that will attract more people of means and good stock." She held up a hand. "Mark my words! In a short time, the village will be a bustling town, and I imagine we will see a few more estates like Amblethorne rising among us."

Georgiana took a sip of her tea. How would Mr. Derrick feel to know of the Gilmours' aspirations? How would any of the villagers feel, for that matter? She almost asked the question of Lady Gilmour. But to do so might be to antagonize Lady Gilmour, or at least to elicit disdain from her, and Georgiana sensed that it would be wise to wait until they were better acquainted to express any such thing. She stood in a much better position to be an advocate for the village if Lady Gilmour didn't dislike her.

"How very ambitious!" she said. "Rushbury is the smallest village I have ever seen, but the picture you paint would mean a very different place indeed. I am curious how you propose to accomplish such a thing."

Lady Gilmour wagged her eyebrows and then smiled widely. She leaned in toward them. "Our first order of business, and the very thing which takes Sir Clyde away from us at this moment, is to attract more business to the village. We have come to learn how very integral wool is to the area, and Sir Clyde had the inspired idea to purchase a few of the newer machines and install them in the uninhabited house at the end of the village lane in the hopes that, in time, a larger mill might be constructed with a great many machines."

Georgiana sipped her tea determinedly. The Gilmours clearly had a vision of Rushbury becoming more like Leeds than the country village it was. She hardly thought that the villagers would appreciate it.

At the end of their visit, Lady Gilmour saw them to the door with a grand sigh. "Ah, ladies. It has been so wonderful to have your company today. I couldn't have dreamed that I would find such amiable neighbors when we first arrived at Amblethorne. Please don't hesitate to call on me at any time, for I already adore you both."

Georgiana and Aunt Sara stepped out into the crisp afternoon air, turning back toward Lady Gilmour.

"Oh," she said, looking at Georgiana with sudden concern, "I meant to say something, my dear, for I must admit that I was quite shocked to see you walking with Mr. Derrick without even a maid to accompany you."

Lady Gilmour clasped her hands in front of her heavily embroidered dress. "You do have a maid, do you not?"

Georgiana smiled, determined not to betray any of her exasperation at the woman's meddling. Lady Gilmour had no business lecturing her. "In truth, I do not, my lady. One of the maids from home accompanied me on the journey, but I sent her back to my family the morning after I arrived. But given that I am hardly in my first blush of youth and then with the size of a place like Rushbury, I admit that I haven't seen the need for a rush to employ one."

"Oh no, no," Lady Gilmour said, setting a hand upon Georgiana's arm. "That won't do at all. Small village or no—and you have heard my assurances that it won't continue so for long—you *must* employ a maid. One never knows what type of people one may come across in such a poverty-stricken place as this."

Georgiana tried to relax her tensing nerves. Lady Gilmour could hardly be much older than she, besides being a near-stranger, and yet she presumed to insist upon Georgiana's employing a maid. "Thank you very much for your kind concern, Lady Gilmour. I shan't make any promises, for I regard my newfound freedom as somewhat of a treasure, but I shall certainly consider it."

Lady Gilmour looked not at all pleased—and ready to say more—but Aunt Sara stepped in. "I assured Georgiana that I would not meddle in her affairs when she came here, but she knows that she is welcome to the services of any of my servants whenever she needs them."

With that Lady Gilmour had to be content, and Georgiana bid her goodbye with the most affable smile she could muster.

Despite there being only three new residents, the pews in Rushbury's church looked much fuller than usual as Samuel gave the sermon. There was something very satisfying about seeing the entire village in attendance, all wearing the finest clothing they owned, with children fidgeting restlessly and the eyes of the adults turned toward him, ready for some encouragement and inspiration during the very short respite they had from their labors.

His eyes traveled to Miss Paige, and he forced them away for what must have been the tenth time. His gaze seemed to seek her out of its own accord, as if she were the most natural resting place for them.

It was silly.

He couldn't deny that he was intrigued by her, for he found her to be somewhat enigmatic. He thought he had pegged her after their first interaction as an entitled, meddling Londoner.

But then she had come to the vestry meeting. And then he had walked her home.

And he found himself having to adjust—significantly—his opinion of her, for she had made him laugh a number of times, and far from being the dismissive Townswoman he had expected, she had listened to his preachiness about the village with obvious interest and concern. She had clearly been struck by the picture he had painted of what life was like for the villagers, and while she seemed intent upon taking an active role in the village, she also seemed to recognize her ignorance and to wish to address it first.

But Samuel didn't dare trust her. His mistrust of outsiders—and the gentry in particular—was deeply ingrained. The seeds planted by his father had been watered over the years by his subtle, disparaging comments on the subject. And when Samuel had chosen to ignore his father's warnings about the McIntyre family—and Miss McIntyre in particular—he had only gone on to prove them when she left Amblethorne not long after, leaving behind her a trail of implied promises of a future with Samuel.

He had no wish to repeat that experience.

As the villagers conversed with him and with one another after the service had ended, slowly filing out of the church, Samuel found that he seemed to be constantly aware of Miss Paige's location. Would she come speak to him?

It was such a foolish thought—the sort of thing he might have felt and asked when he was a youth.

But whether she intended to speak with him or not, she seemed to be intent upon speaking with the villagers, gaining introductions to each of them through the all-too-willing Burke. She remained in conversation until only she, Burke, Miss Paige, and Samuel remained.

"I shan't be more than a minute, Aunt Sara," he heard Miss Paige say before she approached him.

"Mr. Derrick," she said, coming to stand before him. "Thank you kindly for your sermon. I have the very unwelcome suspicion that it was given with me in mind."

He laughed and turned over the book of sermons in his hand. "Not at all, Miss Paige. In fact, it might surprise you to learn that no less than five people have said something very similar to me today. We all have our struggles."

"Ah," she replied with a smile. "You are simply admirably in touch with the needs of your congregation. Bravo."

Samuel glanced at Burke, who was speaking with the elder Miss Paige, though his eyes traveled frequently to where Samuel and Miss Georgiana Paige stood, an approving glint in them.

"In addition to thanking you for your sermon," she said, "I am come to make a request of you."

"Oh?" His defenses were immediately raised.

"Since you were so instrumental in my appointment as surveyor"— she wagged a paper in front of him —"Burke has just delivered this to formalize my position—I thought you might be willing to take me around the parish and show me the boundaries and all the roads so that I might make an account of the state of the roads. I understand that to be one of my duties?"

He nodded, clasping the book of sermons with both hands at his waist. "It is indeed. And I should be happy to do that." Why did his heart jump at the prospect of spending more time with her? It must be a desire to puzzle her out. "Tomorrow I shall be occupied with a few church matters, but perhaps we could plan for Tuesday."

"Certainly."

"Have you a horse for riding? The parish boundaries are quite wide."

She nodded. "My aunt has a horse I can borrow until I am able to purchase one of my own. Shall we meet in front of the church at one o'clock?"

The matter thus settled, Miss Paige and Miss Georgiana Paige went on their way, leaving Samuel with Burke, whose mouth was arranged in a pleasant smile, his hands clasped behind his back as he watched the two women leave.

He turned to Samuel, who met his smiling face—which was a tad too pointed—with a raising of the brows. Burke said nothing, though, his grin only growing wider.

Samuel tugged at his cassock. "Do stop, Burke. If you are to regard me in such a way every time I have conversation with Miss Paige, I shall have to come up with some work for you—to busy your hands and mind with something of more import."

Burke only continued grinning, and Samuel had no choice but to let out a scoff and make his way to the vestry.

CHAPTER 10

Tuesday dawned slightly warmer than the prior days, and Samuel was secretly pleased, knowing that it would give Miss Paige less reason for complaint about Rushbury and its disagreeable weather. If she could only see the place in the summer, she would understand why Samuel could never leave. There was truly nothing like Rushbury and the West Riding during July and particularly August, when the moors were covered in blankets of purple heather.

Spring, too, was a sight to behold, with the happy yellow of daffodils, the varied colors of tulips, the chorus of chirping birds, and the babbling brooks that dropped in small falls over the myriad of crags in the area.

Just a few more weeks, and spring would show itself in full force in Rushbury. Even now, though, Samuel had hopes that they might see some signs of it outside the village itself. The village sat in a small valley that seemed slower to welcome spring than its environs.

But how he loved that valley.

As he guided his horse from the parsonage toward the front of the church, he found that Miss Paige was before him and waiting atop a pretty bay.

"You are early," he said, glancing at his pocket watch and then slipping it back inside his black coat as his horse came to a halt.

"Well," she said with a mischievous smile, "given the state of the roads, I imagine that we will need every last minute available to us to make an account of the problems which need addressing."

He opened his mouth to retort, but her eyes twinkled at him.

"I shan't be provoked today," he said. "Let us be on our way, though, shall we?"

She opened a bag which was secured to the saddle and pulled out a small, leather book and a short, stubby pencil. "I have come prepared."

They proceeded down the village lane, side by side, slowing to greet the villagers who happened to be out and about, as Samuel explained the history of the parish roads to Georgiana.

The village lane was far and away in the best repair of the parish. Frequented as it was by wagons and the few equipages owned amongst the residents, the dirt was packed down and even enough to support the slow traffic that it hosted.

Samuel stopped near the end of the lane, aware that his name was being called.

"Mr. Derrick," cried John Reed, hurrying toward him at a near-run. He slowed once he realized he had the vicar's attention, coming up to stand beside them. He glanced at the last house on the row and jerked a thumb toward it. "Do *you* know what's happening there? We've been seeing Sir Clyde and another man coming in and out of the house for a few days now."

Samuel frowned. It was the only vacant house in the village, remaining so ever since the departure of Mr. Wood to Leeds. It also happened to be the largest house in the village, but due to the change in owners of Amblethorne Park, nothing had been done to fill it.

"I haven't any idea, I'm afraid," he said, staring at it thoughtfully.

"I might know something," said Miss Paige slowly, her eyes also on the house.

Samuel raised his brows, and she looked at him with an anxious expression.

"I had the opportunity to visit with Lady Gilmour the other day, you know," said Miss Paige, "and she mentioned that she and Sir Clyde have great hopes of turning Rushbury into a thriving center of the wool trade." She glanced down at Mr. Reed, biting her lip. "I believe that Sir Clyde hopes to use this house as the beginnings of what will become a small mill in the future."

Samuel's hand clenched at the reins, and he looked at Mr. Reed, whose face had gone pale and his eyes round.

"A mill?" Mr. Reed's voice cracked, and he cleared his throat.

Miss Paige gave a subdued nod and exhaled through her nose. "They seem to have very grand plans for Rushbury and feel that it is somehow their mission and responsibility to bring it current with the technology available."

Samuel reached down and put a hand on Mr. Reed's shoulder. "Don't worry, John."

"Don't worry?" he said, rearing back. "I can barely feed my family as things stand, let alone the new mouth we shall have come September."

"Mary is with child?" Samuel asked, and Mr. Reed nodded, showing no emotion as he rubbed his chin harshly.

"That is wonderful news indeed, Mr. Reed," Miss Paige said with a smile.

He shook his head, staring back at his house up the lane. "Not if the child will starve."

Samuel shared a quick glance with Miss Paige, and he watched her eyebrows draw together.

"We shall come about, John," Samuel said. "You have the

village behind you, you know." He grimaced and looked toward the road that led to Amblethorne. "We won't let Rushbury be taken over by the Gilmours. Not if I have anything to say about it."

Miss Paige nodded. "And I assure you that I will do whatever I can to persuade them against making any drastic changes until they have had a chance to come to know the place."

She looked at Samuel, and he smiled grimly, nodding his understanding. Within her words was an implicit promise that *she,* too, would come to know Rushbury before exercising her influence as surveyor.

Mr. Reed left them looking little comforted by their words, and his gravity seemed to hang in the air with them as they continued forward, winding out of the village and up a hill.

"You must think us fools," Samuel said, gazing at the small buds that were beginning to dot the branches of the trees overhead. He lowered his gaze to her puzzled brow. "For clinging so doggedly to our quaint way of life."

She shook her head. "No. Having spent as many years as I have in London and other such places, I can easily see the value in a place like Rushbury, where time slows down and one can leave the hectic pace of Town life behind. There is something to be said, too, for knowing every single one of one's neighbors. In London, I can avoid people I dislike among the crowds."

"And that is…bad?" Samuel said, incredulous.

She laughed. "It is very convenient at times, to be sure, but overall I think it has an unfortunate effect upon both individuals and society."

"How do you figure that?"

She tilted her head to the side in thought. "It does one good to be obliged to confront those one dislikes or with whom one disagrees. I have often been incorrect in my own judgments, but if I never have occasion to discover it by further interaction with a person, then I remain blind—and likely to become insufferable in the estimation of my abilities as a judge of other people."

Samuel stared at her curiously. What an interesting woman she was. "I quite see what you mean."

A dimple trembled in her cheek. "Then you also see that I have done you quite a favor in forcing you to accompany me today, though I can't promise that your opinion of me shall change in the end. Sometimes one's first impression is altogether too correct."

He narrowed his eyes. "You think I dislike you?"

She shrugged a shoulder. "I would be surprised if you *didn't*, for I was a veritable harpy when we first met, wasn't I?"

He tried not to smile. "You were laboring under a strong sense of ill-usage."

"And used *you* ill in the process." She looked at him, her brown eyes calm but sincere. "Forgive me?"

His heart stuttered as she looked at him, and he forced a chuckle. "I assure you that there is nothing to forgive." He had the uncanny feeling that he would have forgiven Miss Paige for much more than an afternoon's tirade if she looked at him that way again.

Her horse tripped, and he instinctively reached to steady her. Once she and the horse had both recovered, she looked at him impishly. "It will be a miracle if I survive a month here, for your roads seem determined to do me in."

He set a hand behind his saddle and turned to look at the cause of the horse's stumbling—a large rock sticking up in the packed dirt. "They could certainly use some work."

The long incline they had been on began to level out before a bend in the road hid their path from view.

"Oh!" Miss Paige said. "Flowers." She pointed at a little patch of yellow and white at the side of the road.

Samuel's mouth twitched slightly. "Yes. Those particular varieties are lesser celandine—the yellow ones—and then wood anemone which, if you look closely, have pink in the inner part of their petals. However dim and dreary Rushbury may seem, the flowers like it well enough to come back every year."

"How reassuring," she said, a teasing glint to her eyes. "I was beginning to doubt that flowers existed in the North, and *that* would be very sad indeed, for I *do* love flowers."

He raised his brows. "Then you are in for quite a treat and a surprise. In fact…" He glanced at the woods that lined one side of the road, urging his horse toward them as his eyes searched. "There." A narrow path—barely visible unless one knew to look for it and rarely used—wound from the road and into the thick trees.

"What?" Miss Paige said, trying to follow his line of sight.

"Come," he said, hoping with a touch of nerves that his idea wouldn't be for naught. If the flowers beside the road were any indication, though, he had a feeling that Miss Paige would appreciate his idea. "You'll have to dismount, I'm afraid. The branches hang too low in some places to permit riding."

He hopped down from his own horse and looped the reins over the horse's head to hold them in one hand.

Miss Paige eyed him suspiciously but moved her skirts and took the hand he offered, slipping down from the horse where his hands were ready to steady her about the waist. They were close enough that he could smell some sweet but unidentifiable scent floating around her, and he pulled his hands away from her hurriedly to combat his impulse to identify the scent by leaning in.

He slipped the reins around the tangled branches of one of the few bushes that lined the outer rim of the woods, and the horses immediately set to grazing on the short grass.

"Follow me," he said, leading her to the faint trail.

"Please tell me that *this* at least is not one of the supposed roads that fall to my responsibility."

He chuckled. "No. Just a small path I discovered many years

ago." He had found it shortly after the death of his father, and it had become a haven for him during that first year.

They ducked their heads, Miss Paige keeping a hand to her bonnet to prevent its being licked at by the small, mossy branches overhead. The serene quiet of the road they had been on transformed into a heavier silence, broken only by a few, short bird calls and the snapping of twigs that had fallen with the weight of the winter snow.

They walked in silence, for whenever Samuel looked over his shoulder at Miss Paige, she was gazing around, an awed and appreciative light in her wandering eyes. He didn't want to interrupt her enjoyment of a place he loved so well. The last time he looked toward her, her eyes landed on him, and she shut her open jaw, giving an abashed smile. "There is nothing like this in London." She reached a hand toward one of the trees. "Everything here is covered in moss—like a blanket to keep out the worst of the winter."

He helped her over a fallen log, smiling at the picture her words painted.

The trees began to thin out slightly, and Samuel strained his eyes, a little rush of pleasure coursing through him at the sight before him, still masked by the trees. "Close your eyes," he said, stopping and turning toward her.

She narrowed her eyes at him. "If you leave me in these woods as some sort of joke, I shall never forgive you, you know."

He grinned. "I wouldn't dream of it. Come, close your eyes."

She stared at him another moment before obliging. He hesitated as he realized that his plan required him to guide her by the hand. It bothered him how much the prospect appealed to him, but he could hardly tell her "Never mind" without making a fool of himself.

Her eyes were obediently closed, and her face was tipped upward with the slightest of smiles on her lips, as though she were listening closely to the sounds of the forest. He took her hand gently and led her forward, walking backwards himself so that he could secure her safety, while sending quick glances over his shoulder to ensure he didn't trip and cause her to fall as a result.

His smile grew as they came up to the clearing. "We are here," he said, allowing her hand to drop with a mixture of relief and regret. "You may open your eyes."

She obeyed, blinking a few times as she did so, as the light in the clearing was far brighter than it had been among the trees. Her mouth parted and her eyes grew wide as they scanned the scene before them: a small meadow, teeming with color. More celandine and anemone grew in small patches throughout it, punctuated by the pastel purple of violets and a few moss-covered logs.

"Oh my," she said softly.

Samuel smiled, feeling uncommonly pleased at her reaction. "We *do* have flowers in the North."

Her eyes lingered on the scene before moving to his. "You certainly do."

He sighed contentedly as he gazed out at the vibrant meadow. It had been a long time since he had been there. "I had nearly forgotten this place existed."

She looked at him with an ill-suppressed smile. "Ah, yes," she said in a voice of feigned disinterest. "I quite see how you could forget such an insipid place as this. No doubt they are a dime a dozen here."

He chuckled. "Perhaps not *quite* so abundant, but I think you might be surprised. If this place appeals to you, I can assure you that you will be in raptures when August arrives."

She tipped her head to the side curiously.

"Heather," he said simply. "The moors are covered in it."

She took in a large breath and smiled, returning her gaze to the meadow. "I suppose I must at *least* stay until then."

His eyebrows drew together. "Were you thinking of leaving? I was under the impression that you had come to Rushbury to stay."

She took a step forward and bent down to touch a fingertip to the closest patch of anemones. The suspense he felt as he waited for her answer would have been comical if it had not been so aggravating. Why did he care whether she stayed or left? He had been fine before she had come—surely he would be so again if she left.

"You are correct," she finally said, inspecting one of the anemones that was particularly pink. "I was mostly joking about leaving, though my sister Daphne was convinced that I should dislike it here above all things and return as quickly as I came." She smiled down at the flowers. "I do miss Daphne and my family, but it would take a disagreeable place indeed for me to consider returning to London."

Relief washed over him, and his half-smile appeared. Daphne. Was she very much like Miss Paige? He was curious to know more about her family, and yet the prospect frightened him. Miss Paige was easy to be with—too easy, in fact—but she was undoubtedly genteel, and such families did not look upon Samuel with favor. He knew that too well.

"An entire family of Yorkshire skeptics, then," he said, pushing aside his melodramatic thoughts.

"I admit there is a tendency in London and Brighton—and perhaps the South in general—to look down upon those who inhabit the North." She stood and surveyed the scene yet again. "But perhaps that is for the best." She looked at him, and the hair on his neck prickled under her gaze. "I like it better as a well-kept secret."

"Me too," he said simply.

"I feel honored to be let in on it." She glanced again at the field. "How *did* you discover this place? It's not as if it is on a well-traveled road."

He laughed lightly. "No, no it isn't." He pursed his lips, deciding how much he wished to tell her. "I happened upon it walking, actually."

She looked at him incredulously. "Do you make it a habit to go walking in the dense forest, then? You must have a better sense of direction than I." She looked around. "If you weren't here and there weren't some semblance of a path, I would have no idea in which direction the road lay."

He smiled, looking for the spot in the meadow where he had sat for hours one day, his thoughts and prayers meshing together until the sun began to set. "After my father died, I went on many walks and rides, exploring every bit of Rushbury I could. He loved it here, and it felt like a way to honor his memory, I suppose." He glanced at her, wondering how she would receive his explanation.

"It is a sacred space, then," she said, her tone subdued as she looked at him with understanding.

She looked out over the meadow again, as if with new eyes, and silence filled the air again.

"And what of the rest of your family?" she finally asked.

He shook his head, offering something between a smile and a grimace. "It's just me."

"You and the village," she said with a discerning smile, as if correcting him.

He blinked, nodding slowly. "Me and the village."

Their gazes held one another in place, the silence winding around them like forest vines and giving Samuel the impression that they were moving toward one another, even though their feet moved not at all.

He might have convinced himself that it was only his mind tricking him, but he noted the way her chest rose and fell in tightly controlled motions and the way her eyes pierced his.

She swallowed and then smiled, averting her eyes. "I

suppose we should be getting back to the road. Plenty of work ahead of us."

He nodded quickly, feeling the way the tension broke. Had the birds been singing a moment before? It felt as though the forest had stopped with them, but that couldn't be.

He invited her to walk before him, and she glanced one more time at the field before stepping in front of him. "Even if there *were* a parish road running here, I wouldn't change a thing."

Samuel made a disapproving sound with his tongue, furrowing his brow dramatically. "A dereliction of duty, Miss Surveyor."

She laughed, and Samuel's stomach clenched at the way it affected him.

They walked the path back to the main road, Samuel asking questions about Georgiana's family in hopes that it would make him feel less connected to her if it wasn't him sharing bits about himself. But, even though they had lived lives widely diverging in distance and kind, everything she said reinforced to him that in Georgiana Paige he had found a kindred spirit.

He helped her back onto her horse, and they continued around the bend in the road, Samuel pointing out various problem areas where the harsh winter had taken its toll. They stopped every so often for Miss Paige to scribble a quick note in her book, and Samuel couldn't help but smile at the situation. When he had suggested she take on the role of surveyor, it had truly not occurred to him that she would accept. And yet, it pleased him greatly to see her taking her duties so seriously.

He pulled his horse to a stop, pointing at a break in the drystone wall where a wooden fence opened to a dirt path. "The easiest way to address the pockets in the road is to make use of the stone in the old quarry down this path."

She squinted into the distance then turned to him with a hesitant gaze. "Would it trouble you terribly if I took a closer look? You are free to stay here with the horses, of course. Is it very far down the path?"

He chuckled and threw a leg over the horse to dismount. "It is *not* very far, but I certainly won't stay behind. The quarry can be dangerous if you don't know what to look out for—particularly at this time of year when things are thawing."

Before he could make it to her horse's side, she had shifted her leg and slid down deftly. She clearly had no need of his assistance, and he was conscious of a feeling of disappointment.

He looped the reins around the gate post and opened it for her to pass through.

"Are you very worried for Mr. Reed?" she asked, stepping through and then turning to allow him to pass in front of her.

He bit the inside of his lip. "I am worried for all of us in Rushbury, to be quite frank. But John Reed's family stands to lose the most from the endeavor you described. It has already been difficult enough for stockingers in recent years. I imagine you have heard tell of the riots we have experienced here up north."

"The Luddites?" she asked.

He nodded. "Desperate people who can't feed their families and whose labor is undervalued." He shook his head. "I hope we can protect John against such troubles, but what can be done if the Gilmours are set upon bringing a mill to Rushbury?"

Miss Paige was silent for a moment, and he let out a small puff of air through his nose.

"Forgive me," he said. "I imagine our problems are of little interest to you."

She stopped and turned toward him, her eyes narrowed as she searched his. "Do you really think so little of me?"

"No," he said, blinking at the knowledge that he had given offense. She smiled back at him, but it was a quizzical smile. "I only assumed that—"

"What?" she said, a lopsided smile forming on her lips and

eliciting in him the sudden and strange desire to kiss them. He blinked away the ridiculous impulse.

"That I can only be troubled with frivolous things like the latest fashion or how to refurbish a room? I assure you that I care very much for the fate of your villagers." She paused. "And to know what sort of things occupy your thoughts." The humor was gone from her voice, replaced with sincerity. She turned back to the lane, and they rounded the corner leading to the quarry.

"I truly meant no offense," he said. "It is just that, in the past, I have found that those who come to live in Rushbury—who aren't native to it or accustomed to the type of life we lead—they are often bored when confronted with village matters."

They stopped at the edge of the quarry, where the land dropped off steeply into a deep hole.

"I am not offended, Mr. Derrick," she said, smiling up at him. "I'm afraid it takes much more than that to pierce my shell—recall that I have been obliged to listen to comments like Lady Gilmour's for the past eight—or ten, according to her—years. But I can tell you that it is refreshing rather than boring for me to see the way life is lived in Rushbury and to speak of meaningful matters rather than the insipid gossip and polite small talk that I have been accustomed to. I mean what I said at the vestry meeting: I should like to be of help to the village."

They met eyes, and he slowly nodded his understanding. "We are fortunate to have found an advocate in you, Miss Paige. I would be lying if I didn't admit that I feared what type of person might replace Miss Baxter."

She laughed. "Only to have that fear confirmed and *more* when I arrived with a fire lit beneath me, expressing my intention of fixing your roads." Her smile faded. "May I be quite frank with you, sir?"

He nodded, turning toward her attentively and finding his heart picking up speed.

She took in a breath and then looked him in the eye. "We may be able to delay or—with a small miracle—even stop the Gilmours' plans, but I confess myself doubtful that that is the best course." She looked more nervous than he had seen her, and he waited for her to go on, determined to hear her out if only to reassure her that she had nothing to fear from him.

She smiled wryly. "Was it not Heraclitus who said that change is the only constant in life? To resist that change might help people like Mr. Reed in the short-term, but I am afraid that, once it does come to Rushbury—or even to a nearby village—it will hurt him more than it ever would have if he had embraced it and adapted to it in the beginning."

Samuel shifted his weight from one foot to the other, lowering his chin so that it rested on his cravat. She couldn't possibly understand what she was suggesting. She had only been in Rushbury a few days—Samuel had been there for most of his life.

"You love this village and its people dearly," she said. "I have been here only a short time, but *nothing* has been more apparent than that fact—not even the abysmal state of the roads"—she looked at him with such teasing camaraderie that he felt his defenses slide down. "You want what is best for your parishioners, and I admire you greatly for it. I suspect that the best advocate will keep his—or her, in my case—ear to the ground to anticipate whatever changes might threaten the villagers and then find a way to lessen the blow by helping them to adapt." She fiddled with the finger of her glove and then looked up at him, her face so full of understanding that it boggled him how she could possibly comprehend things so far from the sphere within which she had lived her life. It seemed impossible. "You cannot keep them from change, but you can be sure that they are not left behind when it comes. You can take a place at the forefront of that change in order to influence the way that it manifests itself in your particular parish."

His jaw shifted from side to side, and he let out a small chuckle. "If this is your way of persuading me to accept whatever changes you have in mind for the roads...."

She smiled widely. "The merest changes, I assure you! Though it *is* true that the Gilmours' plans cannot succeed with the roads as they now are. They might build the greatest mill in all of Yorkshire, but if a carriage cannot arrive there without falling to pieces..." She gave a shrug of pretended helplessness, and he followed suit.

"Now," she said, turning away from him, "tell me about this quarry."

CHAPTER 11

"Is that all the roads in the parish, then?" Georgiana said, scribbling an unsatisfactory note with the dulled tip of the small pencil she held.

Mr. Derrick let out a short bursting laugh. "No, it is not. We have seen perhaps half of the roads within the boundaries of the parish."

"Good heavens!" she said, looking alarmed. "Who in the world is making use of all these roads? We haven't seen more than one cart since we set out."

He smiled. "You have your London crowds to avoid people you don't wish to see. We have our roads."

"Ah," she said, tucking away the book and pencil in the bag dangling from the saddle. "A much more effective approach, I imagine."

"Perhaps we can finish what we started tomorrow?" Mr. Derrick suggested.

Georgiana looked at him, noting how much the prospect appealed to her. Did it appeal to him too, or did he simply consider this one of the many duties to be carried out in the name of helping the village? "I should like that."

He met her gaze, the hint of a smile on his face. "As

should I."

The next day's survey was without incident, but Georgiana found herself falling slowly in love with the Rushbury landscape. The sun showed its bashful face a handful of times during the ride, and she couldn't decide whether she preferred the somber hues of a cloud-covered sky or the vibrant ones when the sun happened to peek through a small gap in the clouds.

She felt brim full of energy and gratitude as she swayed back and forth on Aunt Sara's bay. Not even the unevenness of the road could detract from her satisfaction with life.

She had learned so much about Rushbury from Mr. Derrick —and she had pieced together a number of things about the vicar himself, as well. Some source of pain lay in his past, and all Georgiana knew was that it was connected somehow with a family who had lived at Amblethorne. She imagined it might be responsible in part for the way he looked askance at the genteel families who flitted in and out of the neighborhood.

That her association with Mr. Derrick was closely connected to the enjoyment she had taken from her time surveying the parish roads was something that had occurred to Georgiana. But it was not something she cared to dwell on. The irony of it was not lost upon her, though—that she should leave London, the Marriage Mart, and its hordes of marriageable gentlemen, only to fall victim to the first man she encountered in a miniscule village like Rushbury.

For she couldn't deny the way she responded to Mr. Derrick —she certainly had enough experience in her eight years on the Town to know that there was something very different in the way she regarded Mr. Derrick. Much like Rushbury, he could appear stern and somber at first. But underneath that façade and underneath his wary demeanor lay a warmth, a playfulness, and a kindness that made her heart yearn for his company. In some ways, she wished that she could prolong the inspection of the roads indefinitely.

"Miss Paige?"

She looked to Mr. Derrick, who was staring at her with an expression of mixed concern and amusement.

Blinking, she laughed at herself. "I am sorry. I was wool-gathering."

"An apt phrase to use in this part of the country," he said, still looking at her. "Whatever it was you were thinking of, it must not have been pleasant." He nodded, indicating her forehead, and she relaxed it, feeling her cheeks pink at the knowledge that he had caught her in the act of thinking about him. She would not have called her thoughts unpleasant, though. Merely troubling.

"No, not unpleasant," she said with a reassuring smile. Hoping to change the subject, she offered, "Well, now that I have taken copious notes"—she flipped through the pages of the book, of which the first quarter or so contained pencil markings —"on the state of all parish roads"—she stopped, looking expectantly at the finger he had raised.

"But you have not—not all the roads. You are forgetting the main road."

She scoffed. "I could hardly forget that road. It is indelibly written upon my memory and shall be for as long as I live. I hope you will agree that I need not revisit it today, for I walked it myself. Indeed, I imagine it will require every last page in this book for me to document my thoughts and feelings on the subject."

Mr. Derrick chuckled, reminding her with the instantaneous lightening of his features why she found such great pleasure in teasing him and making him laugh.

"Very well," he said. "With the time left to us before we

arrive back in the village, let us rather discuss the ideas you have formed after spending a few hours on these roads."

She shifted in the saddle, tilting her head and frowning. "Well, I think that the first concern is whether anything can in fact be done to address the problems that exist. If, as you have mentioned, no one is prepared to pay or to contribute to the betterment of the roads in the way of labor, a list of desired improvements would be pure fancy—and a waste of time."

"Very true," Mr. Derrick replied. He gave a great sigh. "I suppose we will just be obliged to leave everything as is."

She looked at him askance. "How very poor-spirited of you!"

"I prefer to think of it as pragmatic, rather."

She smiled and then suddenly sat up straighter in her saddle. "The Gilmours!" she exclaimed.

He glanced around and then turned to look behind them as if he might see the Gilmours.

"No, silly," she said, reaching for his arm and tugging him back around. "We can apply to *them* for the funds to fix the roads."

He stared at her, his eyes narrowing slightly as he considered her words.

"Just think," she said animatedly. "If they are so set on making Rushbury a hub of activity and trade, they will surely see that the roads cannot be left as they are. An investment in the roads of Rushbury is an investment in its future." She paused, seeing how the lines had only deepened in his forehead. It amazed her how different he could look when he was displeased and when he was laughing. His jaw line was hard, his eyes shadowed by his lowered brows so that they looked almost black.

"What is it?" she asked.

He took a moment before answering. "You wish to persuade the Gilmours to give their money to the repairing and maintenance of the roads, but you wish to do so by dangling in front of them the prospect of the Rushbury they wish for—and that is not the Rushbury I desire. I would sooner leave this place"— he motioned around him at the glowing afternoon landscape —"than see it ruined." His voice went soft. "I will take craters and broken carriage wheels over the vision of the Gilmours any day."

Georgiana was silent. Mr. Derrick's love of Rushbury ran deep. She gazed down at the village, tucked in its small valley at the bottom of the hill they rode down. It was so far distant from any place she had ever lived, and yet she already felt more attached to it than she did to the London townhouse she had spent eight Seasons in.

"I quite see what you mean," she said softly. "I am growing very fond of this little village, provincial or no. I can only imagine what my sentiments might be after spending as much time here as you have." She glanced at him, and his eyes met hers, his face softening and something between a smile and a grimace passing over his lips.

"No doubt you would be wiser than I," he said, staring off at the approaching village and sighing. "You are right about change being only a matter of time—I promise you I see that. And I wish I could welcome it with as much rationality as you do, but...."

"You love it the way it is," she offered.

He nodded, smiling wryly. "Very unsophisticated of me, I know."

She returned his smile, feeling mischievous. "Perhaps you need a bit of an incentive—something to inconvenience you. Might I suggest a fast-paced carriage ride on one of the roads we've just traveled?"

He chuckled reluctantly.

"In all seriousness," she said. "I am afraid that there may be little we can do to entirely prevent the Gilmours from making changes to Rushbury. But if we can delay those changes for a time—using the roads as our method, for I imagine that the task of bringing the roads into good repair will take some time—perhaps we can increase our influence with them and help them to see things from a different perspective?" She rushed on. "I know that it is not ideal, but I think it may be the best option we have."

He looked at her with a glint of wonderment in his eyes. "Why do you put yourself to trouble for us?"

She averted her eyes, feeling suddenly and unaccountably shy. "It is no trouble. I am not so unselfish as you assume."

He continued to stare at her, and she squirmed under his gaze. It was as if he was trying to understand her and believed he could do so by merely looking at her for long enough. "I think you are." He smiled lightly. "You are different."

She swallowed. "Different?" She almost wished she hadn't said anything. She knew she was different. A woman of her family and dowry didn't spend eight Seasons in London without becoming acutely aware that something must be wrong with her.

"Miss Paige," he said with an amused smile. "In the past ten years, we have had no fewer than seven families take up residence at Amblethorne Park. Not one member of any one of those families has shown the interest or concern for Rushbury in their months or years here that you have shown in the past week." He held her eyes. "You are different in all the best ways."

Her throat caught, and she turned her head to blink away the burning at the back of her eyes, mortified at her emotion.

"Miss Paige?" Mr. Derrick said with a hint of alarm. "What have I said? I truly meant no offense."

She kept her eyes away from him as she pulled in a shaky breath to steady herself, widening her eyes in hopes that the cool air would dry them. She put on a smile and turned back to him, shaking her head. "You have not offended me. On the contrary."

He looked at her thoughtfully. "Surely what I said is not news to you?"

She laughed. "I spent eight Seasons in London, Mr. Derrick. Believe me when I say that it is an entirely new experience not to have someone attempting to pinpoint precisely what is wrong with me."

He grimaced, but then one side drew up in a slight smile. "Well, you already know my feelings on the judgment of London folk. I should take their inability to recognize all of your charms as a compliment rather than anything else, if I were you."

Samuel stood at the back of the nave, staring at the stained glass window opposite him. It had been two days since he and Miss Paige had finished their surveyal of the roads, and he felt an impatience to see her.

It struck fear into his heart. He had felt this before, this aggravating and restless need to be with someone. He found himself creating excuses to make a visit to Granchurch House. It certainly would not have been irregular for him to do so—he had spent a great deal of time there since Miss Baxter's passing—but he forbade himself, knowing that his motivations were not on the elder Miss Paige's account. They were almost entirely selfish.

He had been pondering on Miss Paige's words regarding Rushbury and the changes that were threatening it since the arrival of the Gilmours. He felt such a great responsibility for the welfare of the villagers, and her words weighed heavily on his mind. In all his attempts to keep things as they were, to keep Rushbury from changing away from the village they all knew and loved, had he set his parishioners up for disappointment? Failure, even?

Heaven help him if it turned out to be so. Perhaps he had

been too quick to mistrust anyone outside of their little world, but it wasn't without good reason. He had seen small villages like his succumb to the lengthening reach of London, with MPs concerned only with the political power such places afforded them. He had watched as the creeping tentacles of progress in places like Leeds and Manchester had slowly but surely widened their net, leaving behind them a wake of struggling poor whose wages fell even as the cost of food rose.

They had felt it even in Rushbury, insulated as they were in the dales of the West Riding. People like John Reed had been forced to lower the price of their products in order to compete with what was being produced in the mills that were beginning to dot the Yorkshire and Lancashire landscapes—all wool of lesser quality.

A creaking sounded, and he turned his head toward the door.

Miss Paige appeared, and Samuel felt his heart stutter at the welcome sight of her. She wore a short cape over her shoulders, and her blue bonnet was spotted with dots from the rain. One of the maids from Granchurch House followed her in, and Samuel was conscious of a feeling of slight disappointment.

That was ridiculous. And far from proper. But he couldn't help wondering if she had brought a maid along after feeling uncomfortable after the rides they had taken together.

"Mr. Derrick," Miss Paige said, smiling and shutting the door behind her. "I hope I'm not disturbing you."

Entirely aware that he had been lost in a brown study for the last five minutes, during a large part of which his thoughts had been directed toward her, he shook his head. "No, not at all. Please," he gestured to welcome them. "Come in."

"We are on our way to Amblethorne, in fact," she said, brushing at her shoulders with her hands. Little flecks of rain flew off. "I came upon Lady Gilmour yesterday on the village road, and I mentioned to her that you and I had a matter we thought might interest her and Sir Clyde. She insisted that we come speak to her about it today. I wasn't certain if you would be at liberty to come—or if you would wish to—but I thought I would just stop in and check." Her mischievous smile appeared. "And now that I have come on such short notice, you will have a perfectly reasonable excuse not to accompany me if you don't wish to. I know you aren't overly fond of the Gilmours."

He smiled at her stratagems. She was right—a visit to the Gilmours was very near the last thing he wished to do, particularly given what he inferred would be the subject of conversation. He didn't imagine that he would relish hearing the comments that would be made by Lady Gilmour and her husband. "Very thoughtful of you—and slightly cunning, I might add," he said. "I am unsure whether I should be disturbed or impressed. But I think I should come, despite that. Who knows but what, absent my grounding influence, you and Lady Gilmour might not end your visit with plans to construct the next Vauxhall Gardens in the center of Rushbury."

She glared at him playfully. "Come, then. You can exert your provincial influence upon us—what did you call us?—Town folk and stop our evil designs."

"Very good. Allow me to just fetch my hat."

Samuel watched Lady Gilmour's eyes linger on him from where she stood at the window when they entered the drawing room.

"Ah," she said, gliding toward them with outstretched arms. "Miss Paige, Mr. Derrick." She looked to Miss Paige with an approving smile. "I couldn't help noticing your approach from the window, and I see you have employed a maid." She looked highly pleased. "I am very glad that you have taken my advice."

Samuel looked to Miss Paige, curious. He thought he saw the

quickest flash of annoyance cross over her face, but it was gone as quickly as it came.

"Well, to say truth," Miss Paige said, "this is Aunt Sara's maid. I have yet to employ one of my own."

Lady Gilmour's smile flickered. "I must confess that I was very shocked indeed to see you and Mr. Derrick riding together unaccompanied."

Miss Paige's jaw tightened a bit, and her smile was a bit less genuine as she opened her mouth.

But Lady Gilmour continued on, putting up a hand to stop Miss Paige's reply. "Now I know that you think yourself past the age of needing such things, my dear, but I hope you will allow me to be a better judge of the matter. I *did* manage to attract Sir Clyde, after all." She smiled until her eyes nearly disappeared. "One cannot be *too* careful when one's reputation is in the balance." She pursed her lips, looking at Miss Paige consideringly. "I hope you will not think me unkind, my dear, but if you were so free with your attentions in London as you have been here, I suspect it *might* have something to do with your remaining unmarried."

Samuel stiffened. The woman was unbearable.

"Thank you, Lady Gilmour," Miss Paige said, her color slightly heightened. "You are all consideration."

Lady Gilmour looked ready to continue the subject—no doubt to instruct Miss Paige on the methods she used to attract Sir Clyde—but Samuel decided it was time to step in, little though he relished it.

"Lady Gilmour," he said, "we were hoping to speak with you about the survey of the roads you saw us in the midst of completing."

She turned her head toward him, looking as though she had forgotten his presence entirely. "Oh?" she said discouragingly.

"Yes," said Miss Paige. "I was telling the vicar of the hopes you and Sir Clyde had expressed for Rushbury, and we thought it would be worthwhile to talk amongst us about the effect the state of the roads might have upon the future of Rushbury."

Samuel watched in appreciation as Miss Paige navigated the difficult conversation with awe-inspiring dexterity. So subtle and deft was she that Samuel found himself blinking in surprise as they rose to leave, having secured assurances from Lady Gilmour that she and Sir Clyde would put a hold on all of their plans and focus on bringing the roads into good repair—a task toward which they were willing to contribute a significant sum.

As they walked away from Amblethorne Park along the long lane that led to the village road, the maid following discreetly behind them, Samuel turned to Miss Paige.

"I stand quite in wonder," he said.

She looked at him with a perplexed brow.

"You not only managed to convince Lady Gilmour that the idea to improve the roads was hers but for *her* to suggest the idea of paying for the repairs." He shook his head in awe.

She bit her lip. "When you say it like that, it sounds very…conniving."

"Masterful," he replied. "I was terribly wrong to think that you would stand in need of me. I was utterly useless."

"Far from it," she said as she tied her cape around her neck. Her fingers slipped, and Samuel reached for the draping side of the cape and handed it to her. "Thank you—I have fumbling fingers in this cold. But as I was saying, you were not at all useless. You saved me from another five minutes of lecturing on my scandalizing lack of a maid. I hoped she would be satisfied enough by my bringing Aunt Sara's maid along that she wouldn't comment on it at all."

So, she had brought the maid for Lady Gilmour's benefit, not because she meant to keep Samuel at a distance? He glanced at her, but there was no trace of embarrassment on her face at the recollection of Lady Gilmour's unflattering comments. Had she truly become inured to such remarks, or was she simply skilled at hiding how they affected her?

"I was a fool to think that she would let the subject be," Miss Paige continued. "Lady Gilmour is clearly the type of person who must call everyone's attention to the ways in which they fall short of her own standards and then take credit for any positive change she sees." She glanced at Samuel and raised her brows at him. "She will be insufferable whenever something positive occurs in Rushbury, you know."

He sighed. "I imagine so." He paused. "Shall you hire a maid for yourself, then?"

She looked at him significantly. "Lady Gilmour may have a great deal of power to affect change in Rushbury, but I shan't let her control *my* life. I came to Rushbury to *escape* the stiflingly strict rules of propriety in London, not to transport them here with me." She sent a teasing glance at him. "No doubt she is surprised, Mr. Derrick, that you have agreed to spend time in the company of someone as shockingly fast and" —she frowned — "what was it she said?"

"Free with your attentions," Samuel said helpfully.

"Ah, yes," she said. "That. I cannot be considered a good influence upon you or the innocent villagers here."

"I think you are precisely that," he said, stopping as they came to the fork in the road that continued toward the village in one direction and Granchurch House in the other.

She smiled and looked around them, taking in a breath that she let out slowly. "Well, whatever the quality of my influence, I am afraid you are stuck with me, for I am growing much too fond of Rushbury to leave it."

A mixture of pleasure and anxiety rushed through him.

She meant to stay. It meant more time together; it meant coming to know her better; and it meant that Samuel would be forced to confront the rapidly growing admiration and affection he felt for Georgiana Paige.

CHAPTER 12

In the space of just two weeks, the Rushbury landscape had changed dramatically. Mid-April had arrived and with it, the very welcome sight of shoots on the tree branches and flowers ready to burst forth from their buds and add a dose of color to the shades of green, brown, and gray which permeated the village and its environs.

Georgiana walked side by side with Aunt Sara, admiring the grounds of Granchurch House. They were not extensive—only a fraction of the size of Amblethorne Park—but there was a different kind of pleasure for her in becoming familiar with every nook and cranny within them. It made her feel like she belonged there, like it was becoming her home.

"You know, Aunt Sara," she said, her eyes fixed on the arch of vines that led to her favorite spot in the gardens, "I confess that when I arrived in Rushbury I wondered why in heaven's name you had chosen to spend the past twenty years of your life here."

Aunt Sara smiled and sighed, scanning the grounds. "Yes, I imagine that most of the family feels much as you do. It is unfathomable to those who spend the majority of the year in London or Brighton that someone might happily remain in such a small and distant place as this. But I made the decision to come here knowing very well what I would be *missing out on*."

"And have you regretted it? Have you missed life in Town?"

Aunt Sara turned to look at her. "I think it is human nature to doubt our decisions at times. And there *have* been a few occasions when I have wondered what my life might have been like if I had continued attending the Season." She lowered her head and tipped it to the side. "But there came a point when I no longer enjoyed life in Town. The novelty wears off quite quickly, as I'm sure you know, and as the years passed, I found myself yearning for a different kind of life. The only reason to stay was the prospect of marriage, and there was no guarantee that I would marry even if I *did* follow the crowds wherever they went."

Georgiana listened thoughtfully, watching the rhythmic motions of their skirts.

"I decided that I didn't want to wait for life to happen but rather to make it what I wanted. But I had spent so long trying to appease others that I hardly knew what I wanted. So I asked my cousin Matilda—she was just a year younger than I—to accompany me somewhere far away, where we could sort out our desires. Bless her kind and adventurous heart, but she came with me." She glanced behind them at the house. "To this very place. We were only renting at the time, you know. But we came to love it so much—the quiet, slow pace, the fresh air—that, when the owner wished to sell, I determined that I would purchase it with the money that had been left to me by my mother."

Georgiana was silent for a moment. Her own story paralleled Aunt Sara's noticeably, and she wasn't entirely sure how to feel about that.

"Do you wish you had married?"

It might have been considered an offensive question, but Aunt Sara only smiled sadly. "At times, yes. And I knew quite well when I decided to stay in Rushbury that I would likely never marry if I spent my time here." She glanced at Georgiana. "That is not to say that I have not been happy or content, for I am someone who enjoys solitude quite a bit. Indeed, if I ever had married, I think it would need to have been a man whose disposition matched mine very nearly, for I should not at all have liked being married to someone who was forever wishing to hold and attend parties."

Georgiana laughed softly. "In coming here, I fully anticipated that you would be wishing for my company the majority of the day."

She smiled. "My brother has always worried for me so—worried about the amount of time I spent on my own and been convinced that I was lonely. But Matilda and I left each other to our own devices the majority of the time, and that suited us very well. As long as there was conversation at dinner and a few minutes during the day where we could knit together, we were very happy."

Georgiana smiled at her aunt. She, too, enjoyed a certain amount of solitude, but not nearly as much as did Aunt Sara. In fact, she had been stunned by how little her aunt seemed to need—or even wish for—her company.

Going from London, where she was forever in someone's company, to Granchurch House, where she was rarely in *anyone's* company, had been slightly jarring, and Georgiana found herself taking walks in the village for a bit more human interaction or, more often than not, seeking out the vicar's advice on some question or another. She had spent an hour or so each day for the past week at the church, going over the parish records to better understand the history of the village and what had been done by past surveyors.

Mr. Derrick had joined her from time to time between his duties, sometimes assisting her in understanding the records, sometimes merely sitting in companionable silence with her as he made his own recordings in the parish books or prepared for the weekday and Sunday services.

Georgiana would often glance up at him, feeling at war with herself. She recognized the utter contentment her heart and mind found in those moments with Mr. Derrick, and it frightened her.

For years now, she had been trying to convince herself that marriage and romantic love were simply not for her. Her journey to Rushbury had been a leap of faith in that direction. Much like her aunt, she couldn't bear to continue living her life in anticipation of finding a love which became more and more improbable with each passing Season.

It had been much less difficult to persuade herself that she didn't wish to be married when marriage was merely an abstract concept and her husband merely a hypothetical, faceless gentleman.

That she should arrive in Rushbury and find herself yearning not only for love but for love with a specific person—it was irony of the cruelest kind. She could *not* allow her peace to be cut up by Samuel Derrick.

And yet, her heart seemed to function independently of her will, and she suspected that it was already far lost to this country vicar.

With the help of Mrs. Reed, Georgiana slipped on the woolen coat—finally finished—that the Reed family had made for her. Never mind that the day was too warm to necessitate such an item of clothing, Georgiana was in raptures over it, particularly the braiding Mrs. Reed had added at the shoulders and along the openings.

"It is better even than I could have hoped for," she said, touching a finger to the buttons and tracing the braiding beside them. She extended a handful of bank notes to Mrs. Reed whose brows drew together.

"Why, miss," she said, glancing at the money. "This is far more than we had agreed upon." She counted out half of the notes, handing them back to Georgiana.

Georgiana merely shook her head with a smile, continuing to examine the coat. She hadn't missed the desire in Mrs. Reed's eyes as she had held the money.

"I cannot accept this money, miss," Mrs. Reed said, still holding out her hand.

"And nor can I," Georgiana said. She took the woman's hand and pressed it closed around the bank notes. "When I agreed upon the sum before, I hardly knew the exceedingly fine quality of the garment I would be receiving. Please accept this small token of gratitude for a job well done."

Mrs. Reed blinked quickly and nodded. "You are far too generous, Miss Paige."

Carriage wheels rumbled down the road, and they both looked toward them.

A large wagon stopped before the vacant house at the end of the village row, and Georgiana squinted to make out what lay in the bed of the wagon.

Mrs. Reed's hand flew to her mouth.

"What is it?" Georgiana asked, dismayed by the look of horror on the woman's face.

"A spinning machine."

Georgiana's eyes widened, and her heart plummeted. "What? No," she said. "It cannot be."

Lady Gilmour had agreed that nothing should be done until at least a portion of the parish roads had been repaired.

"Excuse me, Mrs. Reed," she said, picking up her skirts and rushing down the lane. Her breath came quickly, and she felt her cheeks begin to warm with the heat the wool coat provided to her body.

"Pardon me, sir," she said to the driver of the wagon and the two young men whose hands were busy untying the ropes that had secured the machine. "What is this?"

"A spinning machine, miss," the driver said. He pulled a crumpled paper from his pocket. "The first of two purchased by a"—he unwrinkled the paper— "Sir Clyde Gilmour," he said, squinting at it. He stuffed it back into his pocket and hopped down onto the dirt road.

"When?" asked Georgiana, following him over to the other two men.

The man shrugged. "I only knows and does what I'm told, miss. I've 'ad enough trouble getting this 'ere in one piece on these roads without troubling my mind over the details."

There was no use trying to get more information out of the man. He clearly knew nothing.

She turned back toward the Reeds' home and saw Mr. Reed standing there, one hand on the door, peering down the street with the look of someone who had just seen a ghost.

Georgiana's heart dropped. Surely for someone who was already struggling to provide for his family, the sight was like unto a death sentence.

His head disappeared into the house, and Georgiana shut her eyes. She needed to *do* something. But what?

Samuel shifted his knees on the small piece of canvas that protected his pantaloons from the dirt of the glebe garden. He straightened himself and looked thoughtfully at the plot he was working on, rolling his shoulders to relieve the aching after being hunched over for half an hour.

He sighed contentedly at the sight of the freshly tilled dirt and the last of the sprouts he had transferred from their place inside the parsonage. It was finally warm enough that they had a decent chance of survival. There was still work to be done—slugs were still to be found in abundance around the garden—but it would do for today.

He raised himself from his knees and brushed off his dirty and worn gloves.

"Mr. Derrick." His maid Jenny appeared, apron sooty from cleaning the grates after a long winter. "Miss Georgiana Paige is here to see you."

"Oh," he said, blinking and looking down at what state he was in. He hesitated a moment. "Please show her into"—he looked up and stopped mid-sentence. Jenny was gone, and Miss Paige stood in her place, hands clasped but fidgeting and an anxious expression on her face. She wore a long, wool coat—one he had never seen her wear before.

"Mr. Derrick," she said. "I am terribly sorry to disturb you, but I didn't know what else to do."

His brows came together, and he walked through the narrow garden paths toward the gate, pulling off his gloves. "You are not disturbing me, Miss Paige. What is it? How can I be of assistance?"

"I have just come from down the lane," she said, glancing over her shoulder toward the village road. "I was out talking with Mrs. Reed when we noticed a wagon stop in front of the house at the end of the lane." She looked Samuel in the eye. "Three men were unloading a machine to take inside."

Samuel frowned more deeply. "What kind of machine?"

"A spinning machine," she replied. "One of two being transported there, the man said. Purchased by Sir Clyde."

"What?" Samuel said, aghast. "Surely not. Lady Gilmour assured us—"

"Yes, I know," said Georgiana, shaking her head in disbelief.

Samuel ran a hand through his hair. "Does John Reed know?"

Georgiana nodded her head, the two small wrinkles in her brow deepening slightly.

Samuel grimaced and set his gloves on the wooden glebe fence. "I must go speak with him. The weight of caring for his growing family weighs on him heavily—I fear what this will do to him."

Georgiana swallowed, rubbing her lips together. "I shall see what I can discover from Lady Gilmour."

Samuel reached for her hand, holding it within his gratefully, making her heart flutter and skip. "Thank you for coming to me."

John Reed had taken it hard indeed. Raw wool littered the floor of the house, the basket that had held it overturned as though it had been thrown in anger, and John sat at the table with a bottle of Samuel knew not what.

Samuel's visit and reassurances had done little to soothe the man's agitation. Things were apparently even more dire than Samuel had realized, and it was only Mrs. Reed's words to her husband which served to calm him.

Samuel could have kissed Miss Paige when he discovered that she had paid nearly double the amount agreed upon for her wool coat. Had she known that it was her generosity which would put food on the Reeds' table for some time?

Word of the machinery's arrival had spread quickly through the village, and Samuel was obliged to answer the questions of a number of people on the short walk back to the parsonage once he had left the Reeds.

He had no answers for the villagers, though, and the only way he found to quell the anxiety he saw reflected in their eyes was to assure them that they would hold a village meeting when they could relay more information and come up with a plan as a community for how to proceed.

It was more than an hour after his return home when Miss Paige arrived back at the parsonage, accompanied again by the maid from Granchurch House.

He welcomed them into the small salon he used to receive guests and was grateful that she began speaking without any need for civil pleasantries to preface the information he most wished for.

"I am sorry it took me so long," she said, untying the strings of her bonnet and sounding slightly breathless, as though she had nearly run the distance to the parsonage. "I had been walking to Amblethorne when I realized that my arrival *sans* maid might not be conducive to a pleasant visit. So I was obliged to return to Granchurch House and find some small excuse for an unexpected visit to Amblethorne."

He motioned for her to have a seat.

"I am afraid the news I have is hardly helpful," she said. "Apparently Sir Clyde found a man selling a few of his spinning machines and simply couldn't resist purchasing them at such a low price. I had been hoping that he merely planned to house the machines in the village while work is done on the roads, but I am afraid he has every hope of putting them to use as soon as possible."

Samuel clenched his clasped hands, dropping his head in frustration.

"I am truly sorry," she continued. "I know that this is not at all what we were hoping for."

Samuel shook his head. "There is nothing for you to apologize for. But no, it is certainly not what we had been hoping for —nor is it what we were promised by the Gilmours. I am afraid that John Reed has taken it very badly. They are in worse shape than I even realized, and that is with help from the parish over the past few months." He looked up at her, remembering her great kindness to the Reeds earlier that day. "If it were not for the coat you purchased—and apparently paid well more than the prevailing rate for, I might add—"

She turned her head away, clearly uncomfortable with her generosity being mentioned.

"—I don't know what John might do."

"Surely there is another way we might help them," Miss Paige said, biting at the tip of her gloved thumb. "I shall put my mind to the matter." She stood, and her maid followed suit.

"Word has traveled through the village, as it always does, and I had no way of quelling the fears that had been stoked without agreeing to hold a meeting at the church later this week."

Miss Paige nodded. "I think it a very good idea. Perhaps we can discuss things more tomorrow? For now, I must return to Granchurch House. It is nearly dinnertime, and that is the one time of day Aunt Sara truly wishes for my companionship."

Samuel could only wonder at a person who wouldn't wish for Miss Paige's companionship all day long, but he agreed to her suggestion without hesitation and saw her out through the parsonage door.

Things were not well in Rushbury, and yet Samuel felt much more calm than he otherwise might have. For once, he had someone to share in the burden of it.

CHAPTER 13

Georgiana looked around the vestry at the villagers before her, the room humming with the low conversations taking place amongst them. Mr. Burke stood beside her as they awaited Mr. Derrick's arrival from tutoring two of the village children. He leaned toward her.

"Anyone might think it had been announced that the next London Season would take place in Rushbury, for all the upheaval two machines have caused."

Georgiana smiled at him. It was true that the entire atmosphere had shifted in the village over the past three days. There seemed to be a closing of ranks amongst the residents of Rushbury, with plenty of narrow, sidelong glances at the house at the end of the lane, particularly when there was any movement there.

Noticeably absent from the meeting were John and Mary Reed. Their oldest daughter Patience sat quietly in attendance, the only one present who seemed to have no interest in whispering with the other villagers. Georgiana's eyes rested thoughtfully on her for a moment.

Mr. Derrick strode through the door, his eyes finding Georgiana, whom he smiled at and came to stand by.

"Good day, everyone," he said, tucking a sheaf of papers under his arm. "Thank you for coming today. We know that everyone has many questions, and I wish we had more answers." He looked to Georgiana and Mr. Burke. "But I hope that we can come together and make some decisions on how to proceed."

"What's *she* doing up there?" Mrs. Green tossed her chin to indicate Georgiana.

Georgiana felt her muscles clench, but she tried her best to smile. It wasn't surprising that the villagers would see her once again as a threat. She had arrived at nearly the same time as the Gilmours, after all, and they saw her as one of their set. They might even believe her responsible in some way for the arrival of the machines—as though any unwelcome change could be attributed to the newcomers.

Besides, with nearly the first words out of her mouth, she had condemned the roads of Rushbury. In time, she hoped the villagers would come to see that she truly meant well and had no desire to upend their lives.

"Now, see here," Mr. Burke said, stepping forward. "Miss Paige is one of us, and the sooner you all realize that, the better it will be for you."

Georgiana felt her eyes sting slightly at the showing of loyalty from the constable.

"Burke is right," Mr. Derrick said. "Miss Paige is not an enemy. I give you my assurance—my word—that you can trust her as you would trust me."

Georgiana turned her head away, blinking rapidly. She knew what it meant for Mr. Derrick to vouch for her in such a way.

When she was confident she could rein in her emotions, she smiled understandingly at the villagers, clearing her throat and stepping forward. Mr. Burke's and Mr. Derrick's words had brought about a change in them already.

"My friends—for I hope you will allow me to consider you as

such—I can sympathize with your wariness at my presence." She looked around at each of the villagers, smiling in understanding. "I hope I can prove to you my trustworthiness in time. I want to assure you that I have every intention of using the small influence I have with the Gilmours to seek the best interests of Rushbury."

There was little response from the villagers, but as no one called out to challenge her, Georgiana felt that it could have gone much worse and stepped back in line with Mr. Derrick and Mr. Burke.

"Thank you, Miss Paige," Mr. Derrick said, smiling at her thankfully. "I know many in this room are struggling already to make ends meet. We are certainly feeling the effect of what has been happening in Bradford, Leeds, and Manchester. We have been insulated from much of the change that has affected others in the wool trade. I think I bear some of this responsibility at least, as I have been a bit, shall we say, *resistant* to change?" He smiled wryly, finding Georgiana's eyes, and her heart skipped as he looked at her. The room relaxed even more with the joke at his own expense. "None of us wants Rushbury to change. But I fear that change is coming, all the same, and we can either adapt to it and turn it to our advantage, or we can flounder as it takes us unawares."

A few heads bobbed up and down around the room.

"Miss Paige has been kind enough to speak with the Gilmours since learning of their plans for our village. She has secured enough money from them to make a substantial difference in the state of our roads without burdening any of you with paying more. However, money is only one part of the equation. We need labor. Thankfully, the Gilmours have provided enough money that we can pay you for your labor this time."

Heads turned and whispers sounded.

"If everyone can come together," the vicar said, raising his voice, "the labor will take a fraction of the time it has in the past. And we will *all* benefit. When the Reeds transport their wool to nearby villages or towns, they will be able to do so faster and more securely, for part of our plans are to cut back many of the branches and shrubbery that have provided concealment for the highwaymen that have plagued the West Riding." He again found Georgiana's eyes, and she narrowed them in an expression of feigned bitterness, though the effect was undoubtedly ruined by the smile she couldn't suppress. "More people will dare a ride into Rushbury for Mrs. Green's famous pastries, where before now they haven't been able to justify the time it takes to travel safely over our difficult terrain. You see what I mean, I think."

Heads nodded.

"We shall have a statute labor day next Monday, then, and we expect—and sincerely hope—that all of you will attend for the betterment of Rushbury."

Mr. Burke stepped forward with a look half-menacing, half-playful. "And if anyone feels inclined to absent themselves, I shall have no choice but to help them—very actively—to reconsider."

The villagers chuckled, and Georgiana sighed her relief at the positive sound.

"So," Mr. Burke said, "who will commit to join us?" He looked around the room, and many hands raised in the air, though a few hung down. "If only Sam and I show our faces to help *yet again*, our early deaths will all fall on your heads!"

More laughter sounded, and a few more hands went up. The hands of Mrs. Green and another woman Georgiana had yet to meet stayed clasped in their laps.

"I'll only help if *she* helps," said Mrs. Green, pointing at Georgiana. "And by *help*, I don't mean standing there in her pretty dress and watching us do all the work."

"Aye," said the woman beside her. "I'll help if she does."

Mr. Derrick looked to Georgiana, a mixture of amusement and apology on his face.

She held his eyes, and her mouth broke into a grin as she lowered her head and shook it from side to side. She had only herself to blame for the situation she found herself in. She had insisted upon involving herself in Rushbury's affairs, and now Rushbury was insisting that she be as good as her word.

She looked to Mrs. Green and inclined her head. "I shall gladly work alongside you, Mrs. Green. And *you,* ma'am." She smiled at the woman beside Mrs. Green."*If*"—she said significantly—"you agree to show me how to do the work."

Both women appeared too stunned to do anything but look at one another and nod, the skin under their chins trembling.

Mr. Derrick stared at Georgiana, looking almost as surprised as the villagers, and she gave a little shrug. There was a sense of satisfaction in astonishing the villagers and forcing them to reconsider their assumptions about her, just as she had been obliged to reconsider her assumptions about them.

Georgiana gazed around herself as she walked toward Granchurch House from the church, admiring the beauty of the emerging Rushbury spring. Each day saw new buds opening and more fresh green filling the tree branches. The sky was often gray and showered rain down upon the village most days, but it seemed much less dreary than when she had arrived weeks before.

She couldn't stifle a smile and a small laugh as she thought of how things had changed in such a short time. It was so very unlike the constant and unvaried months she had spent in London each year.

In Rushbury, there was a rhythm to life and yet, she never knew what each day would bring. Indeed, how could she have known when she set out from London that she would soon be pledging her support—and her hands—to the task of repairing village roads? Her family would no doubt be appalled. And yet she was full of curiosity and butterflies at the prospect. She wanted the respect and friendship of the villagers, and she wanted to help.

She wouldn't be completely honest with herself if she didn't admit that Mr. Derrick had played a large part in her offer of labor, though. She craved his approval in a way she had never before experienced. A smile from him was enough to make her throw caution to the wind. No matter how terrified she felt of her growing attachment to him when they were apart, the moment she was in his presence, the fear fled, and all she could feel was kinship and a desire for more. So much more.

Her brow furrowed as her eyes fell upon a carriage moving toward the stables at Granchurch. Aunt Sara had mentioned nothing about expecting anyone—even Rachel was not expected for another two weeks at least.

She stepped into the small entry hall, and her frown deepened as she strained her ears. A voice resonated from somewhere down the corridor—and it was decidedly male, though too muffled for her to tell any more than that.

She tugged at her bonnet ribbons and removed the bonnet from her head, debating whether to seek out Aunt Sara and her visitor or to go over the surveyor records as she had been planning to: she wanted to be certain that they made the best use possible of the village labor. It would require some input from Mr. Derrick, though, for he was the one who knew which roads would be most important to repair first.

Her curiosity overtook her, though, and she walked the corridor, cocking an ear to listen. Outside of the village, she knew no one in Yorkshire. It was highly unlikely that she would recognize the voice—or the face—of whoever was visiting Aunt Sara.

She paused and then opened the door of the drawing room, freezing and blinking at the sight.

"Georgie! What ho!"

Archibald strode over and wrapped her in a crushing embrace, which she returned after recovering from her shock.

"Archie!" she cried, pulling away and staring at him. "What in the world are you doing here?"

His mouth stretched in a nervous grin. "Needed a repairing lease—been spending the blunt a bit too freely, I'm afraid. Thought I'd come see how you were getting along here!"

Georgiana laughed and embraced him a second time. She had hardly realized how much she missed her family. "Well I cannot say that I am surprised to hear of your financial woes, but that you should choose to come *here* of all places is certainly unexpected."

He frowned at her dramatically. "Ho, now. What a slight to Aunt Sara, Georgie. And to this charming village!" He leaned closer to her, raising a hand in front of his mouth to conceal it from Aunt Sara. "Is there a place for a man to get a decent tankard of ale here? I didn't even see an inn on the drive in."

Georgiana shook her head. "I believe the closest inn is in the next village over. All the more reason for my surprise at finding you here."

"Disappointed, are you?" he said, raising his brows.

"Not at all! Very pleasantly surprised, though I must swear you to a vow of secrecy for when you return to Mama and Papa. I think they would be less than pleased to discover what I have been up to since my arrival."

Aunt Sara waved a dismissive hand. "Oh, they hardly understand how the lines between wealthy and poor blur in a place like this."

Archie looked from Aunt Sara to Georgie, a very curious light in his eyes. "My Georgie become provincial?" he said in a tone somewhere between impressed and doubtful.

"You have no idea," she said on a laugh. She patted him on the arm. "Now that I consider it, I think Rushbury a very good choice for you, Archie. You will be hard pressed to find a place to spend any money here."

"Well that's a start!" he said. "Now I only need to find a way to raise the wind. Papa told me not to show my face until I could pay off at least a fraction of my debts, and that means not until next quarter, saving some place around here where a man might sit down and play some"—he screwed up his face thoughtfully. "What *does* one play in the wilds of Yorkshire? Commerce?"

Aunt Sara laughed heartily. "Come, Archibald. This isn't 1750. We may be far from London, but we in Rushbury can play cards with the best of them! I understand that both Mr. Burke and Mr. Derrick are quite skilled when they choose to engage, which is not often, mind you. But the vicar humored Miss Baxter and me a time or two with a game of piquet, and it was quite obvious that he could have done us in in a trice if not for his being so polite and good-natured."

"The vicar, you say?" Archie said. "Hm."

Georgiana felt her cheeks warming unaccountably, and she busied herself with undoing the buttons of her wool coat. It was likely the last time she would be able to wear it without ruining it from perspiration, since the weather had warmed considerably since her arrival. But she wished for the Reeds to know how much she appreciated it and that her desire to pay them above the agreed upon amount was not merely charity but a reflection of how much use she would get out of the coat.

"Yes," said Aunt Sara, and Georgiana had the uncomfortable suspicion that her aunt was watching her. "Mr. Derrick. You are bound to come to know him if you spend even two days here, for not only is he the centerpiece of the village, he and Georgiana have struck up quite a friendship between them."

Heat emanated from her cheeks, and she was grateful that

one of the buttons was proving more difficult than the rest to undo.

Archie threw his head back as he laughed. "Well, I can't imagine there were many options. Are there any other families in the area?"

Georgiana knew what he meant, but she found that his words irked her. "I believe there are fifteen or sixteen in the village."

His brows drew together. "You know what I mean, Georgie. Other families like ours. Genteel ones."

Georgiana smiled at him. "There is Sir Clyde and Lady Gilmour at Amblethorne Park up the road. You are very welcome to befriend them. I imagine they will be over the moon to know of your presence here."

Archie seemed content enough to know that there was at least one other genteel family nearby. No doubt he would drive over to the nearest inn and meet others soon enough.

Georgiana was glad to see Archie and yet, how would he feel once he knew what Georgiana did with her time there? He had teased her about becoming provincial, but what would he say if he knew she had agreed to labor on the roads with all the villagers?

Archie's presence would add an interesting element to life in Rushbury—for however long he decided to stay. She suspected that he would tire of the place in a week or so, and she had a feeling she might be glad of it when the time came.

CHAPTER 14

Samuel suppressed a grimace at the sight of the Reed family in the pews as he stood to give his sermon. John was absent, and Samuel suspected that he was not doing any better now than he had after the machines had first arrived.

His eyes scanned the crowd and landed upon Miss Paige, as they so often did. She was flanked on one side by her aunt and on the other by an unfamiliar gentleman.

His stomach clenched. Who was he? He was dressed in the height of fashion—or what Samuel presumed that must have been. Having been so long away from Town himself, he couldn't speak to the matter. But he was sitting far too close to Miss Paige to imply anything other than a very close relationship indeed. Had she mentioned a brother? He rather thought she had. He hoped it.

Her eyes met his, and she smiled at him. It was warm and familiar, and he felt his shoulders relax a bit at the sight of it. Was he merely seeing what he wished to see, or was there not something different in the way she smiled at him?

He shuffled the papers in his hands, giving himself a moment to shift his focus to where it needed to be. The village badly needed today's sermon on the dangers of pride—he more than anyone—and he wanted to be sure that he delivered it in the most loving and direct way possible. If they let their pride guide them into making enemies of the Gilmours, he feared what would become of them.

When he had finished the sermon, he stifled his desire to walk straight up to Miss Paige to discover the identity of the newest stranger in Rushbury. Instead, he walked over to the Reeds, whose family required the better part of a pew for themselves. They always sat in the second pew on the right.

"How is John?" he asked after exchanging greetings with them.

Mrs. Reed grimaced, and there was a tight, disapproving turn to the expression. "Drowning his stress in drink, though where he thinks the money for such a thing is to come from when he is shirking his work, I couldn't say. I shudder to think what might become of us if not for Patience's employment." She put a loving hand on her daughter's shoulder, and Patience smiled back up at her.

"New employment?" Samuel asked. "What's this?"

"With Miss Paige, sir," Patience said in her soft voice. "She's taken me on as a maid."

Samuel's mouth opened wordlessly, and he clamped it shut, his eyes wandering to Miss Paige, who stood speaking to Burke with her characteristic smile. She seemed to be introducing him to the man on her left.

She had brought on Patience Reed as a maid? She had been set against such a course, willing even to court the displeasure of Lady Gilmour rather than stifle her freedom. She would not have changed her mind without good reason, and Samuel suspected that it was yet another way of doing what she could to help the Reeds.

He had the overpowering impulse to take her in his arms and show her just how much he loved her kind heart.

"I hadn't any idea of the arrangement," he said, pulling his eyes back to the Reeds, "but I am very glad to hear of it. You will be an excellent maid, Patience, and Miss Paige an excellent mistress."

Patience nodded and smiled. "She already is. I can't imagine anyone kinder."

Nor could Samuel.

Samuel's sermon had seemed to hit its mark, for he was approached by a line of villagers commenting on it after he finished speaking with the Reeds. He caught eyes with Miss Paige a number of times but was always in the middle of a conversation so that, by the time the last of the villagers left, Miss Paige, her aunt, and the mysterious stranger were nowhere to be seen.

The disappointment he felt was only tempered by the knowledge that the following day was scheduled for statute labor, and she had assured Mrs. Green that she would be there. Would the gentleman come along? Somehow he found it difficult to imagine so. Surely Miss Paige was a rarity amongst her set.

"Looking for someone, Sam?"

Samuel turned and found Burke watching him with a knowing smile.

"What think you of the gentleman she brought to church today?"

Samuel considered playing dumb and asking what *she* Burke was referring to. But he knew they were long past that. Burke knew him too well to mistake the way things were trending.

"Who is he?" He tried to sound nonchalant, placing one of the prayer books in its proper spot.

"Wouldn't you like to know?" Burke grinned widely. "I could throw quite a wrench in the works if I lied and told you he was her beau, couldn't I? But I shan't—not after I went to the trouble of seeking an introduction to see in what quarter the wind was blowing." He paused for dramatic effect, and Samuel clenched his jaw in annoyance. Burke loved to tease him. "He's merely her brother. Mr. Archibald Paige."

Samuel nodded slowly, feeling relief flood him and hoping it wasn't as obvious to Burke as it seemed it must have been. "What's he doing here?"

"I believe he's in dun territory and needed a spell away from Town."

"Well," said Samuel, "he's welcome here as long as he doesn't get up to any mischief. He could even make himself useful by coming to help with the roads tomorrow."

Burke laughed. "That would be a welcome surprise."

"I doubt we will see John Reed there."

"No, I don't think we will. But I've been thinking, Sam. Why shouldn't Sir Clyde take on John to manage the mill's affairs?"

Samuel shook his head. "I had the same thought. But he has a man—'a very competent one, mind you,' as Sir Clyde insisted—coming in from Leeds for the purpose, and you know how he looks down upon the villagers. And even if he offered it, John is far too prideful to accept such a position."

"Aye," Burke said. "You're not wrong about that."

Samuel sighed. "I'm afraid we will have to look for a solution elsewhere. I only wish I knew where."

Monday dawned overcast and cool, but the clouds that lay in the sky did so unthreateningly—pale gray and inching along at the leisurely pace of clouds that had nowhere to go.

Samuel and Miss Paige had agreed that the first road to be addressed should be the one that ran from the main highway toward the village. It seemed fitting that the benefit of labor should be first and foremost to the villagers and the road they most often traveled. Assuming anyone else turned up for the labor—and Samuel had his doubts whether that would occur—they would move to the main highway.

He heaved the wheelbarrow, full of stone from the quarry, from the parsonage and up the small path that led past the church and to the village lane. He glanced up as he passed through the church gate, and his eyes met the welcome sight of Miss Paige, attired in a tan muslin dress and holding a shovel in her hand as she walked toward him.

His mouth broke into a grin. She was a vision even in a relatively drab dress, and he suspected it had much to do with what her appearance signified: she was dedicated to Rushbury—so much so that she was willing to dirty her hands in its interests. He had never met anyone like her.

He set the wheelbarrow down with a thud, breathing more heavily than usual. He would sleep well tonight.

"What?" Miss Paige said, looking up and down the village lane. "Just you and me, then? Not even Burke this time?" She tilted her head to the side thoughtfully. "I promised Mrs. Green that I would work alongside her, but as she is not here, I suppose I am under no obligation...." She tossed an arch look at him and turned back toward Granchurch House, taking a few steps and then stopping in her tracks. She turned back toward him. "You seem indifferent on the matter. Am I to take that as a slight to the way you value my ability as a statute laborer?"

He shook his head, still smiling. "No. I merely know you well enough to know you would never leave me to the work myself."

Her lips were pressed together, but they smiled. "Only because you present a very pitiful picture. And you obviously need my shovel." She closed the distance between them, peering into the wheelbarrow.

His brow furrowed as he realized something. "You didn't tell me that you had taken on Patience Reed as a maid."

She prodded at a few of the rocks with her shovel, causing

two to tumble from their place. "I have taken on Patience Reed as a maid, Mr. Derrick."

He chuckled. "Yes, thank you. But why?" He knew the answer, but he wanted to hear how she would account for it. She was not the type of person to draw attention to her own kindness.

"To appease Lady Gilmour, of course," she said, setting her shovel down soundly and leaning upon it. "Why else?" A smile quivered at the edge of her mouth.

He raised a brow. "You fascinate me. You see, I seem to remember you swearing that you would not let Lady Gilmour dictate your decisions."

"I have repented," she said simply, "of my pride, thanks to your sermon."

He pursed his lips. "Believable perhaps but for the fact that my sermon occurred *after* you had taken her on. Besides, if you wanted to appease Lady Gilmour, Patience Reed would certainly not be the obvious or best choice. While she is a very amiable and capable young woman, Patience hasn't a shred of experience to recommend her, besides being far too young to satisfy Lady Gilmour's requirements."

Miss Paige shrugged. "You yourself say she is capable. Why not capable of learning the duties of a maid, then? And I *do* think she was the most obvious choice. Her family is in need, and her younger siblings are growing old enough to take on more of the duties she has been carrying out up to now."

He looked at her for a moment without saying anything, and he thought he saw her begin to squirm a bit under his direct gaze.

"Every time I think that I have your measure," he said, "that I understand just how good and kind you are, you do something even more good and kind, and I am left in wonder."

She met his eyes, her own searching his.

Footsteps sounded, and Miss Paige turned to look behind

her. Her brother was jogging down the hill from Granchurch House.

"Archie?" she said, looking surprised.

He grinned widely and slowed to a stop beside her. "I changed my mind," he said. "What kind of brother would I be if I let my sister labor while I sat inside? Besides, what else am I to do today?" He glanced at Samuel and inclined his head. "Vicar."

"Ah, yes," Miss Paige said. "I meant to introduce you yesterday, but as the entire parish was in raptures over your sermon and Archie's stomach was grumbling loud enough to disturb the family in front of us, it was not meant to be. Archie, this is Mr. Samuel Derrick. Mr. Derrick, this is my brother, Mr. Archibald Paige."

"Just Archie," he said. "Very pleased to meet you, Mr. Derrick. I hope my sister has been behaving herself?"

Samuel looked at Miss Paige and pursed his lips. "Tolerably, I suppose."

She raised a brow at him, and he smiled.

Samuel heard a noise, and he turned to find its source, his smile stretching wider at the sight before him. A dozen and more villagers moved in a pack toward them, carrying various implements to assist with the repairs and led by Burke.

"There are a few stragglers who should be here soon," Mr. Burke said, planting his shovel in the softer dirt that lined the side of the road.

"Well?" Samuel said, looking around at the laborers. "Shall we begin?"

The work was hard and backbreaking. They had the moistness of the dirt, though, to thank for the fact that it wasn't any *more* difficult. The shovels went into the dirt with much less effort than they would have on dry, dusty roads. Unfortunately, it was that same moistness that meant they would have more work to do in a matter of weeks—months if they were fortunate. But such was life in Rushbury.

And even as Samuel's back groaned against the labor, he couldn't find it in himself to complain. The sight of his village working together made his chest swell with pride. And watching Miss Paige wipe her dirt-streaked brow with her forearm, laughing every now and then with her brother or one of the villagers as she threw shovel-full after shovel-full of dirt and stone into the dips and holes that speckled the road—he thought she had never looked more beautiful or desirable than in that moment.

There was no denying it anymore: Samuel was very much in love with Georgiana Paige.

CHAPTER 15

Georgiana's muscles ached in places she hadn't known existed within her. Her dress was covered in a fine film of dirt, with large smudges in places that nearly blended with the tan fabric of the dress. She could only assume that her face looked much the same as did the faces of her fellow workers: streaked with dirt.

Her hands rested on the round top of the shovel handle, arms hanging limp and exhausted as she surveyed the work they had accomplished over the course of the past six hours.

She couldn't remember ever having worked even half so hard, and yet there was a contentedness in her fatigue—a fulfillment that was as new as it was welcome. Gone were the great dips and pockets in the main highway, and the roads branching out from the village lane within half a mile of it were as smooth as anyone could wish for.

"A fine day's work, miss," said Mrs. Green, coming to stand by Georgiana and setting her hands on her hips to survey the road. The villagers were packing up their things and beginning to make their way home, where they would scrape together whatever dinner could be most quickly prepared. They would be hungry from their hard labor, but Georgiana was content that they weren't starving. Aunt Sara had been thoughtful enough to employ the services of the cook and two of the Granchurch House maids, who had put together two large platters of cold cuts and bread for the laborers to eat at midday, conveyed on a small wagon.

Even better, they all went home with money in their pocket.

Georgiana glanced at Mrs. Green, smiling. The woman had warmed up to her considerably over the course of the day, and Georgiana found her to be a delightful surprise. Underneath her thorny exterior, Mrs. Green had a warm and caring heart. More than once, she had demanded the shovel from Georgiana, insisting in tones that brooked no disagreement that Georgiana rest for a few minutes. "Fine genteel folk like yourself aren't cut out for work like this, miss," she had said with only the slightest wink.

Archie strode over to them, his gait slower than usual, no doubt from the day's work. He brushed his forehead with a hand and let out a long, vocal sigh. "What a day, Georgie! Remind me never to agree to one of your schemes again."

Mrs. Green's surliness returned, and she sent a sidelong glance at Archie before striding away. She seemed *not* to have taken to him. At least not yet.

"You were invaluable, Archie," Georgiana said. "Thank you very much."

Mr. Derrick and Mr. Burke approached with the empty wheelbarrow, and Georgiana felt the rush of her heartbeat as Mr. Derrick smiled at her. He had a particularly dark streak of dirt just below his right eye, which endeared him to her all the more, evidence as it was of his willingness to do whatever Rushbury required of him.

Archie clapped his hands slowly at the sight of the lightened wheelbarrow, and both men smiled in response. "What say you, Derrick? Burke? Such a day's work deserves to be followed by a bit of relaxation and a nice game of cards, don't you think?"

The vicar's eyes stayed on Georgiana for a moment, as if he wished to know what she thought of such a suggestion. She didn't know whether to be glad or sorry that he couldn't know how much she envied her brother. She smiled, and his gaze moved to Archie.

"Certainly," he said, "though I will warn you that I haven't played in months and make it a practice only to play for penny points."

Archie laughed and clapped a hand on Mr. Derrick's shoulder. "Even those stakes will be a stretch for me with my pockets to let as they are!"

"Then we are all agreed," said Mr. Burke. He looked at Archie with a slight show of hesitation. "My home is humble, but you're both welcome there if it suits you."

Mr. Derrick shook his head. "You have a wife and children who need their sleep, Burke—and their peace." He sent him a knowing look. "And I know how boisterous you can be when you are losing. Come to the parsonage, both of you."

Archie nodded with a grin. "Then I shall just take a quick jaunt home to clean up. Grant me an hour, and I shall be ready." He looked to Georgiana. "Ready, Georgie?"

She let out a large sigh, thinking how nice a warm bath would feel on her aching back. But there would be time enough for that later. "Thank you, but I shall only be a few minutes behind you. I was hoping to write down a few things in the record books at the church while everything we have done today is still fresh in my mind." She glanced at Mr. Derrick. "Is the vestry open?"

"It is not, but that is easily rectified." He put a hand to his coat, and the metallic jangling of keys sounded.

Why did the knowledge that he would be obliged to accompany her send a thrill through her?

"Georgie," said Archie in a wondering voice, "you are very dedicated to your duties."

Mr. Burke chuckled and nodded. "Never has our parish seen such a fine surveyor—nor any parish, I imagine."

Georgiana shook her head with a small laugh, feeling her cheeks warming. Her duties were much less of a burden than anyone realized, so interconnected with Mr. Derrick's company had they proved to be. "I still have the better part of a year to prove you wrong, you know."

Archie went on his way, while Mr. Burke and Mr. Derrick walked beside Georgiana in the direction of the church, discussing the successes and hiccups of the day as well as the notable absence of John Reed. There was deep concern in the vicar's voice as they spoke of him, and he expressed his hope that paying him another visit on the morrow would prove to be more beneficial than had been his last visit.

Mr. Burke parted ways with them at the church gate, letting the vicar know he would be behind him a half hour, as he needed to spend a little time with his wife and children after cleaning up.

Mr. Derrick opened the latch of the gate as Mr. Burke walked off, inviting Georgiana to pass through before him. Her heart jumped as she brushed by him through the opening. There was nothing like the way she felt in his presence.

"I shall open the vestry for you," he said, "but I hope you will spend only a few minutes recording the day's tasks." He smiled at her as he opened the door to the church. "What you need is a solid meal and a good night's rest."

She returned his smile as they stepped into the nave, where it was so silent that she worried Mr. Derrick might hear her heartbeat echoing among its walls.

He opened the final door for her, ensured she had the quill and ink she needed, and then excused himself, leaving her with a feeling of disappointment. She heavily suspected that her heart would only be content with being near him at all times.

She stifled a sigh as he closed the door to the vestry behind him and, after a moment of staring at it, made her way to the desk and pulled the surveyor book from the drawer.

It took time to record all of the activities of the day. The village had worked very hard indeed, and they deserved every last farthing they had received.

She blew softly on the last page of her entry, noting how the sun was creeping down on the horizon, leaving a warm glow around the furniture in the room. It was time to head back to Granchurch House.

She shut the book and placed it carefully in its place and then left the vestry, pausing for a moment to stare at the stained glass that filled the large windows on the west side of the nave. They were bursting with even more color than usual as the setting sun shone through them, painting the large room with long columns of rainbow-colored light. It was a beautiful ending to a beautiful and exhausting day.

She glanced down at the filthy hem of her dress as she opened the door that led to the outside of the church and then collided with something solid.

Mr. Derrick, slightly breathless, stood before her.

They steadied one another, both putting a hand on the other's arm, a coincidence which brought large, sheepish smiles to their faces.

"I apologize, Miss Paige," he said, leaving his hand on her arm. "I was wondering if you would still be here—hoping for your sake that you would already be on your way to Granchurch, but hoping for *my* sake that perhaps I could walk you there myself before Burke and your brother arrive."

She suddenly felt short of breath and nodded. "I should like that."

Seeming to realize that his hand still held her arm, he removed it and offered his arm to her. His hair was still damp, and she could smell the soap he had used to wash up with at the parsonage. They made their way toward the small lane that led to Granchurch House, surrounded by the glowing colors of the setting sun, which were even more vibrant than she had anticipated.

"Well," Mr. Derrick said, "you have won the hearts of the village, Miss Paige. Even the irascible Mrs. Green is very taken with you, not that it surprises me in the least."

She glanced up at him, but he was looking forward. "I suspect that Mrs. Green is one of those souls who feels compelled to hide her excessively soft heart behind a steel exterior."

He chuckled and nodded. "You are quite right. She has a heart of gold but takes extreme caution before letting anyone see or experience it."

They had nearly reached the top of the hill to Granchurch, and Georgiana tugged at his arm, bringing them around to admire the sunset that provided a backdrop for the village so vivid that it stopped her breath in her chest.

She felt the vicar's eyes on her and chanced a glance at him. He was clean and fresh, and the orange glow of the sunset reflected in his dark eyes as he looked down at her in a way that made her forget how to breathe.

She suppressed a smile and turned her head away, imagining what she must look like in that moment. "I suddenly feel acutely aware of just how covered in dirt I am. It is very kind of you to walk with me in such a state—and to allow me to take your arm." She raised her arm from his and noted the line of dust on his black coat that evidenced where her arm had been. She clenched her teeth together, conscience-stricken. "I am not fit to be seen."

He let out a breathy chuckle, shifting so that he was turned toward her. "And here I had been thinking that you had never looked quite so beautiful as you do now"— he reached a hand to her cheek, a half-smile on his face, and rubbed softly at it

—"covered quite perfectly in evidence of the generous heart you possess."

Her breath caught in her chest at the feel of his warm fingers on her face, and she felt a contradictory chill run through her, as if her body had become aware of just how cold it was everywhere but where his hand rested.

She tried to laugh off his words, but the laugh came out as shaky as her knees felt. "You would love anything covered in Rushbury dirt." She looked at him, and the mischievous smile she wore immediately melted at the sight of his amused one.

"I *am* partial to it," he said, giving a final rub to her cheek before letting his hand drop down.

Her cheek tingled where it had been, and she took in a steadying breath.

He searched her eyes, a look of bafflement in his own. "I can think of no woman in your position who would do what you did today. Each time we meet, you amaze me."

She tried to control her breathing and managed a smile amidst her fluttering nerves. "We London folk are not so terrible as you think, Mr. Derrick." She glanced down at the village below, at the rooftops and doorways of families she could name and describe. "But I have come to love Rushbury and its people."

She looked at him again, wondering if he knew what lay hidden in those words—if he knew just how much she had come to love one person in particular. "For the first time in a very long time, I feel like I *belong*." She laughed and shook her head. "I imagine that must sound silly, for I have been here just a few short weeks, but…." She took in a breath and shrugged. "Rushbury feels like home."

He moved closer to her, taking her fingers and holding them in his hand. He brought her hand—encased in a dirt-covered glove—to his lips and kissed it, closing his eyes as he did so. "You *do* belong here, Georgiana."

At the sound of her name, a thrill burst inside her; a hope no longer able to be contained.

He looked down at her with a half-smile that made her legs feel weak. "From the moment I met you," he said, "I have known that you would change Rushbury." His smile grew. "At first, I thought you my foe—a cursedly beautiful foe, but a foe nonetheless—and one who was determined to conquer this little village." He reached a hand back to her cheek, cupping it in his hand and making her heart race so quickly she could barely hear above its pounding. "I little knew how quickly you would come to be my greatest ally—or how swiftly and completely you would conquer my heart."

She shut her eyes, reveling in his words. They felt too good to be true—like the realization of a million hopes she had been fighting off for years.

"And *I* little realized," she said, sighing and returning his gaze, "how the person my heart had given up hoping for would be found in a small, Yorkshire village, protected and preserved by a dozen little roads too dangerous for any but the most hardy of travelers."

He threw his head back, and she delighted in the sound of his laugh. It was a sound she could never tire of.

When he brought his head back down, his gaze moved to her lips for a moment before he shut his eyes and then turned to look back toward the parsonage and the church. "I imagine Burke is waiting for me already at the parsonage."

"He said that he would be late, did he not?" she said, feeling bold enough to set a hand on his arm and pull him nearer. "And besides, my brother is notoriously late. If he asks for an hour, one must count on one and a half, at least."

Mr. Derrick smiled, looking intrigued, and his eyes moved down to her lips again, his chest rising and falling more heavily. The scent of almond soap filled the air between them, and she felt herself move closer to him as if her body was moving of its own accord.

A door closed and footsteps sounded somewhere behind Georgiana. "That will be Archie," she said, listening as the foot-steps grew louder. She sighed, moving away from the vicar reluctantly. "Prompt for the first time in his life, I think."

Mr. Derrick took her hand in his, placing it between them so that no one looking on would be the wiser. "May we continue this conversation tomorrow?"

Georgiana nodded, holding his eyes as if she might will him to understand everything that hadn't yet been said. But there would be tomorrow. And many tomorrows after that, she dearly hoped.

"Derrick!" Archie said, jogging up to them.

Mr. Derrick dropped Georgiana's hand, his eyes lingering conspiratorially on hers for a moment before he turned to Archie.

"Shall we?" Archie said, glancing at Georgiana and then at the vicar.

Mr. Derrick held her eyes a moment longer, the promise of tomorrow's conversation burning in them, then turned toward Archie and nodded.

Georgiana watched them walk off down the hill as dusk lay its blue blanket over the countryside. Her heart skipped two beats when Mr. Derrick turned to look over his shoulder at her midway down the hill. She couldn't be sure, but it seemed that he wished as much as she did that they could choose to spend the evening together as easily as Archie had arranged for them to do.

But at least there was tomorrow.

She sighed in mixed contentment and longing and turned toward Granchurch House.

CHAPTER 16

Samuel thought he might have given his right arm to be able to continue with Georgiana as they had been. It was all he could do to keep his voice calm and his responses sensible as he spoke to Archie when exhilaration was coursing through him from his conversation with her. The feel of her warm cheek under his hand, the tingle of anticipating their lips meeting....

But it would have to wait. He hardly knew how he could stand the promise of what the morrow would hold.

He rolled his shoulders, forcing himself to focus on the conversation at hand.

Archie Paige was extremely personable and easy to talk to, but it didn't take long for Samuel to see how he had come to find himself obliged to "rusticate," as he referred to it. He had very little of Georgiana's responsibility and far too much spirit to stay out of the scrapes of which London provided more than enough.

Once they arrived at the parsonage and were joined by Burke, Archie drank freely from the bottle that Samuel's maid had placed upon the table, which only led to his cheerfully dominating the conversation.

"...And *that* is how I come to find myself here with you

amiable chaps," Archie said with a grin, pouring himself another glass of brandy and kindly refilling the nearly full glasses of Samuel and Burke—both of whom had only taken a few small sips since they had begun.

"I imagine your sister and aunt are thrilled to have your company," said Burke, discarding from his hand.

"Well," Archie said, peering at his cards through narrowed eyes and the slightest swaying of his head, "I told Georgie she was mad to come all this way, but she was determined."

"Why?" Samuel couldn't keep from asking. He couldn't wrap his mind around the good fortune that had brought Georgiana Paige into his life.

Archie and Burke both looked at him curiously, and he shrugged. "I am simply curious why she should choose Rushbury of all places, when she undoubtedly could have visited friends or family somewhere less remote."

"Ah," Archie said, resting an elbow on the table and pointing at Samuel. "But there was no fortune to be had in such places."

Samuel frowned. "What do you mean?"

Archie laughed and tossed a card onto the pile. "Georgie hopes to gain the favor of Aunt Sara, since Aunt Sara can leave Granchurch and her money where she will."

Samuel's hands paused in the act of rearranging his cards. His eyes met Burke's.

"Is she in need of a fortune?" Burke asked.

"Isn't everyone?" Archie said with a lopsided smile. "I have considered trying to beat her out for it." He laughed and took another large gulp from his glass.

Samuel forced a smile, but his muscles were tight, his stomach clenched. Could it truly be money that had brought Georgiana to Rushbury? Of course, Archie's words were true to an extent: one had to be practical, and everyone needed a way to support their life. It didn't change what he knew about her and what he had witnessed of her character.

But it didn't sit entirely well with him. Perhaps he had idealized her too much and that was why the possibility that it had been pure self-interest that had brought her to his village bothered him.

Or perhaps Archie was simply wrong and his tongue so loosened by drink as to be unreliable. If forced to choose between believing idle words and his own personal knowledge of Georgiana, he would certainly choose the latter.

The morning crept by at a snail's pace, and Georgiana found herself wondering yet again when she would have the opportunity to speak with Mr. Derrick.

With Samuel.

He had called her by her Christian name. She would call him by his.

They had agreed that they would continue their conversation that day, but they hadn't made any arrangements for how that might be made to happen.

However they managed to find one another, it wouldn't happen until the afternoon, she imagined. So she tried to while away the hours of the morning by writing a letter to Daphne and then walking the grounds of Granchurch. She smiled as she spotted a patch of celandine, thinking back on their walk to the meadow. If she could have chosen a place for them to continue their conversation, it would have been there.

The weather was warming, and Georgiana couldn't think of a more hopeful spring than this one. New life was everywhere—in the leafy tree branches, in the musical chirping of birds, in the budding of new and colorful flowers, and in the delightful bleating of new lambs in Rushbury's fields. But nothing filled her with more hope than the prospect of her own life and what it might hold.

She had come to Rushbury ready to lay to rest the idea of marriage and companionship—to embrace life as a spinster. Never had she considered that her life might find rebirth there—in the harsh and somber Yorkshire landscape where she had arrived.

Stepping back into the house, she pulled off her bonnet and set it on the entry hall table, making her way to the breakfast parlor. To her surprise, Archie entered shortly after her. Quelling a desire to ask him a dozen questions about his evening with Mr. Burke and the vicar, she settled for asking him how he was doing.

He winced as his fork clanged against his plate. "I've got a headache."

She smiled sympathetically. Archie was not known for his temperance. "Yes, I suspected you might, which makes it all the more surprising to find you here at this early hour. I imagined you would be in bed until much later."

"Well," he said, taking a gulp of black coffee and grimacing, "apparently it is not only the dinner hour that is pushed early in the countryside. In Rushbury, it seems that *everything* ends hours earlier than it does in London, including a game of cards. I was home by midnight."

She smiled. She wasn't surprised to hear that Samuel did not stay up till all hours of the night, particularly after the strenuous day they had all had yesterday. "Not everyone has your appetite for entertainment, Archie. I imagine the entire village slept quite soundly after their hard work."

Archie frowned and set down his cup of coffee with a noncommittal grunt. He leaned back in his seat, folding his arms across his chest. "Do you know *everyone* in the village, Georgie?"

She tilted her head from one side to the other. "Nearly, I think. Some better than others, though."

He nodded, his eyes still narrowed in thought. "Who lives in the house with the extra tall chimney stack?"

Georgiana pictured the village in her mind. "The third house? On the north side?"

"Yes, I think that's the one."

She stirred her tea and nodded. "That would be John and Mary Reed. Why do you ask?"

Archie shook his head. "Just curious, that's all."

"How long do you intend to stay at Granchurch?" Georgiana had expected that a couple of days there would have been more than enough to give Archie a distaste for the place, but he hadn't communicated any plans to leave yet.

He shrugged. "I haven't decided yet. Burke and Derrick are pleasant fellows and don't seem to mind playing for penny points, and that's all I can manage until quarter day comes."

The thought of simply refraining from cards was unthinkable to Archie. Georgiana was pleased, though, to know that her brother had taken a liking to the vicar.

There had been two thoughts lurking behind her contentment and joy since those precious moments with the vicar. One was a slight nervousness that her family would not approve of her marrying a country vicar.

The other was the unwelcome fear that the entire situation was simply too good and wonderful to be true, and that it might all come crashing down around her at any given moment—that the vicar would realize his error and realize that she was *not*, in fact, worthy of his attentions. Eight years of being overlooked had not given Georgiana confidence in herself, and she knew the smallest desire to run away before her heart could be broken, before Samuel could realize what had been obvious to everyone in London: Georgiana was not meant for marriage.

But she couldn't run. Her fears were far eclipsed by that stubborn hope that she had tried in vain to extinguish over the past eight years: hope that there was something more for her than the solitary life she watched Aunt Sara and other spinsters lead; that she might fall asleep and wake to the familiar presence of someone whose happiness mattered to her more than her own; that there was someone whose heart would respond to hers in perfect reciprocity.

Her time in Rushbury had fanned that little hope to a raging fire within her—one her fears were entirely unequipped to snuff out.

It had been quite some time since Samuel had slept in past six o'clock, and even when he rose from his bed with the small hand of the clock tipping toward seven, his movements were more sluggish than usual. His body fought against his wishes for movement, his arms and back aching, the skin on his hands feeling tight with the promise of blisters. He was sincerely glad he had refrained from following Archie's lead in drinking more than one glass of brandy—he couldn't imagine adding a throbbing head to everything.

A quick, urgent knock sounded at the front door, and Samuel's brows drew together as he tied his cravat. It was far too early for any callers.

A knock only slightly less urgent sounded shortly after on the door of his bedchamber. "Come in," he said.

His maid appeared in the doorway. "It's Mr. Burke, sir. He says it's urgent."

Samuel nodded and shrugged on his coat, following his maid from the room and taking quick strides toward the front door.

Burke was looking down at the floor, spinning the hat in his hands distractedly. His head came up at the sound of Samuel's footsteps.

He grimaced and shook his head. "Bad news, Sam."

"What is it?" Samuel said, gesturing for Burke to precede him into the study.

"The Gilmours' machines. Someone took an ax to them—broke the window to get into the house and then went to work destroying the machines."

Samuel's mouth opened as his muscles tensed. "Luddites?" He shook his head, rubbing his mouth. "How could they have received word of the machines so quickly?"

It had been a few months since any news had reached them of Luddite violence, and Samuel had secretly hoped that the riots and uprisings were a thing of the past—an unfortunate but short-lived blemish on the histories of Yorkshire and the surrounding counties. He sympathized with the men, of course—they were desperate to feed their families and guard their livelihoods—but the fear and havoc they had spread across the North had been palpable.

Rushbury had been mercifully unaffected by it all. As a village slow to embrace progress and technology, there had been no reason for the Luddites to come there.

Burke pinched his lips and brows together, holding Samuel's eyes as if he wished for Samuel to understand something without speaking it.

"What?" Samuel said.

"I don't think that word *did* travel so quickly, Sam."

Samuel sucked in a quick breath and clamped his eyes shut as he let it out. "John Reed." The man had been impossible to catch since the arrival of the machines—he had brushed off Samuel's attempts at conversation, usually drunk when he did so. John knew what it would likely mean for him and his family. More hardship. Lower wages for the same work. And all with a growing family.

"I don't have proof," said Burke, "but I highly suspect it was he. He hasn't been sober in a week, and you know how he is when he's been drinking."

Samuel nodded, running a hand through his hair. John had abstained from drink for some time before this when he had realized how unhinged and violent it made him—and how it had affected his children to see him that way.

Burke shrugged helplessly. "The Gilmours are insisting I put up a sign calling for information—offering a hundred pounds for the identity of the person responsible."

"A hundred pounds?" Samuel said incredulously. He let out a gush of air. "That's more than twice the normal reward."

A hundred pounds come by without any work was a sum unimaginable to most of Rushbury's residents.

But they wouldn't turn on one of their own. At least not willingly.

Burke nodded. "A servant has already been sent to order the printing of the signs. I reckon I'll have them in hand by noon. And the Gilmours want them up without delay."

Of course they did. They saw this act as a threat to all their plans for Rushbury, and Samuel suspected that they would be merciless with the offender. They would make an example of him.

"I must find John," said Samuel. "I *must* speak with him and help him see reason. No one will inform on him—I am confident of that. But he cannot think to get away with such a crime with no repercussions."

Burke slapped his hat against his leg softly. "Then what? What are you proposing?"

Samuel grimaced. "I have no idea."

There were no good options. He couldn't watch as one of his closest friends was tried and transported—or worse, hanged—for a decision made out of desperation. It was a terrible decision—there was no arguing that—but he didn't deserve to die, and his family didn't deserve to be left alone, worse off than ever and deprived of a father and husband.

He would need to speak to John. But first he needed a plan—

something to force John to come to his senses and see that he was hurting no one more than his own family. He was putting the village in a terribly difficult position. If the Gilmours were intent upon finding the criminal responsible, they had the ability to tear Rushbury apart by putting pressure on the villagers to tell what they knew.

He suppressed the desire to swear. He couldn't sort through this on his own. He needed to speak with Georgiana. Perhaps she would know what to do.

CHAPTER 17

By twelve o'clock, Georgiana was feeling too anxious to sit inside anymore. Fortunately, she had remembered two or three things which she had forgotten to detail in the surveyor records the day before. They were small matters, but whoever took up the position once her year of service was over would surely be grateful for her meticulous documentation.

It sounded like a frail excuse even to her, but she took it, nonetheless.

Patience helped her into her light blue spencer and handed her bonnet to her. She had only been acting as maid for a few days, but she was looking more tired than usual. Georgiana couldn't help but wonder if she was trying to help her family as well as performing her duties at Granchurch. Georgiana had purposely given her flexibility, insisting she only needed her at certain times of day, but she was beginning to doubt the wisdom of this. What had been intended as an act of charity and consideration—and a way to safeguard her own freedom—might instead be taken as an excuse by Patience to overwork herself, devoting her time and attention between Granchurch *and* home.

Georgiana would have to see if she could draw Patience out. She was a very kind and amiable young woman, but Georgiana had the impression that she kept her thoughts and feelings close and shouldered burdens heavier than someone her age should have to bear alone.

Georgiana tingled with anticipation as she stepped outside, and her heart quickened as she passed the spot where she and Samuel had stopped yesterday evening, the memory bringing a warmth to her cheeks. She was only halfway down the hill, though, when she spotted the vicar himself striding toward her. He was looking at the ground and seemed to be frowning.

Her heart stuttered. Had he already thought better of things? Was he coming to clarify that he hadn't meant anything by what he had said and done the day before?

He finally looked up, and the frown melted away, the corner of his mouth tugging up slightly as he slowed and then continued walking toward her more quickly.

The slightest sigh of relief escaped Georgiana, and her mouth broke into a smile. "Samuel," she said, feeling her nerves flutter at her forwardness. She had meant to let his behavior dictate her own, but she hardly felt in control of herself.

He came up to her, taking her hands in his as a vestige of the frown reappeared on his brow. "I have bad news, I'm afraid."

She clasped his hands more tightly. "What is it?"

"The Gilmours' machines," he said. "Someone vandalized them last night." He glanced over his shoulder toward where the village lay, and his mouth drew into a line.

"Good heavens," Georgiana said.

He looked her in the eye and then shut his, shaking his head. "I am fairly certain I know the culprit."

Her mouth parted, and her stomach clenched. "John Reed?"

He nodded. "Burke is under orders by Sir Clyde to post signs all over the village and those nearby, seeking information about the act in exchange for a reward." He paused, his nostrils flaring. "One hundred pounds."

Her eyes widened. One hundred pounds was of little note to someone like Sir Clyde. But to one of the villagers….

"You think someone will inform on him?" she asked. "Were there any witnesses?"

Samuel shook his head. "Not that I can discover. The village was very quiet last night. Everyone was to bed earlier than usual, exhausted from the day's work, I imagine." He looked into her eyes, increasing the pressure on her hands. "I feel confident that none of the villagers would inform on him, even if they knew. The only person I am unsure of is…your brother."

Archie. Would he do such a thing? She couldn't imagine him even taking notice of the dealings of Rushbury.

She shook her head. "No, we needn't worry about Archie."

He frowned. "Perhaps I should speak with him to be sure."

She smiled wryly. "Quite unnecessary. My brother is lamentably true to the portrait painted by people like Mrs. Green: he thinks himself above the dealings of the village."

He looked at her with uncertainty. "Are you sure?"

She nodded. "If you wish, I will speak with him, but Archie is not nearly observant enough—or interested enough—to concern himself with such matters."

Samuel nodded with a little smile. "Opposite from you, then?" He looked down at her fingers, fiddling with them distractedly. "When I heard the news, you were the person I wanted to speak with." He looked up at her, and the somberness in his eyes led her to put a comforting hand to his cheek. "I *cannot* let John—or his family—be ruined by this. But neither can I turn a blind eye to his reckless and foolish choices. Besides, from what I know of the Gilmours, they won't rest until they find the person responsible and make him pay."

She nodded. "I very much fear you are right." She paused, taking in a breath. She wanted to lift Samuel's burden however she could. "I will speak with them."

He put a hand to her cheek and looked at her in a way that

made her feel that, no matter how unpleasant it might be to speak with the Gilmours on the matter, it would be well worth it.

"You will take your maid, I trust," he said, a glint of humor lighting up his grave expression for a moment.

"I wouldn't dream of jeopardizing things by neglecting to do so," she said.

They stood smiling into each other's eyes for a moment before Samuel sighed and Georgiana's smile faded, the weight of the situation settling back in on them.

"I would like to continue our conversation from yesterday," he said, "but I wish to do it without the necessity of brevity and without John Reed's future hanging over our heads."

She swallowed and nodded, her heart flapping against her ribcage.

"I must first ensure that John doesn't take his recklessness any further—or alternatively, succumb to his conscience and confess all before we've had the chance to decide upon a plan."

"Go," she said. "Ensure his safety. In the meantime, I will try to discover from Lady Gilmour what they intend to do in the event that no information is brought forward"— she rubbed her lips together nervously —"or in the event that it *is* brought forward."

"Bless you, Georgiana," Samuel said. "You are an angel." He put a hand behind her head, leaned in, and set a soft kiss on her forehead.

Stifling the desire to wrap her arms around him and prevent him from going, she merely smiled sadly and shook her head. "If there is anything more I can do to help, please let me know."

He nodded, pressing her hand in his, and then turned on his heel.

Samuel frowned as he closed the Reed's door behind him. John was not well. Defensive and almost belligerent, he had refused to acknowledge that what he had done was wrong.

As Samuel had suspected, he had been drinking too much before making his way toward the house at the end of the lane, but John insisted that he would have done the same thing sober. How he could claim such a thing was difficult to understand, since he still smelled too strongly of drink to lay any claim to sobriety.

And yet, Samuel had seen the fear in his eyes and the way his gaze flicked to his wife and her rounding midsection when Samuel spoke of what would be in store for him if he was arrested.

Mary had been painfully quiet during the visit, going about her duties in the kitchen silently and with a defeated and resigned quality to her movements. Samuel sensed that he was merely repeating what had already been said to John by her.

It had been all Samuel could do to extract a promise from John not to do anything more to jeopardize his or his family's safety. The man was desperate, after all, and he could only see the ruining of the machines in a positive light, so sure was he that he would not be found out.

John saw the Gilmours' bringing the machines into Rushbury as the breaking of a promise—one that needed to have consequences.

Samuel grimaced as he caught sight of the reward sign hanging on the nearest tree. He sincerely hoped John was right about there being no one who could—or would—claim the reward. In time, John would see the error of his ways, but Samuel was still at a loss for how he could make amends without confessing and risking his own death or transportation.

Preoccupied by the dilemma for the entirety of the day, Samuel found himself wondering whether Georgiana had already spoken with the Gilmours and what she had discovered. If they wouldn't listen to Georgiana, there was little hope for John, he feared. It would only take the detective work of a novice to discover that, not only was John the one with the most motive for breaking the machines, he'd had opportunity to do so. If Mary was interrogated as to his whereabouts on the night in question, she would be forced to choose between lying and setting the seal on her husband's fate.

Samuel was no closer to thinking of a solution when a knock sounded at his door as he prepared himself for bed. He paused in his shirtsleeves, straining his ears to hear who had come to the parsonage at such an odd hour. Recognizing the distinctive quality of Burke's voice, he tossed his cravat onto the bed and strode down the corridor, dismissing the maid and welcoming Burke in.

Burke's face was grave as he followed Samuel into the study. Samuel pulled the door closed behind them and took in a breath, trying to prepare himself. He had never seen his friend look so somber, so completely without the customary good humor that lined his eyes and mouth. Unbidden, memories of a similar late evening visit came to his mind, when Burke had informed him of Miss McIntyre's marriage.

He pushed away the thoughts. "What is it?" He took the brandy from the liquor cabinet and poured two glasses.

"Information has been brought forward against John," Burke said, his eyes fixed on Samuel.

Samuel's face fell, hand pausing in the act of passing a glass to Burke. "What? Already? The signs have only been up a few hours."

Burke said nothing, merely shrugging.

It wasn't fair. He'd not had enough time yet to come up with a palatable solution to the problem. He had never imagined anything would happen so soon.

He clenched his jaw. He so desperately wished he didn't have to ask the question on his lips, but it was no use. He would discover the identity of whatever villager had betrayed John, one way or another.

Was it the Mitchells? They had passed a particularly difficult year, and he could well see how a hundred pounds might be too tempting an offer. "Who came forward?"

Burke paused, his lips compressing into a tight line as he watched Samuel carefully. "Archibald Paige."

Samuel's breathing stilled, and he blinked once.

Burke nodded. "He came to me just half an hour ago with a name and description of John Reed."

"How? How would he know?"

"Seems he saw John exiting the house at the end of the lane with an ax in one hand and a bottle in the other just after we left here the other night."

Samuel swore softly, rubbing his chin. "I don't understand. Georgiana assured me he wouldn't interfere—and she promised to speak with her brother in order to ensure it." He lifted his shoulders. "He's not even met John to *know* his name."

Burke tipped his glass from side to side, lips pressed into a line. "Well he knows it well enough now. And so will the Gilmours."

Samuel tried to suppress the fear and unease that was making his throat feel blocked and tight.

Burke hadn't touched the brandy in his glass. "I told him it was too late in the evening to collect the reward from the Gilmours—that I would communicate the information in the morning." He shrugged his shoulders helplessly. "I don't see what else I can do. My hands are tied."

Samuel nodded. It wouldn't be fair to ask Burke to withhold information or evidence from the Gilmours—not when it was his job as constable to see that the law was followed in Rushbury. He began pacing the short distance of the study. "What will happen to John?"

Burke looked down, not meeting Samuel's eyes. "Nothing good. It will depend upon the Gilmours, though you know how seriously the justices treat followers of General Ludd."

Samuel stopped, tossing his hands up in frustration. "He's *not* a follower of Ludd! He's a man desperate to feed his family, for heaven's sake!" The anger was building inside him, and he could feel his hands beginning to shake, jostling the liquid in his glass. He tossed it off, throat burning and eyes watering, then slammed the empty glass down on the nearby table.

"I know, Sam," Burke said. "John is my friend too."

Samuel glanced at Burke and let out a gush of frustration. "You're right, of course. I'm sorry, Burke. I just can't bear to see John meet the same fate as those bands of ruffians."

"Nor I. But the justices won't care about that. They only care about making an example of anyone inciting violence or rebellion. You know that as well as I do."

Samuel ran a hand through his hair, pacing again.

"I must get home now," Burke said. "Molly is sick, and I promised to put the children to bed."

Samuel sighed and nodded. "Yes, of course. Go." He put a hand on Burke's shoulder. "Thank you for coming to tell me."

Burke shook his head. "Never did I think to bear such news, Sam. I always thought you were foolish to regard people like the Gilmours and the Paiges with such caution. But you were right. In the end, it all comes down to money for them." He drained his glass, set his wide-brimmed hat atop his head, then turned and left.

Samuel tossed and turned for the better part of the night, his mind taken up with so many contradictory thoughts, he thought he might be going mad.

He had considered going to John after Burke left—telling him to take his family and run. But he only considered the idea for the merest second. The Reeds had no money to sustain the life of fugitives. And with Mary increasing, such a course would be even more dangerous than usual. Besides, Samuel's conscience balked at the idea of engaging in such subterfuge.

As much anger as he felt toward the Gilmours and Archie Paige, he found that most of it was directed inward. He could have prevented all of this.

He had let Georgiana into the village, had vouched for her to the villagers and promised them they could trust her, had befriended her brother.

He had let her into his heart.

He had been a thoughtless, selfish fool, in fact. It had been his weakness for her, his blindness that had led to all of this. Why could he never learn to steel his heart to these newcomers?

Never would he have trusted the word of the Gilmours or agreed to play cards with Archibald Paige if he had not first allowed himself to trust Georgiana.

He had known it was foolishness when he had first met her, but he had ignored his instinct instead, and it had all led here: to a man's likely death.

CHAPTER 18

Georgiana's visit to Amblethorne Park had been a waste. Lady Gilmour and Sir Clyde were not at home and were not expected to be until far into the evening. She fretted all day long, unable to find distraction in any of her usual activities.

Archie was not at Granchurch, and it was from Aunt Sara that Georgiana discovered his intention of riding into the nearest village to see whether any entertainment was to be had there. When he returned after dinner, his high spirits provided a great contrast to Georgiana's.

"I take it you found Pickton to your liking?" she asked.

"Well, no," he said, "not really. It is only slightly less sleepy than Rushbury, as it turns out."

"Then what are you grinning about?"

It felt strange to see his wide smile when things were at such a crossroads in the village. But Archie was blissfully unaware of what was happening, and she could hardly explain it in a way that would make him understand. He had not come to love the village and its people as she had. The goings-on were a matter of indifference to him, naturally.

"Just the very unexpectedly productive and fortunate morning I have passed," he said, rubbing his hands together in a satisfied gesture. "I shall now be able to pay one of my most pressing debts and may not have any need to remain here quite so long, after all. Particularly if I can turn what money I now have into more money, which I fully intend to."

Gambling. She might have known that it would be success in such an arena which had brought up his spirits so.

He turned to leave the room, and she almost let him leave without saying anything. It almost seemed foolish to bring his attention to the situation. But she had promised Samuel.

"Archie," she said. "I had been hoping to speak with you about something."

He turned back toward her and raised his brows, waiting for her to continue.

"There has been an incident in the village—a terrible decision made by one of them—and while I know that you aren't involved in things here as I am, I merely wished to ask that you refrain from concerning yourself with it in any way. It is a very delicate situation."

He stared at her wordlessly, as if seeing through her, and then opened and shut his mouth. He cleared his throat and nodded. "Anything else?"

She shook her head, and he shot her something between a grimace and a weak smile before leaving her to herself.

The wind howled as Georgiana lay in her bed later that evening, trying in vain to fall asleep. The windows creaked with each gust, and the fire in the grate was nearly extinguished a number of times, so drafty was the side of the house where her room sat. The eerie groaning and whining of the wind made her skin prickle. Whatever little buds had managed to burst from their enclosures on Rushbury's trees and flowers, their strength was certainly being put to the test.

She didn't know when she finally fell asleep, only that it felt as though she tossed and turned for hours, with flashes of dreams coming and going until she lost consciousness. When she awoke in the morning, the wind had stopped entirely, and she could hear a bird chirping its morning call outside her window. The thought of trying to pass the hours until she could make a call to the Gilmours without seeming rude chafed her.

She rang for Patience. A walk into the village might calm her nerves, and perhaps the Reeds would be glad for a loaf of fresh bread from Mrs. Green.

She rang the bell again, and it was a few minutes before rushed footsteps sounded in the corridor outside Georgiana's door. Rather than Patience appearing, it was the chambermaid. "I am very sorry, miss, but Patience hasn't been seen today. Would you like me to help you dress or bring you a tray?"

Georgiana frowned. Patience had been very prompt in her short service, and it was unlike her to be missing at this hour, particularly since Georgiana had slept later than usual.

"Just some tea, thank you," she said. She would dress herself.

The morning was bright, and Georgiana felt her nerves settle a bit as she stepped along the track down to the village, holding her empty basket and gazing at the way the morning sunlight shone through the passing clouds intermittently. Mornings always provided so much more hope than dark nights, and Georgiana felt a sense of calm about the future as she stepped into the village. They would find a way to help John and the Reeds. Something would occur to her. And perhaps the Gilmours' hearts could be softened to the plight of people like John.

As she approached Mrs. Green's, the smell of fresh-baked bread met her nose, and she couldn't help but smile at the inviting scent. She bought three loaves from a grumbling Mrs. Green, who was very clearly not at her best in the mornings. Georgiana felt a gush of appreciation and affection for the woman. She wouldn't have changed a thing about Mrs. Green.

Much like the baguettes she sold, she had a firm and crusty exterior that made her interior feel all the softer.

She thanked her kindly and left the bakery, stepping out into the street and glancing up toward her destination. Her heart stuttered as she noted both Samuel and Mr. Burke standing at the door of the Reeds' home, speaking with Mrs. Reed in the doorway. An unfamiliar equipage stood in the street, its two horses fidgeting as Samuel held their reins.

No one noted Georgiana's presence, and as she neared the group, it became clear that the tone of the conversation was somber. This was hardly a surprise, though, given the situation the family was in.

She hesitated slightly. Should she leave them to their conversation?

But Mrs. Reed's eyes moved toward her, and Georgiana raised the basket in her hands, a few traces of steam rising into the air. Mrs. Reed closed her eyes and turned her head away, and Georgiana's face fell.

Mr. Burke and Samuel followed Mrs. Reed's gaze, and their jaws both unmistakably hardened upon seeing Georgiana. Her stomach clenched, but she took in a breath and stepped toward them.

"Good morning," she said. "I don't mean to interrupt, but I thought I might bring you a loaf or two of bread—and see how Patience is doing." She held up the basket slightly to display the bread.

Mrs. Reed still didn't look at her, and an unwieldy silence filled the air. It was Mr. Burke who finally spoke.

"I am very sorry for the inconvenience it may cause you, miss, but I imagine Patience wishes to be with her family this morning."

Georgiana blinked. Mr. Burke's tone was brittle, a hard quality piercing through the civil words.

She nodded quickly. "Of course. I shall just leave this basket with you, then," she said to Mrs. Reed.

Mrs. Reed finally turned her gaze back to Georgiana, and Georgiana swallowed at the look of pain mingled with anger that emanated from her tear-filled eyes.

"Why?" Mrs. Reed said, her voice hoarse.

Georgiana looked to Samuel for any sort of explanation, but he turned his gaze away. Her stomach clenched, and her breath came more quickly, her heartbeat quickening even more, twinging and aching at the thought of Samuel being angry with her.

She blinked away the thoughts that rushed her mind, anticipating rejection from him—the rejection she had been terrified she would open herself up to by allowing him into her heart.

She couldn't fathom what was happening, what had caused such a shift. She looked back to Mrs. Reed, raising her shoulders and shaking her head slowly. "I am terribly sorry, but I don't understand."

Mr. Reed appeared behind his wife, his face drawn and lined with a resoluteness that inspired a strange panic inside Georgiana. His eyes passed over her briefly, and she wasn't even sure that he recognized her. They landed upon Burke, and Mr. Reed inclined his head once, the slightest tremor in his bobbing throat.

"It is time, John."

Mr. Reed looked to Samuel with pleading eyes. "I shouldn't have done it, Sam. But with the kids hungry and another one on the way" —his voice broke— "I lost my head."

Samuel said nothing, only grasping at Mr. Reed's shoulder in a kind but bracing manner, his throat bobbing beneath his cravat.

"We will give you a moment to say your goodbyes," said Burke, stepping away from the door and turning his back to the Reeds. Samuel followed suit, and Georgiana stood rooted to the spot momentarily, watching as the Reeds turned toward one another and Mrs. Reed's body began to shake.

Georgiana turned away, feeling as though she had just witnessed something terribly intimate, something never meant for her eyes.

She stepped toward the vicar and the constable. "What has happened?"

Samuel wouldn't meet her eyes, his nostrils flared and jaw hard. "He is being taken away for trial. Information was laid against him."

"What?" She glanced at the Reeds again, wide-eyed. She couldn't imagine that any of the villagers would serve the Reeds in such a way. "By whom?"

Samuel's jaw worked for a moment. "By your brother."

Georgiana stared.

The world spun around her. Archie? Surely it wasn't true. She felt a sickening thud in the pit of her stomach as she thought on her conversation with Archie. He had boasted of his newfound ability to pay one of his debts.

"It couldn't be," she said, eyes still unblinking. "He assured me that he would not interfere with the situation." She shook her head. "No, he wouldn't do such a thing." Would he?

"Much as you assured *me* that we needn't worry about him involving himself," Samuel said, a bite to his tone.

Her breath caught at the hard words, and she lowered her head, hoping to conceal how they had affected her.

"He informed on John last night," Samuel said, his words softer now, as if he were trying to temper his frustration.

"But Archie has never even met Mr. Reed. How could he possibly know…?" She trailed off, feeling the color drain from her face as she remembered his offhand inquiry about who lived in the Reeds' home.

Samuel scoffed lightly. "Your confidence in your brother is inspiring, but the fact remains that he laid information against

John. He was able to identify him by name and correctly identify the house he had seen him enter after the crime was committed. He came by that information somehow."

Georgiana's heart sank, and she shut her eyes. No wonder he was angry with her. She had assured him more than once that Archie thought himself above the happenings of a small village like Rushbury. She hadn't accounted for his financial situation.

"He came by it by me." She hardly dared open her eyes to face Samuel, but she forced herself to, stifling the desire to flinch at the look of disappointment he wore. "He had the information by me. Though I swear I had no notion why he was asking."

The way he looked at her, eyes full of betrayal and hurt, felt like something from a bad dream.

"I *trusted* you. You assured me…" He looked away toward the Reed home, where Patience stood in the doorway, tears streaming down her face as she held one of her younger siblings on her hip. "It hardly matters. The damage has been done."

And it is your fault. He didn't say the words, but they were implied in what he was saying.

And he was right. She had immediately dismissed the idea of Archie doing anything. If she had taken the possibility seriously, she might have prevented all of this.

"Excuse me," Mr. Burke said gravely. "I must take John." He left Samuel's side and strode over to the Reeds, putting a hand on John's shoulder and grimacing at Mrs. Reed.

Georgiana couldn't bear to watch. "Samuel," she said in a pleading voice. "You know I would never do anything to—"

He put a hand up, his other gripping at the bottom half of his face. "Please. Do not." His hand slid down his chin harshly, and his eyes moved back to the Reeds. Georgiana could see the pain and helplessness in them as he watched the family.

"What can I do?" Georgiana asked, feeling desperate to put an end to the nightmare she was caught in.

"You have done enough," he said. He watched the Reeds a moment longer, then shut his eyes and let his head fall. "Please just leave us in peace." He turned away and moved toward Burke.

It must have been a full minute before Georgiana realized that she was standing still, the basket in her hand trembling along with her fingers. The smell of the warm bread was long gone, and no steam rose from the basket. Samuel, Mr. Burke, and the Reeds conversed in low tones, seemingly oblivious to her presence. It was as if she had ceased to exist, merely a ghost looking on.

She dashed a tear from the corner of her eye and turned away toward Granchurch House, forcing down the small sob that threatened to escape her.

Samuel couldn't stand it a moment longer. He turned to look over his shoulder, but it took time before he spotted the retreating figure of Georgiana, beginning the ascent up the lane toward Granchurch House.

His heart writhed within him, aching with one beat, pounding angrily the next. He hurt deeply for the Reeds—at the prospect of losing someone he loved so dearly—and while he knew that it was Archie, not Georgiana, who had informed on him, he found himself unable to deny her a portion of the blame. Perhaps it was simply his way of shifting the blame anywhere but himself.

But if she had never come to Rushbury, Archie would never have come; if she hadn't provided John's identity to Archie so thoughtlessly, he wouldn't have had the ability to lay the information. Without the Paiges, he could have arranged things—arranged them so that justice was served, but mercy too. The

Gilmours might have been repaid, and John need not go to prison.

But deep down, Samuel knew his anger was directed at himself. For believing he could trust anyone from Georgiana's world and for assuring the village—the people who trusted *him* —that they could trust her as well.

He could plead with the Gilmours, and he would certainly do that, though he harbored little hope that it would do any good. He could fall on his knees and pray that God would soften the hearts of whatever justices would hear John's case. But he was familiar enough with the fates of those guilty of similar crimes to have little hope there either.

He felt entirely helpless, and as he watched Georgiana disappear around the bend in the lane, he felt the first shadows of despair engulf him.

He was alone.

Georgiana blinked as she faced the door of Granchurch. She hardly remembered the walk there.

She felt numb, but as she wiped the back of her glove on her face, it came away wet from tears. She entered the house, setting down the basket of bread upon the entry table and letting out a large gush of air as she set a soft hand atop the towel wrapped around the bread. All the hope from earlier that morning had vanished and left her feeling almost dead inside.

Her first inclination was to go upstairs and lie upon her bed, begging sleep to submerge her so that she needn't relive what she had just witnessed, what had just been said to her.

Please just leave us in peace.

She winced and strode through the doorway and up the stairs. She couldn't sleep, but she could ride.

Shedding her dress for one more appropriate for riding, she

fiddled with the buttons, grateful she could do so without the assistance of a maid. The thought only brought on a fresh wave of eye-watering. No wonder Patience had been absent. She was about to lose her father.

So far from sounding hopeful as it had that morning, the chirping of birds outside felt discordant to Georgiana—as though the creatures were purposely ignoring the tempest raging in Rushbury and in Georgiana's heart.

The effects of the windstorm were apparent on the grounds of Granchurch—a few fallen branches, flowers absent their new petals.

She tossed the reins, signaling Aunt Sara's horse to move down the hill at a quicker pace, as if she could escape the chirping by putting more distance between her and Granchurch. But the chirping followed her.

At the crossroads at the bottom of the hill, Georgiana tugged on the reins for a moment, then turned the horse to the right. She couldn't face the village. She couldn't pass through it right now. Indeed, how would she ever face anyone there after today? They hardly knew Archie—to them, he was merely an extension of her. His choice to inform on John would be taken as a betrayal by Georgiana herself—just as Samuel had taken it to be.

She would not be welcome in the village anymore—that had been quite clear from her interaction with Samuel, Mr. Burke, and Mrs. Reed. Her presence would be painful to the people of Rushbury—a reminder of what had happened to John Reed. She didn't think she could bear seeing that in everyone's eyes. Certainly not in Samuel's eyes.

She gave the horse a kick, and they were off in the direction of the main road at a much higher speed than Georgiana would have felt comfortable adopting prior to the work the village had just done. Yielding to a desire to be alone, she followed a small trail that led through the trees just short of the main road and found it looping her around the back side of the village, coming out onto one of the small roads she had surveyed with Samuel just a few weeks prior. It took her five minutes of riding to discover just where she was, and when she did, she winced.

Just a hundred feet in front of her, another trail led off the road, nearly invisible. It was the path that led to the meadow.

It was a self-torturing decision, and yet Georgiana couldn't prevent herself. She slid down from the horse and led it into the trees. She could only imagine how the path would look when the leaves were fully grown, how intimate and protected it would be. She had meant to see it in every season. To see it with Samuel in every season.

The path seemed longer without someone to pass the time conversing with, and when she reached the end, where the trees opened up and the sky reappeared, she stopped and shut her eyes.

Gone was the field full of colorful blooms she had seen so recently. Ravaged by the windstorm overnight, there was no color to punctuate the green of the grass.

It was nothing to provoke tears—it was the natural order of things, after all—and yet Georgiana found herself staving off a desire to weep.

She stooped down, picking up two stray petals that had not been swept into the woods by the gusts. She gazed at them and rubbed them between her fingers: evidence of what used to be and of what she had come to the meadow hoping for again. But it was gone, and she could not summon it back.

Like the meadow, Rushbury had been an unexpected haven for Georgiana. She had not come there expecting to love the people. It had merely been a means of escaping the life she had come to loathe—of embracing spinsterhood on her own terms.

But she *had* come to know and love the people there. She had even fallen in love, opening herself up to the possibility of marriage for the first time in years.

But all that was gone—swept away as quickly as the flowers

in the field had been by the windstorm. The bliss was never meant to last, and now Rushbury would forever hold painful memories of what might have been—a taste of the life she hadn't dared admit—even to herself—that she wanted.

Nothing would be more painful or unbearable than to stay in Rushbury, amongst people she cared for who now viewed her with hostility; to be forever seeing Samuel and knowing that he wished her elsewhere.

She turned away from the meadow and rested her head against the horse's neck, closing her eyes and then cringing. She could hardly stand to think of returning to London. But London would be more bearable than Rushbury now—perhaps her parents would permit her to return to the family estate rather than staying in Town or following them to Brighton.

She didn't know if she could bear waiting to leave Rushbury until Archie was ready.

CHAPTER 19

"Georgie?"

Georgiana blinked and raised her eyes from the spot they had been trained on for the past ten minutes.

Archie stood just inside the doorway of the drawing room, looking at her with a furrowed brow. "I've just told you that I am for London at the end of the week, and you don't so much as blink?"

"London?" she said, sitting up and looking at him with sudden alertness.

He nodded, still watching her with a slightly wary expression. "Well, not to London precisely. I swore to Father that I wouldn't set foot there until quarter day, you know. But a friend is hosting a party at his estate near Richmond." His smile widened. "Barlow has promised to be in attendance, and he is by far the worst whist player I know, yet he always insists on playing for the highest of stakes. I hadn't thought to attend, my pockets being to let as they have been, but now…." He put a hand to his coat with a smile.

Georgiana felt a wave of nausea rush over her. He meant to gamble with the money he'd had in exchange for informing on John Reed. She suspected that it was that same money which would allow Archie to make the journey at all. She debated confronting him—part of her wanted to tell him just how terribly he had ruined everything with his thoughtless, selfish actions. But she feared if she attempted it right now, she would lose hold on her emotions, and nothing would send Archie running faster than a bout of crying.

"I was thinking of going to London myself," she said, her voice trembling slightly. She was so very angry with him, yet sorrow was what threatened to overcome her.

He reared back slightly. "London? For how long?"

She tugged at her glove seam. "I'm not certain that I shall return to Rushbury." The words settled deep inside her, weighing her down in her chair. She couldn't stand to stay, but the thought of never setting foot in the village again made her eyes burn.

A knowing smile appeared on his face. "Devilish dull place, isn't it?"

She couldn't manage any words in response, her throat sticking so that she could hardly swallow. Rushbury was the place where she had hoped to spend the rest of her life. He didn't understand how her heart ached at the thought of leaving. It was only just more bearable than the thought of staying.

"What of Aunt Sara?" he asked.

Georgiana took in a large breath. "I am sure it hasn't escaped your attention that Father has a warped idea of her fragility. She *likes* her solitude. And besides, Rachel will be here at the beginning of next week. She hardly needs me." She had no reason at all to stay.

He nodded. "Well, you're welcome to come with me, of course, though we shall have to part ways at Richmond, you know."

She nodded with an attempt at a smile. "That is quite all right. And I insist upon paying for the journey." She would pay twice as much for it if only it meant they wouldn't be using that hundred pounds.

His eyebrows shot up. "But why?"

She shrugged, not caring to tell him the real reason. "I couldn't make the journey without you, so it is only reasonable. Consider it my way of thanking you for your trouble." She was feeling more sick by the moment as she thought on the prospect of departing in just two days.

Archie frowned and narrowed his eyes. "You look blue-devilled." He walked toward her. "What's the matter?"

She hardly knew what to say. He couldn't possibly know what he had done, what pain he had caused for the village, for Samuel, for the Reeds. For her.

He had acted thoughtlessly, with no concept of the lives his actions were affecting. But that was the problem. It was precisely what the villagers thought of people like Archie and Georgiana—thoughtless, selfish creatures who couldn't be bothered to concern themselves with anyone they thought below them.

And he had lied to her about it. That, more than anything, brought the bile into her throat.

"I know you informed on John Reed, Archie," she said, turning her head to gaze through one of the windows. It was easier than looking at him, and if her anger took the form of tears, at least he wouldn't see them.

There was a long pause, and she heard the floorboards creak beneath him as he shifted his weight. "I was under the impression that my identity would be kept confidential. I suppose I should have known better in a place like this where one cannot so much as step out-of-doors without the entire village becoming aware."

Georgiana turned toward him, regret sweeping over her at the utter lack of understanding he was displaying—just as she had anticipated he would. "You assured me that you wouldn't interfere!"

He raised up his shoulders in a gesture meant to convey innocence. "What would you have had me do? I hadn't any notion that you were aiding and abetting law-breakers, Georgie! And it was too late by then."

"At the very least you might have *told* me. But you didn't." She bit at the inside of her lip. "You lied—and you did it to save your own skin."

"I did," he said waspishly, not mincing matters. "And I take full responsibility for doing so. Maybe it was a cowardly thing to do, but dash it! The man looked fit for Bedlam with how bosky he was, and swinging his ax about, no less! If I'd suspected you kept company with the likes of him, perhaps I would've given a second thought to laying the information, but I had no idea." He tossed his hat onto the nearest chair and put his hands on the back of it, gripping it harshly and letting out another sound of displeasure.

Georgiana clenched her hands into fists. "Why must you always be gambling away your money? Always so focused on what the next entertainment is? Have you no thought at all for anyone but yourself?" She let out a frustrated breath. "The man you informed on," she said, turning toward him, "he is a friend, Archie."

Archie looked up and stared at her. "But…he's a drunkard. A violent drunkard."

Georgiana shook her head, pressing her lips together. "He isn't, though. He is a man who has fallen on hard times through no fault of his own. And because *you* wanted a bit more money in your pockets—to fritter away—he will likely hang."

Archie paced, putting a finger up and shaking it. "I know what I saw. An innocent man doesn't do what that man did."

How could she possibly explain it to him? He hadn't been raised to concern himself with people like John Reed. "You know what it is like to be at your wit's and pocket's end—to need money desperately."

He nodded, frowning.

"Well, imagine that there *is* no quarter day to look forward to. Imagine that, if you cannot find a way to raise money, Aunt Sara and I should starve; and that someone more powerful than you has taken your only hope of making that money."

His brow was still knit together in displeasure, but his throat bobbed.

"*That* is but a peek into the life of John Reed and what led him to the desperation you witnessed. Those machines will forever change his life and the lives of his wife and children."

He grimaced and let out a breath. "I had no idea." He looked at her, apology written in his eyes. "And I *am* sorry."

She felt a desire to relieve some of her frustration on him, to tell him that his being sorry did *nothing*. But she clamped her jaw shut to prevent any words from escaping. What good would it do, after all? What was done was done.

"I *must* do something," she said softly, chewing on the tip of her thumb.

She glanced at the ticking clock, and her eyes widened when she realized that it was nearly two. She could make a visit to the Gilmours now—and pray that they were home this time.

But what would she say to them? Even less than Archie would they understand the plight of John Reed. He had cost them a significant amount of money, and she suspected that such a concern would outweigh all others.

But she had to try. Before leaving, she had to do whatever she could to untangle the mess she had made.

Samuel clenched the brim of his hat in his hand, feeling every muscle in his body tighten as he watched Lady Gilmour sip her tea unconcernedly. One would have thought they were discussing something as banal as the weather rather than the life of a man hanging in the balance.

"He sincerely regrets what he did in a moment of passion and despair, Lady Gilmour."

She set down her tea gently, then looked at him as though he were the most pathetic figure she had ever encountered. "I am afraid my hands are quite tied, Mr. Derrick. You must understand, surely, that Sir Clyde and I cannot allow such a crime to go unpunished. We would merely be setting ourselves up for future occasions of violence."

Samuel's fingers tightened even more around his hat. Violence? She spoke of John's choice as though it had put her personal safety at risk. "I am not asking you to turn a blind eye to what he did—merely that you seek lesser charges against him. A fine perhaps?"

She smiled at him so that wrinkles appeared at the edges of her eyes. There was no kindness in the smile, only more pity and condescension. "I do not pretend to any expertise in matters of the law. I feel confident that justice will be carried out much better without my interference. I understand that we are to consider ourselves fortunate that it was the work of only one man rather than one of the bands of criminals who have committed such crimes in other parts of the North."

Samuel had never been one to condone the means used by the Luddites, but he found himself in sympathy with them more than ever. After all, what could one do to combat the utter indifference people like Lady Gilmour displayed toward the difficulties of those who enriched them with their labor and skill?

He inclined his head. "Thank you very much for your time, my lady."

"Not at all, vicar," she said, rising from her seat to go ring the bell. "It was my pleasure."

"I shall see myself out," he said with a bow, unable to summon a smile, despite his best efforts.

He hadn't expected much from his visit to Amblethorne, but there was always that stubborn shred of hope inside him, and as he strode purposefully down the corridor toward the entry hall, he felt a little wave of panic begin to wash over him.

There was nothing he could do to stop the wheels that had been set into motion by Archie Paige—set in motion due to his *need* to pay off whatever ridiculous debts he had accrued. More than likely, he would take his reward prize to some greasy-haired moneylender in London, only to be in the same position in a few months' time.

Lady Gilmour's refusal to do anything at all to show mercy to John was entirely in line with what Samuel knew of people like her. If something did not add directly to their comfort, it was not worth the energy or effort to pursue. The Gilmours obviously did not view Samuel as someone whose opinion bore serious consideration—he was merely one of the lowly villagers they were obliged to tolerate.

If there was anyone they would listen to, it would not be him. It would be Georgiana.

"Thank you," he said as the door was opened for him by a servant. He took long strides down the wide path that led away from Amblethorne.

The thought of requesting help from Georgiana made him shut his eyes in consternation. He shook his head. Rushbury didn't need more interference from outsiders. He should know by now that it only led to more trouble in the end. More hurt. Besides, what could she possibly say to Lady Gilmour that he hadn't already said?

The Gilmours were set on doing things their way—they had made that abundantly clear when they had purchased the machines, despite having given their word not to move forward with their plans.

When he reached the parsonage property, he glanced at the garden, grimacing and then striding toward it. He had been neglecting it.

He squeezed through the creaking gate and bent down by the vegetables, squinting at them. Fresh bite marks lined many of the leaves—far more than had the last time he had come out to pull weeds—and he took off his hat and threw it at the ground with a gush of frustration through his clenched teeth.

So much for Burke's beetles. They were nowhere to be seen. Whatever Burke said, the critters didn't belong there. It looked like they had made things *worse,* if anything.

He stood and picked up his hat, dusting it off more harshly than was warranted. A few short days ago, everything had been going his way. But now? Fate seemed to have turned against him and the village.

An image of Georgiana's smile swept across his mind, making his heart feel sore inside him, as if thoughts of her pressed directly on a fresh bruise.

But it didn't matter how he felt for Georgiana Paige. No matter how much they had managed to pretend it, they were not of the same world. John's arrest had acted as a cold glass of water over Samuel, awakening him from the illusion and fantasy he had been entertaining for the last few weeks.

He wouldn't let his heart—and a woman well outside of his world—put Rushbury at risk again. She might sincerely wish the best for the village—indeed, Samuel believed that she did—but at the end of the day, she didn't know what the best looked like. And how could she? She hadn't lived her life amongst people and problems like those in Rushbury. She would never truly understand it—not like Samuel did.

It had taken all of Georgiana's resolution, reaching into the most courageous and kindest parts of her will and heart, to knock on the door of the Reed's house before going to Amblethorne. All she could see in her mind was how her feet stood in the precise spot as had John Reed's earlier that day when he had embraced his family for perhaps the last time.

The thought made her sick, but it strengthened her resolve. Woolen items sat just inside the window, as they had done on Georgiana's first visit, and she glanced down at the coat she wore. It was too warm for the coat, but it was a necessary discomfort.

The curtain moved to reveal the face of Mrs. Reed, and Georgiana swallowed. She was undoubtedly the last person on earth Mrs. Reed wished to see. The door opened slowly, creaking at the hinges, and the face of Patience appeared. Had Mrs. Reed sent her daughter to respond to the knock after seeing who it was?

"Patience," Georgiana said softly, extending a hand toward her.

Patience glanced at the outstretched hand and hesitated. She took in a quick, uneven breath, and then her face convulsed, a hand coming up to cover her mouth. She offered her other hand to Georgiana, tears beginning to spill from her eyes.

Georgiana pulled her into an embrace, shutting her eyes tightly. "I am so terribly sorry," she whispered into Patience's hair.

Patience sobbed into her shoulder, and Georgiana held her, blinking rapidly but failing to keep her own tears at bay.

They stayed that way as the minutes passed, and when Patience's breath began to come more evenly, Georgiana pulled away, putting her hands on the maid's arms. "You are under no obligation whatsoever to help me in what I am about to ask of you, but I wanted to offer you the opportunity."

Patience nodded, taking in a large, trembling breath and wiping at her cheeks.

"I have no reason to think that anything will come of this—I know the Gilmours well enough to harbor sincere doubts—but I must try."

Patience looked at her questioningly, eyes swollen and red.

"If your mother agrees to it," Georgiana said, "I would like to take a number of your products with me to Amblethorne Park."

Patience's brow wrinkled, and she pulled back slightly.

"I think that the Gilmours will be struck by the quality of the work your family does, and I am hopeful that we can turn that to your father's account." She raised up her shoulders. "It may be far fetched, and I sincerely understand if you don't wish to accompany me—or even if you don't wish for me to go at all. But I cannot help trying if there is even the slightest possibility that it will do any good at all."

Patience stared at her for a pregnant moment and then nodded slowly. "I will just speak with Mama."

Ten minutes later, they made their way to Amblethorne Park, both carrying a basket of woolen items on their arms.

Sir Clyde was not at home, but Lady Gilmour welcomed them into the drawing room, looking on the presence of Patience with a slight raising of the eyebrows followed by a curious scanning of the baskets on their arms.

After exchanging the required civil inquiries, Lady Gilmour looked at Georgiana expectantly.

"The purpose of my visit is likely to seem strange and perhaps even a bit uncomfortable, I fear." She took in a fortifying breath and continued. "You are aware, no doubt, of the arrest that has been made in connection with the destruction of the machine you and Sir Clyde purchased."

Lady Gilmour nodded, her mouth drawing into a prim line. "Yes, we were very pleased to have a resolution to the issue so quickly."

Georgiana suppressed the impulse to glance at Patience. She couldn't imagine what it would feel like to hear her father's likely death being referred to as a *resolution*.

She cleared her throat. "I must inform you, Lady Gilmour, that Patience—my maid—is the daughter of the man arrested for the crime: Mr. John Reed."

Lady Gilmour stiffened.

Georgiana sent an encouraging smile at Patience, who looked ready to shrink into the chair she sat upon. "I asked her to accompany me here for a number of reasons, one of which was to assist me with these baskets." She offered the basket handle to Lady Gilmour, who took it with some reluctance.

"The Reed family has been in the wool-spinning trade for generations," Georgiana said, rising to sit beside Lady Gilmour. "I have never seen such fine products in all my life." She extended her arm to display her sleeve. "They were kind enough to make this woolen coat for me after discovering that I had arrived ill-equipped for Yorkshire weather."

She watched Lady Gilmour's expression carefully, as it shifted ever-so-slightly from skepticism to reluctant admiration. She ran a finger along the braiding that lined Georgiana's coat.

"Very fine indeed," she said, pulling her finger away and sending a sidelong glance at Patience as she shifted in her seat, as though she didn't wish for the girl to see her admiring the family's work.

"I think Patience would be the first to admit that what her father did was wrong," Georgiana offered, and Patience nodded, keeping her eyes down. "But I beg of you, Lady Gilmour, to have mercy on him."

Lady Gilmour said nothing, keeping her hands folded primly in her lap.

Georgiana decided to press the point. "I think that, given the chance, you would come to see what an asset John Reed is to

Rushbury—particularly to the vision you and Sir Clyde have for the village."

Lady Gilmour let out a skeptical laugh. "I hardly see how a man who destroyed the very beginnings of that vision could be an asset to carrying it out."

Georgiana nodded. "I quite understand what you are saying. Allow me to explain what I mean." She shifted in her seat so that her knees pointed toward Lady Gilmour, feeling the importance of how she handled what she was on the verge of communicating. "The same passion which led John to damage your machines might quite easily be channeled into the future of Rushbury. No one knows wool like John Reed. Patience will be able to speak more to this than I, but I understand that he is known all over the West Riding for his skill and knowledge."

Patience nodded again. "People pay more when they know that John Reed spun their wool."

Lady Gilmour paused, looking thoughtful. "What are you suggesting, then, Miss Paige?"

"What if," she said, resisting the urge to swallow anxiously, "John Reed were to oversee your efforts at expanding the wool trade in Rushbury? To act as a manager?"

Lady Gilmour reared back slightly. "Put him in charge of all the machines—the very things he ruined?"

Georgiana nodded once. "It is a risk, I know, but I think that it is one well worth taking. I give you my assurance that he can be trusted, as long as he knows that he is valued and can act in the best interest of the mill—which means balancing the interests of both you and the workers, for the mill will suffer if the workers are unhappy and undervalued. John Reed will have invaluable insight not only into the making of wool but into what will bring out the best work from the employees. It was his desperation which drove him to drink—Patience can attest to that."

Patience gave a somber but firm nod.

Lady Gilmour ran her thumb along the woolen stockings in her hand.

"I will not pretend to be a disinterested party," Georgiana said, "for I consider the Reeds to be friends, just as I consider you a friend. But please know that I would not suggest it to you if I did not think that it would be to your benefit. It would be to everyone's benefit, in my opinion."

Silence reigned.

"Will you at least think on it, Lady Gilmour?"

Lady Gilmour nodded, setting the stockings back in the basket. "I will speak with Sir Clyde, though I cannot promise anything. He has been very upset by the entire situation, feeling very betrayed."

Georgiana nodded. "I quite understand. I would be more than happy to talk with him about things if that would be helpful—to vouch for Mr. Reed."

"That won't be necessary," she replied, rising from her seat. "But thank you."

Georgiana rose slowly, suddenly filled with doubt about Lady Gilmour's intentions. Would she truly speak with Sir Clyde? Or would this be another instance where the Gilmours didn't feel compelled to be true to their word?

"I shall just leave a few of these items with you to show Sir Clyde the quality of work of Mr. Reed, then, for I think that will be of interest to him." She indicated the baskets and then saw the dismay in Patience's eyes.

With her father gone, every single item they could sell was undoubtedly precious—not only for its financial worth but for its sentimental value.

"Perhaps we could leave you with the stockings and my coat?" she suggested.

She began undoing the buttons, and Patience came to her aid, sending Georgiana a look full of gratitude and relief.

"I can send one of the servants to retrieve them when you

have had a chance to show Sir Clyde," Georgiana said, setting the coat on the arm of the chaise longue.

"Oh," said Lady Gilmour, looking at the coat with uncertainty. "I wouldn't wish to deprive you of your coat, Miss Paige."

"Not at all! The weather has turned quite nice, and there is no better demonstration of the Reed family's skill and reliability, for they were very swift indeed in the making of this."

Lady Gilmour took the stockings with a polite smile, and Georgiana stifled a disappointed sigh. The likelihood of her making a case to her husband for John Reed's release seemed very slim indeed.

CHAPTER 20

Samuel sat at the table at the parsonage, his food growing cold as he stared at it, sitting back in his seat, with his hands clasped in his lap and a frown on his face. He had no appetite. He couldn't manage even the simplest of life's tasks without feeling haunted by thoughts of John Reed.

It felt wrong to go about life, enjoying a full and hearty meal, when John was in chains. Samuel had visited him in the Wakefield gaol, and it had been all he could do not to shut his eyes at the sight of his friend in such a place. And John would sit there for the next few weeks, awaiting the assizes—weeks of anticipating and wondering whether his fate would be to hang or to be transported to Australia. If he was transported, it would be for fourteen years at least.

In the dank and dark gaol, John's remorse and regret had descended upon him like a heavy blanket, nearly suffocating him. He was full of questions about his wife and family, and it grieved Samuel terribly to have to inform his friend that the Gilmours refused to show mercy to him. John had given an infinitesimal nod, his throat bobbing as he looked at Samuel resolutely.

A knock sounded on the parsonage door, and two minutes

later, Burke appeared in the kitchen, his eyes moving to the untouched plate of food.

He pulled out a chair and sat across the table from Samuel. "You must eat, Sam. Starving yourself helps no one."

Samuel picked up his fork, only to put it down again. "I can't stomach it, Burke."

Burke pursed his lips and set his hands on the table. "Is this about John? Or is it"—he searched for words—"*more* than that?"

Samuel's head snapped up. "What do you mean?"

"Come, Sam," he said. "I'm not blind. I know as well as you that you've fallen headlong in love with Miss Paige, and I saw your falling out. A thing like that doesn't happen without making a man feel half-mad."

Samuel pushed away his plate. "It is hardly worth speaking of. And certainly not when John Reed sits in prison." In truth, he didn't know if he *could* speak of it. His throat already felt thick just thinking on Georgiana's face and the hurt in her eyes.

"Very well," said Burke. "We need not speak of what happened, but I think we must speak of the way forward. What will you do?"

Samuel felt a flicker of anger. "What *can* I do? We are from different worlds, she and I. I was a fool to entertain the idea for even a second. I should know better by now."

Burke watched him thoughtfully. "I understand what you're saying, Sam. And I agree that you and Miss Paige are not of the same world. But you'd be a fool to put her in the same box as Miss McIntyre."

"Would I?"

"Yes, Sam. You would. They're different as night and day. You know I was never an admirer of Miss McIntyre—or whatever her name is now. If not for the pain I saw you in, I would have been thrilled to see her family leave Rushbury for good." He leaned his elbows on the table, and Samuel reluctantly met his gaze. "But Miss Paige is worth a hundred of Miss McIntyre."

Samuel stood abruptly. These were hardly the words he needed to hear. "Make up your mind, Burke! Just yesterday you were telling me I had been right all along about outsiders like her. Now you seem determined to persuade me that I was, in fact, *wrong* all along."

"I was angry, Sam. Just as you were. But time—and a little food in the belly"—he pushed Samuel's plate toward him —"brings reflection and wisdom. Don't misunderstand me. I could wring Archie Paige's neck for what he's done. But neither he nor Miss Paige intended ill."

"Precisely," Samuel said, letting the fork drop onto the plate with a clank. "They are so far removed from the lives we lead that they can't help but cause problems, even when they intend to help." He shook his head. "It was a fool's dream to think that Georgiana Paige and I could ever be more than passing acquaintances. We are simply too different."

His heart didn't believe that, but if he said the words enough, perhaps he would come to accept them in time. He couldn't allow himself to entertain the thought of a future with Georgiana, much as his heart urged him to grasp at the possibility.

Burke stared at him, his lips jutting out as he sighed and stood. "Different you may be, Sam, but the difference between two people is as short as their willingness to bridge it, and I don't think it's Miss Paige who's unwilling."

He set a hand on Samuel's shoulder and then left the room.

Samuel sat still, listening for the familiar thud of the front door.

What if Burke was right? Was Samuel wronging Georgiana by seeing in her the same things that had caused him so much pain years ago? Was he remaking her in the image of Miss McIntyre, when she had given him every reason to believe the best of her?

His thoughts and feelings felt so jumbled that he began to

doubt everything about Georgiana—the good and the bad he had come to believe. The only thing that might bring clarity to his mind and heart would be to see her again..

In the chaos of John Reed's plight, Georgiana had entirely forgotten about the items of business she had meant to record in the parish books the day following statute labor. She wished to leave the records as tidy and complete as possible before departing for London—and she needed to inform Samuel that she would no longer be able to fulfill her role as surveyor.

It was an obligatory post—she knew that. She knew *he* knew it. But she also knew that he would likely accept her resignation willingly, given how little he wished for her presence in Rushbury. One of the other villagers would take over the position, and Georgiana's short stint in the role would become a distant memory—the kind one begins to doubt was real.

She was equally terrified and anxious to see Samuel. She couldn't leave Rushbury without seeing him once more, no matter how painful that encounter proved to be.

The days were lengthening as May emerged in Rushbury, and as Georgiana left Granchurch with the church as her destination, the sun was dipping lower on the horizon. Its golden rays pierced through the few wispy clouds that sat low in the sky, and as she walked down the hill, Georgiana's heart throbbed at the sight of the village below, bathed in golden rays. This place which, upon her arrival, had looked so dreary and gloomy nearly took her breath away now.

There were only a couple of villagers out in the streets, and Georgiana felt their eyes following her, their harshness intensified by the lack of greeting she received. It hurt her deep inside, reconfirming her decision to leave. Rushbury would be a happier place without her there.

The church door was unlocked, and it made the same echoing creak as she pushed it open and then closed again. She sat down quickly at the vestry desk, hoping that she could write down the necessary things before the light faded enough to require a candle. She flipped through the pages of the record book, watching as the script within changed from the clumsy scratches of her predecessor to her own neat handwriting.

It was only five minutes before she was done and, as soon as the ink had dried, she closed the book, rubbing a hand over its battered leather front, remembering the notebook she had carried with her on the rides with Samuel as they surveyed the parish roads. She would give anything to return to that time.

But that was impossible.

Her heart pounded against her chest as she left the church and took the small path that led to the parsonage. How many times had Samuel walked that same path? How many times would he yet walk it? He would live and die in Rushbury. Georgiana had no doubt of that. And she envied him terribly for it. Rushbury wouldn't be Rushbury without Samuel Derrick.

She clenched her eyes shut and walked faster to outrun her dreary thoughts.

She had only been to the parsonage once before—to Samuel's home. It seemed strange, for she had come to feel that she truly knew him. But she hadn't any idea what kind of house he kept: how many servants, what his favorite room was to read in, what books he owned.

They didn't truly know one another. And he had already implied that he regretted what he *did* know of Georgiana. He didn't want her in Rushbury—he wanted her to leave.

. . .

P*lease just leave us in peace.*

She let out a gush of frustration that trembled with suppressed pain. Would those words haunt her for the rest of her life?

She reached the doorstep of the parsonage and, for a moment, she considered leaving the record book there and avoiding the painful encounter with the man she loved so much.

Forcing her hand to the door, she knocked three times. It would be cowardly to leave the book there, and whatever Samuel now thought of her, she would not allow his last memory to be of her cowardice.

The door opened to reveal a maid, middle-aged with kind eyes and a heavily lined face.

"Is Mr. Derrick at home?" she asked.

The maid nodded. "He is just eating his dinner right now, miss. I shall just inquire with him."

Dinner. Georgiana had entirely forgotten about it in her preoccupation. "I don't wish to disturb him," she said.

The maid waved a dismissive hand and smiled. "I won't be but a moment."

Georgiana's heart picked up speed again, and the smell of roast mutton and potatoes drafted through the door as the maid's departure shifted the air.

The first face she caught sight of was Mr. Burke's. He preceded the vicar to the door, tipping his hat and inclining his head at Georgiana as he reached her.

"Good evening, miss," he said. "I am just on my way out."

The reserve and coldness of manner of which she had been the recipient the morning before were gone.

She smiled at him, turning her head to watch him as he passed by her and left her to face Samuel alone.

She tightened her grip on the record book before turning her head to the vicar at the last possible second. To her surprise, the anger and hardness were absent in his gaze, and all that remained was a cautious glint in his eye.

"Miss Paige," he said.

She didn't miss that he had reverted to addressing her more formally, and it surprised her how much that one word stung—the wall it represented between them.

She extended the record book toward him. "I am very sorry to disturb your dinner. I only wished to bring you this."

He looked down at it and took it from her slowly, his eyes searching hers as if for understanding.

She smiled sadly. "I wish to offer my resignation as surveyor of the highways and leave these records in your care."

He opened his mouth to speak, and she put up a hand to request his silence. He nodded for her to go on.

"I understand that the position is obligatory, but I hope that there might be some allowance made in this case."

He frowned. "And why is that?"

She took in a fortifying breath, averting her eyes from his face. Nothing would weaken her resolve more than looking into his eyes and seeing all of the hope and warmth that had been there before suddenly absent. "I believe that someone from the village—someone more well acquainted with the area—can better fulfill the duties of surveyor than I have done. Perhaps more importantly, I shan't be able to attend to the obligations all the way from London."

He had been rubbing the front cover of the book with his thumb—just as she had done at the church—but his head came up abruptly at her words. "From London?" His voice cracked slightly on the words.

She nodded. "I will be journeying there with my brother"—she resisted the urge to look away as she said the words, knowing how much havoc Archie had wreaked in his short time there — "in two days."

Samuel's jaw hardened and his nostrils flared. Was it hurt or anger in his eyes? "I see." His eyes moved away from her face and down to the book in his hands.

"I believe the records are complete," she said, swallowing down the hurt in her throat and indicating the book with her head. "I hope that they will be of use to whoever takes my place."

He said nothing. She wished he would have said *anything*, given her any indication of his thoughts. Was he angry? Apathetic? Hurt?

She cleared her throat, unwilling to dwell on that last possibility. The hope would crush her. "I also wished to apologize sincerely for the consequences of my time in Rushbury." She suppressed an impulse to take his hands in hers and force him to look at her. "I never meant to cause any harm." She looked down. "I have come to love Rushbury as I have loved no other place. It feels like…home." She bit her lip and shut her eyes. "But I don't belong here."

She wanted to. Oh, how she wanted to. And for a brief time, she *had*. But no more.

She brought her head up to look at Samuel. "Thank you for taking me in and making me feel welcome here. I know it has come at great cost to you, and I shall never forget your kindness."

I love you.

The words stayed on her lips, eager to take flight. But she couldn't allow them to. She couldn't face the rejection that would follow them. She had lived with rejection for years—there was no rejection as implicit or constant as eight years in London without a single offer of marriage.

But to tell Samuel her feelings for him would invite a rejection much more acute—one so loud that it would ring in her ears and reverberate through her heart, perhaps for the rest of her life.

"I wish you well on your journey to London," he said,

standing straighter and meeting her eyes.

The small distance between them felt wider than eternity, and Georgiana wanted nothing more than to close it—to remember what it felt like to be in his arms as she had been so briefly, to see him look at her the way he had.

She hesitated, clenching her eyes shut, delaying the moment when she would step away from his doorstep—for he hadn't invited her in.

This couldn't be goodbye with Samuel. It was so cold, so distant and formal. She let out an involuntary gush of frustration. This was her last chance with him. What would she regret more: telling him how she felt? Or failing to do so?

"Samuel," she said, clasping her hands in front of her and swallowing down her fear.

He looked up at the sound of his name, and there was no mistaking the hardness that had reentered his eyes.

She froze at the sight, unable to get any words out.

"Goodbye," she finally said, turning on her heel and stifling the involuntary sob that rose in her throat.

CHAPTER 21

Samuel stood rooted to the spot, watching Georgiana's back as she retreated farther and farther down the path leading to the main road.

She was leaving.

And he didn't know whether to throw the book in his hand and yell or slump down on the ground and weep.

Frustrated as he had been with her and with himself, he had harbored a shred of hope still inside him—a hope to be proven wrong, to be shown that she wasn't like Miss McIntyre.

But she was leaving. Leaving him. Leaving Rushbury.

All her talk of plans to stay there indefinitely had been nothing more than idle words. She had stayed while it was convenient, and now that there was real trouble, she was leaving.

He smacked a hand against the door frame, clenching his eyes shut and cursing his foolishness. How had he let himself fall in love with her? As if he hadn't known better. And so far from showing the caution that would be reasonable for a man with his history, he had fallen much deeper this time, with no one to blame but himself.

He looked at the book in his hand, holding it so that the pages flipped until he stopped them with a thumb.

His throat felt thick as he scanned the lines Georgiana had written during their survey of the parish roads.

Particularly rocky stretch going from the base of Rush Hill to the meadow path.

He could still remember the way she had hesitated as she wrote, tilting her head to the side and asking him how to refer to that particular hill. She had been so anxious to learn about Rushbury, her brow furrowed thoughtfully as he had related his knowledge to her. He remembered the way she had looked upon opening her eyes before the meadow of flowers.

However he had felt for her before then, those two days had solidified his feelings. It had been the point of no return for his heart.

He shut the book with a snap and tossed it onto the table just inside the door. Stepping back outside, he pulled the door to the parsonage closed behind him, making his way toward the garden.

Stooping down once within, he inspected the leaves of the lettuce and cabbage plants. The distinctive lamb ear silhouette was punctuated with crescent-shaped bite marks. He pulled the fragile leaves to and fro, making his way down the line, his breath coming faster and harsher with each step.

Not a beetle in sight.

He stood and rubbed at his mouth, clenching and unclenching his jaw, then kicked at one of the plants. Dirt flew in front of him, and he strode out of the garden. This would clearly not be the year he succeeded as a gardener. Or as anything, it seemed. He had failed John Reed; he had failed the parish.

He had failed himself.

Georgiana's valises and portmanteaux sat open on her bed, with only a bit of space left for the few items still to pack.

There were dresses she had never worn, meant for warmer weather. She had intended to stay in Rushbury indefinitely, after all.

Suddenly the amount of clothing she had packed seemed ludicrous. Hadn't Samuel commented on it when she had first arrived? Had he known then that her stay would be so short?

She let out a soft, sad chuckle as she thought on that first meeting with the vicar. She had probably appeared deranged to him. Little had she realized how she would come to care for him, to crave his company.

A knock sounded on her door, and she turned toward it, opening it to reveal Archie's face.

"Will you be ready to leave in the next two or three hours?" he asked.

She nodded, biting her lip. "But I wondered," she said, "if you might do me a favor on our way?"

He narrowed his eyes. Archie was always wary of committing to anything.

"I wish to visit John Reed in the Wakefield gaol on our way." She said the words unapologetically. She would go with or without Archie, but it would certainly be less unpleasant if he accompanied her. She had never visited such a place and suspected that she would cause a bit of a stir going on her own. She needed to reaccustom herself to requesting chaperonage whenever she went out.

She stifled a sigh at the thought.

He pursed his lips, finally nodding. "I will accompany you if you are set on going, but gaol is no place for someone like you, Georgie."

He had said something similar when he had first discovered

her intention of coming to Rushbury. What place *was* for someone like her? She belonged nowhere.

"First, I must make a visit to the Gilmours." She set a folded shawl inside a portmanteau. "I shall be back within the hour."

She made the walk to Amblethorne Park with a heart both nervous and heavy. Everything she did felt laden with significance in her last moments in the village. Even a place like Amblethorne that Georgiana had mixed feelings about became a symbol of lost opportunities.

She breathed a sigh of relief when she discovered that Sir Clyde was at home. It was a bit forward, what she was about to do, and yet the knowledge that she would never see him or Lady Gilmour again gave her confidence and courage.

Sir Clyde smiled at her as he entered the drawing room. "Miss Paige, what a surprise. What can I do for you?"

She returned the smile, hoping that his kind welcome was an indication of being in good humor. "I am very sorry to arrive in such an unexpected manner, Sir Clyde, but I am very glad to find you at home. I came to retrieve the items I left with Lady Gilmour, hoping that she had the chance to show them to you." Her voice ended on a questioning note.

Sir Clyde's brow furrowed. "It must have slipped her mind," he said, "for I cannot think to what you are referring."

Georgiana's muscles clenched in frustration. She should have known Lady Gilmour would fail to convey her request.

"Oh," she said, trying to sound less disappointed than she felt. "Well, perhaps it is for the best. I was hoping to speak with you myself, in fact, but you were not at home when I came the other day. Do you have a few minutes to spare?"

He nodded, inviting her to sit down and taking the seat across from her.

Trying to strike the balance between appealing to Sir Clyde's business interests and his heart, she spent the next five minutes explaining her request and the benefits she saw him reaping from complying with it. His brow was wrinkled in thought as he contemplated her words, and she felt encouraged by the questions he asked. He expressed the same hesitation and doubts as had his wife, but unlike her, he seemed to be seriously considering Georgiana's words—a fact she attributed to the careful way she had made the case for John Reed's potential as a manager.

"I think," she said, "that you might set the mill quite apart from the others in the region by doing what others have not done: placing a high value on the well-being of those you employ. If you can gain the trust and respect of those people, they will make up for any extra costs you sustain through their hard work and loyalty."

Seeing him nod, she was encouraged to go on. "Rather than grudging labor, you will have people eager to please you and live up to the high standards you set for the mill."

She straightened, making the final push—the part that might well determine the future of John Reed. "And I truly believe that the key to that is employing someone like John Reed, who not only understands wool better than anyone in the region, but understands what will inspire better work from the laborers since he has been one himself."

He stared at his clasped hands in his lap thoughtfully, his lips turned down in a frown. "You make a very good case, Miss Paige, I must admit. If you had told me ten minutes ago that I would be considering requesting the release of the man who destroyed my machines, I would have laughed in your face—or perhaps shown you the door." He chuckled. "But I see the value in your proposition. It is a risky one, though."

She nodded. She needed to make Sir Clyde feel safer in submitting to her request—she needed to make it seem like less of a gamble. "What if you were to offer Mr. Reed a trial period? Say, two months, to see whether the arrangement suits?"

His brows went up, acknowledging the wisdom and appeal of her suggestion.

"And please don't think I have forgotten the cost you have incurred with the destruction of the machines." She sent him an understanding grimace. "I imagine that Mr. Reed would gladly agree to forgo some of his wages in order to make payments toward the replacement of the machines."

This was perhaps the greatest hurdle of her argument, for it would take years of accumulation for a fraction of Mr. Reed's wages to replace the machines, and there was no guarantee that John Reed would even agree to any of this. He was a prideful man, and she knew how much he valued his craft—one he believed machines devalued and undermined.

Sir Clyde let out a sigh, and his head bobbed up and down thoughtfully. "I surprise myself by saying this, but I am inclined to agree with everything you have said."

She nodded, feeling a sliver of hope for the first time since witnessing John Reed's arrest.

He stood and began pacing the room.

"I will give the orders for Mr. Reed to be released from gaol," he said, turning toward her and stopping as she held her breath, "on one condition."

She waited, feeling the hope expand inside her.

Sir Clyde's face became stern and grave. "If I have any problems with Mr. Reed—if he shows *any* tendency at all toward the violence he showed in destroying the machines, I will call again for his arrest. And there will be no mercy shown him then."

She nodded quickly, feeling the hairs at the nape of her neck stand on end at his words.

She hoped that Mr. Reed would live up to the assurances she had given Sir Clyde of him. But that was not within her control. She could help him to water, but she could not make him drink it.

"I think that is a very fair condition, sir," she said. "And I admire you greatly for the kindness you are showing to a man who has wronged you. It says much about your character."

He clasped his hands behind his back and bowed slightly to accept the praise. "I confess I am unsure what should be done now."

Georgiana could hardly contain what she was feeling inside, feeling full to bursting with a desire to speak with John Reed immediately. "I think," she said, forcing herself to speak in a calm, level voice, "that you might write a note requesting the release of Mr. Reed. I had intended to go there myself—accompanied by my brother, of course—and I imagine that Constable Burke would be happy to come with us to handle any of the official or legal matters which might arise."

He nodded. "Very good. Grant me five minutes, if you will, and I will send you with the note."

CHAPTER 22

Archie was waiting for her when Georgiana returned, their belongings already loaded into the basket behind the traveling coach. The letter Sir Clyde had written rested safely in the pocket of her woolen coat. She had returned the wool stockings to the Reed home, desperately wanting to tell them to expect the return of their husband and father, but too nervous to do so before everything was settled.

Aunt Sara stood outside, watching the preparations and smiling serenely at Georgiana as she approached. She put out her hands, and Georgiana took them gladly.

"Can we not convince you to come with us, then?" Georgiana asked.

Aunt Sara shook her head. "I had enough of London to last me a lifetime, my dear. I am quite content here." She looked around with the same smile of satisfaction with which Georgiana had looked upon her surroundings just a few short days ago.

How she envied Aunt Sara.

"You needn't worry about me," Aunt Sara continued, a teasing sparkle lighting up her eyes. "Rachel will be here

Monday or Tuesday at the latest, and I think that the quiet, slow life here at Granchurch will suit her very well."

Georgiana nodded, removing Sir Clyde's note from her coat and slipping it into her reticule to mask the tears.

"I worry more for *you* than I do for me," Aunt Sara said.

Georgiana worried what her father would say upon her unexpected arrival home, too. She worried about what the future held and sincerely hoped that her parents would not ask her to continue attending all the events that Daphne would attend. Surely they could see that she was past that and no credit at all to Daphne. It would make most sense—and be most merciful—if she could return home to their estate.

In time, if Georgiana had her way, she would find a suitable female companion to share with her in the renting of a cottage near the sea.

With a heartfelt embrace, Georgiana bid her aunt farewell and instructed the coachman to take them first to Mr. Burke's home and then to Wakefield gaol. She climbed into the coach with a final glance at Granchurch House. She would always miss this place.

Archie ducked into the coach and seated himself across from Georgiana. The coach rumbled forward, and Georgiana gave a final wave through the small window.

"I think we can make it as far as Rotherham tonight," Archie said, "as long as you don't intend to spend an inordinate amount of time in Wakefield."

Georgiana shook her head, feeling the strangest mixture of contentment and sorrow as Granchurch disappeared from view behind the hill. "Just a short conversation with Mr. Reed will do, but I must first request the company of the constable."

When Mr. Burke opened the door, he smiled kindly upon her. His eyes flitted to the carriage in the road, and his brow pulled together slightly.

"Miss Paige," he said, pulling his eyes from the coach. "Good day to you."

"I am sorry to disturb you," she said. "But I believe your presence may be required—or at least prudent—for the errand I am on."

His brow wrinkled more. "How may I be of assistance?"

She glanced back at the coach and saw Archie standing on the steps, watching her, his foot tapping. He was determined to make it to Rotherham, where he had apparently enjoyed the most delicious meal in all his travels, and the detour to Wakefield might set them back if it was not accomplished speedily.

She pulled Sir Clyde's note from her reticule, handing it to Mr. Burke. "I need to deliver this," she said, "and I think that your presence may be necessary."

He opened the note and scanned its contents, his jaw slackening, and his eyes widening with every word. His eyes traveled to hers. "How did you manage this?"

"I can explain it on the way to Wakefield if you are agreeable?"

He nodded quickly and handed her the note again. "Of course," he said, reaching for his hat on a nail in the wall.

"Unfortunately, my brother and I will not be returning this way afterward," she said. "Could I accompany you in your wagon on the way there?"

A horse was quickly readied and attached to the wagon, and Mr. Burke helped her in. There was a rushed energy to his movements that spoke to his impatience to better understand what had happened to elicit such a development.

Archie's carriage went before them, and Georgiana was grateful that she would be journeying to London in it rather than in Mr. Burke's rickety wagon.

Explaining her visit to Lady Gilmour and the subsequent one to Sir Clyde, she watched Mr. Burke listening carefully, his eyes on the road but his ear cocked toward her.

"God bless you, miss," he said in a hoarse voice when she had finished. "God bless you."

She shook her head, feeling her cheeks warm at the praise. She watched the passing countryside around them. "John Reed wouldn't even be in this situation if it wasn't for me."

Mr. Burke shook his head. "It is not your fault, miss. Don't think it."

"How can I not?" She lowered her eyes and shut them. "Everyone else does."

"In such situations, everyone is looking for someone to blame," he said. "It makes them feel as though they can avoid similar hurt in the future, if only they can pinpoint where the fault lies. It takes time for people to come to their senses—but they will. You have only tried to help us—and gone far and beyond what anyone expected in order to do that." He indicated her reticule with a tip of his head. "That note is yet more evidence of that fact."

She swallowed the lump insistently rising in her throat.

Mr. Burke glanced at her, hesitating a moment before he spoke. "Do you know any of the history of Rushbury, miss? Our experiences with the tenants of Amblethorne?"

She shook her head. "Mr. Derrick mentioned that it has been frequently occupied and then abandoned."

Mr. Burke nodded slowly and thoughtfully. "That it has. We have gone through periods of neglect—where no repairs could be made for months due to the absence and indifference of Amblethorne's tenants—and then periods of interference—where sudden changes were made at great cost to the village, only to then have the residents leave abruptly. It has not endeared members of your class to the village, I am afraid." He cleared his throat. "To Sam, least of all."

She thought she saw Mr. Burke steal a glance at her out of the side of his eye.

So that was how Samuel still viewed her? As another meddling busybody?

"He became quite close with one of the families that lived in Amblethorne for a time," Mr. Burke continued. "This was years ago—five or six, I believe. There was a young woman there in whose company he was frequently found. I believe Sam thought that they had a future together—we all did. But one day she and her family left without a word."

Georgiana pulled her lips between her teeth, fighting off the jealousy that pricked her already-sore heart. "What happened?"

"We found out weeks later that she had married a baronet in Derbyshire."

Silence reigned for a moment as Georgiana thought on the light the information shed upon Samuel's bias against outsiders. Did he still love the woman? Was it a broken heart that was fueling his distrust? The thought brought a hand to her stomach, which felt sick with aching want.

"Sam's father was a doctor, you know," Mr. Burke continued. "Moved to Rushbury not long after he married, buried his wife and two children in the village cemetery, and stayed here till he died a few years ago. He had a great mistrust of the Quality, despite being educated at Oxford himself."

Mr. Burke scanned their surroundings with a sigh. "He preferred to live here over anywhere else, despite the inconvenience to his duties as doctor, insisting that he would take a man or woman from Rushbury over a duke any day." He glanced at Georgiana. "Sam inherited that same mistrust, and when Miss McIntyre left so suddenly, it only confirmed it to him. I was very happy indeed when he took to you so quickly after your arrival here—it seemed like he was healing. But..."

She shut her eyes. She and Archie had ruined everything, giving him even more reason to distrust outsiders.

"Don't be too hard on him, miss. He is hard enough on himself."

The town of Wakefield came into view, and along with it, the noise and bustle. Georgiana was grateful for the distraction it caused, requiring Mr. Burke's concentration, since she didn't know if she could have spoken. Her heart ached for Samuel and what he had experienced—it ached to show him that she was not like Miss McIntyre.

She shut her eyes and cringed as she thought on her own arrival in Rushbury and how it must have appeared to Samuel—yet another stranger intent upon changing the village. She smiled wryly as she thought of his attempt to teach her her place by offering up the role of surveyor and how she had surprised him by accepting it.

Whatever his first impressions of her had been, he had been unfailingly kind and helpful to her despite her clumsy attempts to belong.

But knowing Samuel's history did nothing to change what he had expressed: his regret at Georgiana's ever having come to the village. It didn't matter how she felt about him if he couldn't return her regard.

As the coach pulled in front of the gaol, Georgiana felt her stomach churn. The stone building was small and cramped-looking, with puddles of old stagnant water lining the road around it. A wooden board extended over one of the larger puddles leading to the door.

"Shall I come in?" Archie asked, meeting them in front of the board. "With Mr. Burke here, I thought perhaps my presence might not be necessary."

"If it isn't too much trouble, sir," Mr. Burke said, "I think it would be best for you to accompany Miss Paige. I must go speak with the powers that be to show them Sir Clyde's instructions."

Archie nodded with a bit of reluctance, and Georgiana extracted the note from her reticule again, handing it to Mr. Burke. "I hope it will be sufficient," she said.

Mr. Burke assisted her in stepping across the board and then spoke with the man who answered his firm rapping at the door.

They were led down a narrow, dark hallway with ceilings so low Georgiana was obliged to remove her bonnet and then crouch slightly. Mr. Burke seemed to know his way around, though, and he left them at an intersection of the dark corridors, turning to the right where more light illuminated the way.

The prison guard ushered Georgiana and Archie farther into the gaol, finally slowing and saying, "John Reed. Visitors."

He turned to Georgiana and Archie expectantly. Georgiana handed her bonnet to Archie and opened her reticule, taking out her small coin purse and setting a coin in the guard's hand. She thanked him, her eyes watching the emerging form of John Reed.

The cell where he was being kept was dark as night, with no candles that Georgiana could discover. Only the beams from a small tallow candle in the walkway between cells illuminated the area.

Mr. Reed looked at Georgiana and Archie warily, his eyes full of a dark despair Georgiana hoped was merely accentuated by the dim lighting in the prison.

"Mr. Reed," she said, suddenly feeling a wave of nerves wash over her, causing her hands to tremble. She gripped her coin purse more tightly to still the shaking. "I imagine that we are the very last people you wish to see, but I hope that you will grant me a few moments of your time."

He gripped the bars of his cell, giving them a jostle. "Even if I didn't wish to, I don't have much of a say in the matter, do I?"

"No," she admitted. "But I am not so unkind that I will force you to listen to me if you don't wish to. Mr. Burke is here and may convey the information to you if you prefer it."

He shook his head. "Go on, miss."

"First, I wish to convey my deepest regret at what has occurred. My brother"— she indicated Archie with a hand, and he shifted uncomfortably—"hadn't any idea what he was involving himself in when he laid information against you."

Mr. Reed's eyes moved to Archie, and Georgiana braced herself for the inevitable anger, but he only frowned. "I don't blame anyone but myself for where I am today. I was a selfish fool, and I'm paying the price. I and my family." His voice cracked on the last word, and Georgiana laid a gloved hand on the fingers he held curled around the iron bars.

Archie lowered his head beside her, his hands clasped in front of him, holding his hat.

"We all make mistakes, Mr. Reed," she said. "And I don't believe that yours should cost you your life or your family. I have come to offer you hope in that regard."

He looked up at her, and even in the dim light, she could see the sheen of tears in his eyes.

"It will require great humility on your part," she said.

He nodded, inviting her to go on.

"I have spoken with Sir Clyde Gilmour, the man who purchased the machines you destroyed. I made a proposition to him regarding your future, and he has accepted it, on a few conditions. It will not give you back the life you had before, but it *will* give you a new opportunity—to support your family more easily than in the past, but also to take a front seat in guiding the changes which will be taking place in Rushbury."

Mr. Reed's brows knit together, but he watched her with alert eyes.

"If you can demonstrate to Sir Clyde that you will be a loyal and dependable worker, he is willing to consider employing you as the manager of operations in the mill he hopes to grow in Rushbury."

Mr. Reed's mouth opened and fingers slackened on the bars, sliding down a bit before he resumed his tighter grip.

"It will be a probationary period initially," she said, "with the potential for permanence—as long as you can demonstrate your value and dedication to him. You would be a go-between of sorts, reporting to Sir Clyde and ensuring that the mill functions to the standards he wishes to maintain, while also acting as an advocate for the mill workers, to make sure that they can produce the best work under fair conditions and pay."

Mr. Reed looked at her wonderingly, blinking as if he thought he was hallucinating. "But…but…why?" he stammered. "Why should he do such a thing?"

Georgiana took in a breath. "Because I assured him that he would not regret it. And I rely on you to make good on my word." She smiled, and he nodded quickly, hope shining from his eyes through the tears.

"I won't disappoint him, miss. Nor you. I'll do anything —*anything*—to be with my family again."

She nodded, her own eyes filling so that the dark cell quivered and blurred. "You *will* be obliged to forgo a percentage of your wages in order to reimburse Sir Clyde for the expense of the machines."

He dashed away tears with the back of a dirty hand, nodding rapidly. "I will work twice as many hours until it's paid—plus interest."

Georgiana gave a watery chuckle, relief flooding her at Mr. Reed's reaction. His time in gaol had softened and humbled him. She knew some people whom it might have hardened instead.

She clasped her hands together. "If I might make a suggestion, I believe that a small gesture on your part might go a long way in helping Sir Clyde feel at peace with his offer," she said. "An apology—a recognition of wrong and a promise to make restitution."

"Yes, yes, of course," Mr. Reed said quickly.

Georgiana smiled at him. "I pray that Sir Clyde will see the wisdom of it and the potential within you."

She looked at Archie, who had been silent the entire time,

and noted his deeply furrowed brow and the way his mouth turned down at the sides. Was he feeling uncomfortable, seeing this softer side of Mr. Reed? He had been certain that the man was an angry drunkard. It couldn't be pleasant to see the results of his choice to inform on the man.

She turned back to Mr. Reed. "I wish you the very best, Mr. Reed. Mr. Burke is speaking with the authorities right now. Provided everything is in order, he will be able to escort you home."

A little sob escaped him on her last word, and he nodded, screwing up his mouth in an expression that spoke volumes of his gratitude and emotion. "Thank you, miss." His voice broke, and he took a moment to regain control over himself. "I shall never forget your kindness."

"It was the least I could do for a friend." She smiled and sniffled softly, turning away.

"Wait." Archie was looking down at the floor, but his head came up to meet Mr. Reed's gaze. He drew in a breath and then searched in his coat pocket, drawing out a handful of bank notes.

He looked at them for a moment and then extended them toward Mr. Reed. "Take those."

Georgiana stared incredulously.

Mr. Reed hesitated, looking at Archie with wide, uncomprehending eyes. He shook his head. "I couldn't."

"Take it. You need it more than I do, and I don't want it." He shrugged. "It's not enough to pay back Sir Clyde, but it will give you a decent start."

Mr. Reed's lip trembled and he took the notes slowly, entirely unable to speak for the emotion that had overcome him.

"Good luck, my friend," Archie said with a nod.

CHAPTER 23

Samuel swallowed the last gulps of ale in his tankard, glancing at the record book that sat on the table. His eyes found it no matter where he put it, drawn to it whether it sat by the front door, on the chair in the study, or on the table in the kitchen. It was just a book, but he couldn't look on it without seeing Georgiana, without thinking of her.

The parsonage was set back far enough from the main road that he often couldn't hear passing equipages, but his ears had been straining for their sound all the same.

Today Georgiana and Archie would leave for London, and Samuel found himself anxious and restless. He had bolted through the front door twice at the sound of wheels, but both times it had just been villagers going about their daily activities.

He pushed open the side door that led to the garden. He needed to busy his hands or he would go mad thinking of her, fighting the desire to beg her to stay.

But she wanted to leave, and he wouldn't stop her from pursuing what she wanted. No doubt her few weeks in Rushbury had been ample time to make her see that she didn't wish for the life she had been living here. She belonged in a fine London townhome, not a small, dirty village like Rushbury.

He knelt on the garden dirt, and his knees settled into the soil, which was much softer than it had been a few weeks ago. Surveying the small garden and its neat rows of growing plants, he sighed. The plant he had kicked at leaned awkwardly toward its neighbor, a dent in the dirt surrounding it. He scooped some loose soil from nearby and filled in the furrow.

He was not angry anymore. He was simply in pain.

He had hurt before—the passing of both his parents had brought him down into the depths of sorrow; Miss McIntyre's departure had wounded his pride *and* his heart. But he had never known his heart could physically ache so that nothing he did distracted him from it.

Pulling off a few leaves that had been almost entirely consumed by the slugs, he startled as a large, black beetle emerged from beneath the leaves.

He let out a relieved breath, watching it toddle over the uneven soil. "So you *didn't* leave," he said softly. "I thought you had taken a look at the state of things here and abandoned me."

He lifted a few more leaves, looking for signs of slugs. He saw none. "It appears I underestimated you," he said as the beetle disappeared under one of the cabbage plants. "You and your friends have been doing good work. I should have trusted you, shouldn't I? Perhaps we can yet salvage some of this garden together." The beetle disappeared entirely, and the garden was silent. He pursed his lips and rose to a stand. "Perhaps I should stop talking to insects."

He stared thoughtfully at the plants and then at the place where he had stepped on the first ground beetle he had seen a few weeks ago. Perhaps his garden would be in a much better state if he hadn't killed the thing.

He had always been wary of outsiders—one of his duties as a small child had been to inform his father whenever anyone new appeared in the village—and that wariness had served him well in the past. But perhaps he was too quick to mistrust the unfamiliar, to assume ill intentions.

It had certainly been his approach to Georgiana when she had arrived in Rushbury. Had he not classified her as an intruder, an enemy to what he was trying to accomplish and protect before he had even seen her?

He had been wrong then, too. Or at least he had seemed to be. She was leaving, though, just as he had feared she would—abandoning Rushbury. Abandoning him. Like so many of her class, she didn't care enough about Rushbury to remain there.

And yet he had seen the way his words had hurt her. He hadn't meant them. He *didn't* regret her having come to Rushbury. Her time there had been the most joyful weeks for him in years.

He had feared for John Reed, though. His arrest had shown Samuel just how quickly things could change—how swiftly someone he loved could be lost or taken from him. And in the anger and fear of the situation, he had sought distance between himself and Georgiana. He had pushed her away. And the conversation he had promised her? They had never had it.

He leaned against the garden gate, rubbing his forehead harshly. What would Burke say if he were here?

Samuel let out a wry chuckle. That was easy. Burke would tell him what a blockhead and a hypocrite he was being, accusing Georgiana of abandoning them when Samuel had abandoned *her* in his own way.

He let out a groan and ran his fingers through his hair. He wanted more than anything to finish his conversation with Georgiana, to let her know that he wanted her here in Rushbury, that the prospect of the village without her made him feel bleak and hopeless. She might still choose to leave, and if she did, the pain would be unbearable. But he couldn't let her leave without telling her how he felt.

He might already be too late. Heaven forbid.

The muffled sound of carriage wheels met his ears, and his eyes widened. He took in a large breath and then pushed it out through tight lips, turning and swinging the gate so quickly and so wide that it came off the hinges.

Running toward the village road, he tried to peer through the trees which blocked his view. His breath came quickly as he reached the road, slowing to look toward the main highway, but there was no carriage there. He turned to look the other direction and his eyes met with the view of Burke's wagon and a crowd of villagers surrounding it.

Seeing him from afar, Burke squeezed through the group and jogged toward him.

"What is it?" Samuel said, trying to see whoever the villagers were congregating around. They seemed to be taking turns embracing someone.

"John Reed," Burke said, grinning more widely than Samuel had ever seen. "He's been released."

Samuel's round eyes jumped back and forth between Burke and the congregated villagers. "But how?"

Burke clapped him on the shoulder. "Who do you think?"

Samuel stared.

"Who else has shown herself capable of surmounting even the greatest obstacles we face in this village?" He smiled knowingly. "She spoke with Sir Clyde. Convinced him to take John on as manager over the planned mill for a trial period."

Samuel blinked. "As manager?" He looked toward the crowd, searching for Georgiana's face. "Where is she?"

Burke's smile morphed into a tight-lipped grimace. His shoulders came up. "Gone. She and her brother left for London directly from Wakefield."

Clenching his eyes shut, Samuel dropped his head. He was too late.

"Samuel!"

He lifted his head. John Reed was striding toward him as

quickly as he could, flanked as he was on either side by his children, who had their arms wrapped around his legs and were giggling at his attempts to walk.

Pushing aside the defeat and anguish, Samuel summoned a tortured smile for John and wrapped him in an embrace, his eyes filling with tears. "I thought we had lost you," he said into John's ear, his voice gruff.

"And it would have served me right," John said, letting go of him and stepping back. He shook his head. "I am sorry, Samuel. Sorry for all of it."

Samuel took John's hand between his and pressed it. "Let us put it all behind us and look to the future." His mouth turned up in a half-smile. "A future managing Sir Clyde's business, Burke tells me."

John's chin trembled slightly. "An opportunity I don't deserve, but one I will work to do justice to. All thanks to Miss Paige and her brother."

Samuel swallowed at the sound of her name but tilted his head, frowning. "Archie?"

John nodded, but he was struggling to keep his emotions at bay, and one of his young daughters tugged on the leg of his trousers.

Burke wrapped an arm around John's shoulders with an understanding expression. "It seems Archie gave John the reward money from Sir Clyde—to put toward replacing the machines. Here now, little Miss Jane," he said, picking up John's daughter as John attended to the other. "I hear your mother calling for you." He turned back toward the village only to pause and look once more at Samuel. "I thought perhaps you might wish to know that the Paiges intend to spend the night at Rotherham." And with a raising of one brow, he was gone, and John Reed with him.

CHAPTER 24

The landscape of the West Riding passed—or rather jolted—by slowly through Georgiana's window. Archie's head was tipped back, his mouth open and his breath coming in faint snores. How he could rest with such violent bumping, Georgiana hardly understood. He had fallen asleep just twenty minutes outside of Wakefield, leaving her to a confusing mixture of thoughts ranging from the melancholy to the euphoric. The former seemed to be winning the day, though, perhaps helped along by the throbbing headache she was battling from the bumpiness of the roads—and perhaps a few silent tears shed once Archie had succumbed to slumber.

She was thrilled for John Reed and for his family. It was the bright, silver lining to her departure, and she would never forget the look of unalloyed gratitude and relief on his face when he had understood the reason for her visit. She hadn't been entirely certain what to expect from him—he was stubborn and opinionated enough that there had been a real possibility he would want to spit in her face for suggesting he oversee the beginnings of a mill.

Samuel might still feel that way, in fact. He wanted no mill in Rushbury, and Georgiana's act had all but made it inevitable. She had made a muddle of everything.

She sniffed softly into her handkerchief, hoping not to wake her brother. He always panicked when confronted with tears, and she wanted to indulge herself a while longer.

"Stop!" a muffled cry rang out. The carriage slowed precipitously.

Georgiana stabilized herself with two hands on the sides of the carriage, her heart suddenly racing, while Archie startled awake, sliding forward on the seat until he put his hands out to stop himself.

She hurriedly reached for the pistol in the velvet pocket of the carriage, straining her ears in vain to understand the muffled conversation occurring between the driver and whoever had caused him to stop.

Archie blinked as he watched her. "What are you doing?"

She cocked the pistol, breathing in deeply to prepare herself, her cheeks still wet. "I was set upon by highwaymen on the journey here and sent them on their way. I don't intend to let them succeed this time either."

"Are you *crying*?" Archie stared at her.

"Of course not," she said impatiently, keeping her eyes trained on the carriage door.

Footsteps drew nearer, and she moved so that she could point the pistol straight at the carriage door, gripping it to keep it steady, ready to confront whoever had the audacity to interrupt her journey—and the cry she had been needing for days now.

The door rattled, sticking for a moment.

"Give it to me," Archie hissed, motioning for her to hand over the pistol.

She shook her head. It was time for her to tell these Yorkshire types just what she thought of them. She wasn't about to leave that to Archie.

She put out a hand to push open the door, but it gave way before she reached it, and she fell forward, stumbling out of the carriage as a shot sounded and she tumbled into the arms of the highwayman. She pushed off of him, regaining her grip on the pistol and pointing it at him.

At Samuel.

The pistol smoked lightly, and Georgiana realized with wide, blinking eyes that *she* was responsible for the gunshot. Dread filled her as Samuel put both his hands up in a gesture of surrender, looking every bit as surprised as Georgiana.

"Samuel?" she croaked. She scanned his body quickly, looking for evidence of a bullet hole, then dropped the pistol.

He kept one hand up and his eyes on her, using the other to point toward a nearby tree. A small hole marred the otherwise smooth bark.

Archie's head appeared in the doorway of the carriage, scanning the scene before him. He swore. "You've not shot the vicar, Georgie, have you?"

"No," said Samuel, lowering his hands slowly, with the slightest flicker of a smile on his lips. "But not for lack of trying."

Georgiana shook her head, horrified. "It was a mistake, I assure you. If you hadn't pulled the door so hard, I shouldn't have lost my footing, and"—she stopped and, realizing that he was teasing her, averted her eyes with an embarrassed smile.

Suddenly realizing that she was entirely in the dark regarding the reason for his presence there, she looked at Samuel. The outside air made her cheeks tingle where the tear trails stained them, and she brushed at them to hide the evidence of her crying.

"What are you doing here?" It wasn't the kindest way to ask the question, but there it was. If she tried to be kind, she might succumb to tears again, for seeing the vicar before her now intensified her anguish, sending a pang through her heart every time she looked at him.

Samuel glanced at Archie, still standing in the doorway to the carriage. "Could you give us a moment, Archie?"

Archie blinked, as if it had never occurred to him that the vicar and his sister might need to be alone.

"O-of course," he said with a stutter, and his head disappeared into the carriage, followed by his hand pulling the door shut.

Georgiana swallowed, her heart galloping.

"Will you take a walk with me?" Samuel said, his eyes flitting to the driver sitting on the box at the front of the carriage.

She nodded, though she secretly wondered whether her legs would cooperate. They felt wobbly and unsure beneath her.

He offered her his arm, and she took it somewhat stiffly, knowing that every point of contact between them added a thread to the connection she felt with him. She hadn't any idea why he wished to speak with her, and it was all she could do to keep the hope at bay.

They stepped into the trees that lined the road, but the way was so narrow that Samuel extracted his arm from hers and held her hand instead. Georgiana felt lightheaded at the touch, trying to ignore a wish to remove her glove so that she could really feel his hand holding hers.

Nothing but a few snapping twigs filled the air as they came to a slight widening in the trees.

He stopped and turned toward her, looking at her with something between a smile and a grimace. "I think I deserved that you should shoot at me. I have been the very worst of fools."

She shook her head, thinking of the tree with the bullet hole and cringing as she thought where the bullet could have ended up. It made her stomach contract, and she pushed away the images in her head. She had *not* shot him, thank heaven.

"Georgiana," he said, taking another step toward her so that there was only a foot between them. "I know you are on your way to London, and I wouldn't blame you if you never wished to set foot in Rushbury again, but...." He scanned her face, his brows drawing together. "Have you been crying?" he asked, touching her cheek with a soft thumb.

The touch sent a shiver through her, and she shut her eyes, scared of what she would feel if she looked into his. But shutting them only heightened her senses so that she could feel the path his finger traced on her cheek.

"Only a little," she lied, opening her eyes and smiling pathetically.

His mouth turned up at the side. She had missed his smile terribly over the past few days.

"Stay," he said, leaving his hand on her cheek. "Please don't go."

She put her hand over his, shutting her eyes again. How she had longed to hear those very words.

"Rushbury needs you."

She opened her eyes, her brows knitting, and she bit her lip. "I know that the village means the world to you, Samuel. I have come to love it dearly myself. But"—she swallowed and looked him in the eye. "I don't wish to be desired for what I bring to Rushbury."

He blinked and shook his head, looking dismayed. "Georgiana." He let his hand drop from her cheek, staring into her eyes intently. "I don't wish for you to stay for Rushbury's sake. I wish for you to stay because I cannot imagine my life without you—I don't *want* to imagine it. Please forgive me for being such a fool."

He took her face in both hands, staring down into her eyes with such earnestness that she had to force herself to breathe. She nodded quickly.

"Rushbury is the only real home I have ever known," he said.

"And though I would love nothing more than to be there together, I could make a home anywhere, as long as you were by my side. *You* are my home."

Eyes burning at his words and under his gaze, she wrapped her arms around his neck and pulled him down until their lips met, soft and warm, familiar and yet entirely novel.

All the despair of the past few days vanished with his arms around her and their lips locked. And once those feelings had gone, eight long years of discouragement and loneliness began to dissolve with every passing second.

And she knew. She knew that she would live those eight years thrice over if it meant finding what she experienced in those moments of bliss with Samuel.

She pulled away slightly so that their lips parted, her own widening in a mischievous smile so that, when he tried to kiss her again, his lips met her teeth. "If I stay, you know I shan't rest until all the roads in the West Riding are seen to."

She felt his lips spread into an answering grin, their noses touching and his breath bathing her face in warmth. "And until every highwayman—or innocent vicar—has seen the barrel of your pistol?" he asked.

She let her head fall back and laughed, reveling in the feeling of being so close to him that he could feel rather than just hear her laughter.

"Precisely," she said. She relaxed into him, resting her forehead against his and letting out a contented breath.

"I love you, Georgiana," he said softly, pulling her more tightly against him. "More than anything in this world."

"And I you," she said. "I have never wanted to belong anywhere so much as I have wanted to belong with you." She pulled away and looked him in the eyes, seeing herself reflected in them.

His brows pulled together. "I am so sorry that I ever made you feel anything but completely and utterly wanted. Like a fool,

I let my fear overcome my faith at the first sign of trouble—I feared we were too different."

"What changed?" she asked.

He let out an airy laugh. "Burke. He told me that"—he squinted his eyes—"what was it? The difference between two people is as short as their willingness to bridge it." He cupped her face with two hands, staring down into her eyes. "We *are* different, Georgiana. Are you willing to bridge that distance together?"

She flared her nostrils and nodded quickly, a smile stealing into her eyes. "Are you proposing some sort of statute labor for this bridge?"

His lips stretched into an appreciative smile. "Yes. I suppose I am. A lifetime of statute labor together, I imagine, for who knows what kind of maintenance the bridge will require."

She reached up to kiss him again. "You bring the wheelbarrow, and I shall bring the shovel."

EPILOGUE

Surrounded on all sides by cheering and clapping, Samuel helped lift his wife into the open carriage, his cheeks aching from smiling and grains of rice falling from his hat onto the village road already covered in it.

Georgiana settled into the carriage, looking around and smiling at the villagers, glowing so much that Samuel took a moment to admire her before climbing in to sit beside her. She was radiant and so utterly perfect. He wished his father could be there to see the woman he had married. Like Samuel, he would have been forced to reform his opinions of outsiders after meeting her.

Georgiana looked at him, her smile somehow brightening even further as their eyes met, and he took her hand in his, drawing it to his mouth to kiss it.

Burke handed the reins up to him. "A happier day than this would be difficult to imagine, Sam." He indicated the villagers behind him with a toss of his head.

Everyone was wearing their best attire, complemented by the smiles on their faces. Sir Clyde had agreed to John's request to let the mill workers—all five of them, two of whom were new to Rushbury—off work early to attend the wedding. The vicar from the nearest parish stood serenely at the back of the crowd, a Bible clasped between his hands and beside him the entire Reed family, including Mary, whose hand rested on her round stomach.

Georgiana's family stood near the carriage, smiling up at them, Aunt Sara most of all. Georgiana's parents had been far more kind and accepting of a lowly country vicar than Samuel could have hoped for—a fact Georgiana teasingly attributed to their relief at her marrying at all. But the truth was, they loved Samuel—Daphne in particular was elated at the match, declaring that she would be furious if her own husband was hiding out in a village somewhere when she had been scouring London for him.

"An afternoon off work," Burke said, "a sunny summer day, and the union of the two best-loved people in Rushbury." He clapped a hand on Samuel's knee. "No one deserves happiness more than you and Mrs. Derrick, my friend."

"We wouldn't be here without you, Burke," Samuel said.

"Off with you two, then!" Burke said, stepping away from the carriage.

Samuel tossed the reins, and the carriage rumbled forward. Georgiana linked her arm through his, turning to wave at her family and the village as they took the road north out of Rushbury.

Georgiana glanced back at the village as the road climbed a hill, putting a hand to her bonnet to keep it in place. "The village is growing, Sam."

He sent a quick glance behind them, noting the two village homes being built at the end of the row to make room for more mill workers. Sir Clyde and Reed seemed to be working well together, and as the mill showed its potential in Reed's capable hands, Lady Gilmour was slowly warming to him—a vast improvement over her horror at the first news of his employment.

"Do you dislike it terribly?" A small frown wrinkled Georgiana's brow.

He let out a long breath, then looked down at her with a wry smile. "Change has never been easy for me."

"This I know." She smiled and reached up to kiss his cheek.

"But," he said, "the villagers are happy, and the roads are better than they've been in years." He winked at her. He transferred the reins to one hand, wrapping an arm around her shoulders and pulling her closer. "What matters to me is *you,* my love. If you are happy, I am happy."

Georgiana rested her head on Samuel's shoulder, and he sighed contentedly, planting a quick kiss upon her bonnet.

They spent a few minutes in silence, both content to admire the passing countryside. Samuel had never realized what joy there could be in mutual silence.

Georgiana's head came up as they took the right fork at a crossroads. "This is not the way to the inn, Sam."

He smiled. Georgiana took her duties as surveyor very seriously. At this point, she knew the parish roads as well as Samuel did.

"I hope you won't mind if we take a detour on our way," he said.

She turned her head to look at him, an intrigued glint in her eyes. "A detour?"

He nodded, smiling down at her. His wife. He had come so close to losing her, and somehow that made his joy all the more potent.

The carriage slowed as the horses struggled to make their way up the steep hill, taking them out of the parish boundaries. This was new territory for Georgiana, and he felt a thrill at the prospect of showing her something he knew she would marvel at.

"Do you remember when we went to the meadow the first time?" he asked.

"I shall never forget." She squeezed his arm and looked up at him.

Nor would he. He had fallen in love with her that day. "I promised you that you would love Rushbury even more in the summertime."

"And so I have. But I seem to remember you promising me fields of heather as far as the eye could see."

The carriage crested the hill, and he pulled the reins, the horses slowing to a stop.

"And when have I ever lied to you?" He inclined his head, inviting her to look at the view in front of them.

Her hand came up to her mouth slowly, her head moving to take in the scene: a flat expanse of purple heather, covering every inch of the earth before them as far as the eye could see, until the ground dropped off into the next valley.

"What do you think?" he asked.

She turned toward him, eyes still wide. "What do I think?" She shifted back toward the fields. "I think that I have spent far too many summers in Brighton and far too few here. I am seriously considering taking up residence in this field."

He pulled her even closer, so that she fit snugly under his arm, then pushed her bonnet back and rested his mouth against her head, smiling into her hair. "I think you might regret that decision when the snow comes, my love."

"Hmm. Perhaps so." She sighed. "I suppose I shall have to content myself with living at the parsonage. With you."

He made a clucking sound with his mouth. "A very dismal prospect indeed."

She turned toward him, reaching her hands to his coat lapels and pulling him down toward her. "It will be unbearable," she said, unable to hide her smile.

Another tug, and their lips touched, lightly at first, then, as she pulled him closer, the kiss became more insistent.

There was a new sense of thrill in the knowledge that he had a lifetime to enjoy the woman in his arms—to memorize every inch of her face and ensure that the wrinkles that would form there would tell the tale of their joy together. No matter what adversity life brought in the years to come, no matter what changes came to the village, they would face them together, finding happiness in moments like this—moments that nothing and no one could take from them.

The End

Read the next book in the series: A Forgiving Heart by Kasey Stockton

AUTHOR'S NOTE

While women in the Regency era were severely limited in the ways they could participate in the civil process, they had much more ability to do so at the level of local governance. The extent to which they could do so varied depending on the needs and attitudes of their parish, with some parishes choosing to restrict their participation and others welcoming it. There are documented cases of unmarried or widowed women taking on some of the duties at this level, including that of Surveyor of the Highways, and also records of legal contestations of those appointments being upheld by higher courts. If one declined to take the position, one was liable to be fined, as the position was obligatory—and unpaid until the 1830s.

SEASONS OF CHANGE SERIES

Book 1: The Road through Rushbury, by Martha Keyes

Book 2: A Forgiving Heart, by Kasey Stockton

Book 3: The Last Eligible Bachelor, by Ashtyn Newbold

Book 4: A Well-Trained Lady, by Jess Heileman

Book 5: The Cottage by Coniston, by Deborah Hathaway

Book 6: A Haunting at Havenwood, by Sally Britton

Book 7: His Disincline Bride, by Jennie Goutet

Other Titles by Martha Keyes

Tales from the Highlands

The Widow and the Highlander (Book One)

The Enemy and Miss Innes (Book Two)

The Innkeeper and the Fugitive (Book Three)

Families of Dorset

Wyndcross: A Regency Romance (Book One)

Isabel: A Regency Romance (Book Two)

Cecilia: A Regency Romance (Book Three)

Hazelhurst: A Regency Romance (Book Four)

Phoebe: A Regency Romance (Series Novelette)

Regency Shakespeare

A Foolish Heart (Book One)

My Wild Heart (Book Two)

True of Heart (Book Three)

Other Titles

Of Lands High and Low

The Highwayman's Letter (Sons of Somerset Book 5)

A Seaside Summer (Timeless Regency Romance Book 17)

The Christmas Foundling (Belles of Christmas: Frost Fair Book Five)

Goodwill for the Gentleman (Belles of Christmas Book Two)

The Road through Rushbury (Seasons of Change Book One)

Eleanor: A Regency Romance

Join my Newsletter to keep in touch and learn more about British history! I try to keep it fun and interesting.

OR follow me on BookBub to see my recommendations and get alerts about my new releases.

ACKNOWLEDGMENTS

There are always a few key people who are instrumental to the creation of a novel.

I couldn't do any of this without my husband. He ensures I have time to write, edit, research, and all the other tasks involved in the running of an author business. He listens to unsolicited facts as I research and has become a very helpful troubleshooter as I run into barriers during the plotting and drafting process.

My mom is always the first to read my early drafts and offer feedback and encouragement.

Thank you to my little boys, who are graciously still napping, and who put up with my distraction every day.

Thank you to my editor, Jenny Proctor, for her wonderful feedback—I'm so glad I have you!

Special thanks to Kasey, Jess, Emily, and Evelyn. You are the best critique partners a girl could ask for! Much love to my fellow Sweet Regency Romance Fans author team. I love rubbing shoulders with all of you as authors and friends.

Thank you to my Review Team and my beta readers for your help and support in an often nervewracking business.

ABOUT THE AUTHOR

Martha Keyes was born, raised, and educated in Utah—a home she loves dearly but also dearly loves to escape whenever she can travel the world. She received a BA in French Studies and a Master of Public Health, both from Brigham Young University.

Word crafting has always fascinated and motivated her, but it wasn't until a few years ago that she considered writing her own stories. When she isn't writing, she is honing her photography skills, looking for travel deals, and spending time with her husband and children. She lives with her husband and twin boys in Vineyard, Utah.

Made in the USA
Columbia, SC
21 June 2021

40801907R00148